THE THIRTY-THIRD OWL

The Thirty-Third Owl

Jane Burnard

Gwasg Carreg Gwalch

Published in 2021

ISBN: 978-1-84527-830-4

Published with the financial support of the Books Council of Wales

Cover design: Eleri Owen
Cover image: Elin Manon Cooper
Graphic novel: Efa Blosse-Mason

Published by Gwasg Carreg Gwalch,
12 Iard yr Orsaf, Llanrwst, Wales LL26 0EH
tel: 01492 642031
email: books@carreg-gwalch.cymru
website: www.carreg-gwalch.cymru

Printed and published in Wales

I Gareth

For Gareth

Dear Mum

I've written a story. It's about what happened that week – the last week of the summer term.

Every word of it is true. I want you to read it, because there's something we need to do, together. And when you get to the end of the story, you'll know what it is.

So, here it is. It's called The Thirty-Third Owl.

Thanks, Mum.

Love always, Rose

PS Some of the conversations happened in Welsh. Because you don't understand much Welsh, I've shown them by putting the first sentence in Welsh, then translating it all into English.

Maybe one day you'll learn Welsh too, and we can speak it together? 😊

1

A giant green tortoise, as big as a small car, was creeping in short, jerky movements over the grass. Then it stopped, and it seemed to brace itself before making a huge leap, actually coming off the ground. When it came back down, its back collapsed with a *whumph*, and the tortoise turned into a billowing green jellyfish.

A head poked out of its edge. It had brown hair, which fell into its eyes, and it wore a big grin on its face.

It was, in fact, a twelve-year-old boy named Ianto.

Nearby was a twelve-year-old girl called Rose. She was laughing so hard that she had fallen on to all fours, and tears were streaming down her face.

'Stop it, please,' she begged, head down. 'You're killing me.'

'What's the matter with us?' asked Ianto, still grinning. 'This is supposed to be the easiest tent to put up, ever.'

It was early evening, just a week before the beginning of the summer holidays, and the clearing where they were trying, and failing, to put up the tent was in the middle of a wood, that was in a valley, that was in Cymru – Wales.

'Forget the tent,' said Rose. 'Let's drink hot chocolate instead.'

She rummaged in her backpack and pulled out a flask. Then she poured the steaming, milky drink into two cups and passed one to Ianto, who untangled himself from the tent and plonked down next to her on the soft grass.

The hot chocolate was sweet and thick, and the sun shone warmly on their faces, though it was low in the sky now and about to dip behind the hills. They swallowed the hot drink gratefully, both going 'Mmm,' then turning to each other and laughing again.

Fortified by hot chocolate, it was not long before they were tackling the tent once more – slotting together then threading in its backbone, pulling tight the guide ropes and hammering down the pegs with a stone, making sure that the inner tent, with its groundsheet, was stretched out properly.

And then, like a miracle, it stood before them – a welcoming, green igloo. Ducking inside, they discovered a warm, muted space, with its own particular smell – like grass and balloons.

Rose said, 'I love camping.'

'You haven't done any yet,' noted Ianto. 'You have to wait till morning before you say that.'

The plan was to spend the night here. Ianto had been given the tent at Christmas, and he wanted to try it out before camping in it at the National Eisteddfod, which was coming up next month. He usually slept in his family's caravan when they went to the Eisteddfod, but it was always a bit cramped – so this time he would be branching out on his own.

Rose had been looking forward to this for ages. She loved this wood. She'd been coming here since she was little, exploring, climbing trees, paddling in the stream and watching, quietly, for its birds and animals to reveal themselves. More recently, she'd enjoyed taking photos here – of trees, mostly. Some she took close up, of patterns in bark and lichens and mosses. Others she took from a distance – trying to capture the spirit of the whole tree.

Lately, she'd found the wood a comforting place, somewhere to forget her troubles for a little while. Being amongst the trees was like being surrounded by old friends – accepting and peaceful. She often stayed out here till the sky grew dark, but she'd never spent the whole night in the wood. Now she could hardly wait for night to fall to feel at one with the night animals – the owls, the foxes, the badgers – amongst the trees. And with her best friend, Ianto.

Ianto was reaching into his backpack and pulling out a map. He spread it out on the ground in front of the tent. 'Look,' he said, pointing at it. 'Here we are.'

Rose saw the whole valley and the village translated into coloured lines, shapes and words on neatly creased paper. There was the mountain that rose before them at the head of the valley. There was the track up to Mr Williams's farm, and there was the tiny rectangle which showed his farmhouse. *Fferm Bigfelen*, said the map.

'I never knew Mr Williams's farm had a name,' said Rose. '*Pigfelen* – that means yellow beak, doesn't it?'

'Yes. It's another word for *aderyn du*, or blackbird.'

'Fferm Bigfelen. Blackbird Farm.' Rose looked up at the farm buildings, huddling halfway up the mountain.

It was as if a stone ship, caught in a storm, had ploughed into the side of the mountain centuries ago and flung its cargo all about. The buildings were tumbledown and ancient, falling apart, and a lot of rusting farm machinery lay about in the yard in front of them, like flotsam and jetsam. At the end of the drive which joined the track to the farmhouse stood a flagpole, from which flew the Welsh flag, resplendent, its dragon a vivid flash of red on the mountainside.

There was no sign of Mr Williams or his sheepdog, Del. Rose could see sheep in the fields above the farm, moving in single file down the zig-zag paths that led to the scrappy hedgerow where they spent the night.

Looking at the map again, Rose followed the track down the mountain with her finger; followed it all the way out of the valley and into the village.

Mr Williams's farm was the only building on the track. The only building in the valley.

'Wait a minute,' she said. 'Where's our house?'

Ianto bent to examine the map and shrugged. 'It's not there,' he said. 'This map's pretty old. It was probably made before your dad built your place.'

Suddenly, Rose felt stunned. The house that Dad had built was not on the map. As if they weren't supposed to be here. As if they didn't exist. To her alarm and surprise, tears sprang to her eyes. And with the mention of Dad, the thought of Dad, her insides felt as if they had been opened up, and she was suddenly teetering on the edge of a deep, dark abyss of panic . . .

Ianto noticed her silence. He glanced at her. Then he said, quickly, 'Hey, don't worry! Your house'll be there when they draw up the next map.' He gave her a gentle nudge, and drew her attention back to the map. 'Look – here's the wood.

You can even see this lumpy thing.'

He gestured to the long, raised hump in the middle of the clearing, not far from their tent. It was a kind of dyke or mound from which, in places, large pieces of rock jutted through the turf – turf which was nibbled short and smooth by rabbits, so that it was like a piece of green velvet, draped over a bony, sleeping giant.

Rose gulped down her panic and looked in fascination at the tiny, round shapes on the paper, marking the mound's place.

Then she looked at Ianto, absorbed in his map. Mr Williams, the owner of the farmhouse on the mountain, was Ianto's great uncle. Ianto's family had lived in this area all their lives, for generations and generations. And they were Welsh-speakers – they had all spoken Welsh from birth.

Does Ianto know how lucky he is? she wondered. Compared to him, she felt like the girl from nowhere – especially now that Dad wasn't with them.

Rose could speak Welsh too – she had learned it at school. But she didn't speak Welsh with Ianto. Just English. It was somehow hard to start, after all this time. She hoped that maybe, one day, they would speak Welsh together, naturally.

As the light faded, Ianto carefully folded his map and put it back in his backpack. Now the sun had sunk behind the hills and the valley was starting to darken. The sky was a deep blue, like the sea, and the moon a slim, white sickle, floating above. One or two stars shone brightly already.

Then, from out of the dusk, burst a long, loud, breathy hoot: '*Hoo hoo-hoooo hoo-ho-ho.*'

Stunned into silence, they waited, wide-eyed. Looking

around slowly, Rose could see nothing but the indistinct shapes of the trees.

Then, from closer by came a sharp, excited '*Ke-wick! Ke-wick!*'

It was a pair of tawny owls. They were calling to each other.

Ianto and Rose sat motionless, holding their breath for more.

Suddenly, without warning, Ianto piped up: 'Hoo-hooo, hoo-hooo!'

Silence. Then, from the darkness, '*Ke-wick!*'

'Ianto!' Rose hissed, turning to him with wide eyes. 'She replied!'

Ianto looked as surprised as her.

'OK, I'm going to try now.' She cleared her throat and raised her voice, her heart beating fast, for some reason: 'Hooo-hoo-hoooo! Hooo-hooo!'

They held still and waited.

But this time there was no answer. Nothing except the sound of the wind, whispering through leaves.

Soon they began to feel the cold so, fully dressed, they got into their sleeping bags and lay inside the tent with their heads poking out, looking up.

Now it was properly dark. The milky way spread across the sky above them like a great, silvery brush-stroke, and every now and then Rose and Ianto gasped to see a shooting star appear then fizzle out in the time it took to point and say '*Look!*'

In the end, they lapsed into silence and became absorbed in the sky above. Until Rose began to feel dizzy, as if they were lifting upwards into the sky; or as if they were upside down now, and the stars were shining below them, so they were falling downwards, amongst the stars – into sleep . . .

The next instant, she was in a dark place, trapped under something heavy and immovable. Panic filled her, and she struggled to free herself, desperately moving her arms, her legs, trying to turn her head. Something was wrong with her body.

Her open eyes strained against the pitch black, but she could see nothing. Her arms, brushing the stone that confined her – cold, hard, heavy – were no longer arms. They felt strangely strong, and seemed covered in something soft and protective, so that the rough stone did not graze her skin. And what was wrong with her legs? Where her arms were stronger, her legs seemed weaker. Were they even there at all?

She scrabbled with them, painfully, against stone. Yes they were. But they felt weak, and scratchy, and short. Her ears were working differently too – so that every sound she made was amplified and sharply defined – almost deafening in her head.

Her heart was beating faster than she thought possible. *Am I having a heart attack? Am I going to die, trapped down here, wherever I am?*

At that moment, the stones around her shifted suddenly, dropping slightly, as if an earthquake had taken place, and she heard a creaking, grinding sound of stone on stone. She shifted with the rocks, helpless – pushed to one side, crushed further. Then came a scraping above her as a rock swivelled swiftly away, and before she knew it she had pulled herself free, leaping upwards with her arms spread out, through the gap in the rocks and into the air.

And somehow, she was flying. She turned her head to take in brown, thickly-feathered wings, beating silently and determinedly on either side of her. She was high in the air already, because she was looking down on the stony clearing, and it was like an island surrounded by the dark sea of the wood. And there was the tent, a small round mound on the grass.

The stars shone brightly in the black sky, but Rose was astonished to realise she could see as well as if it were day. Better, even. She circled the clearing, her eyes piercing the darkness well beyond the wood – out to the village and the landscape all around – the mountain, the hills either side, the great bog beyond . . .

She sped on through the air, over the trees now. Over her house – the little bungalow that Dad had built on the edge of the wood, where Mum was sleeping now, all on her own. She turned her head to take in the overgrown back garden. And when she turned her head, she *really* turned her head – almost all the way around.

She felt a surge of exhilaration, then her beak opened, to cry 'Ke-wick! Ke-wick!'

Circling her house, she flapped back over the wood to the clearing. The canopy of the trees below swayed and crashed in the breeze like waves in a dark, stormy sea.

The clearing appeared beneath her again – a bare, pale expanse, studded with rocks that stuck up out of the grass. She plummeted down to land on the ground at the edge of this jumble of rocks, dropping with wings held backwards and upwards. Her clawed feet met short grass, and she was suddenly stationary. She swivelled her head to make sure that she was safe. Nothing moved around her. No sounds but the whispering of the wind in the trees.

She folded her wings and waited. What for, she had no idea.

The wind dropped, so that the whole wood was silent. But only for a moment. Then the stones before her shuddered, breaking up through the turf with a great booming noise. A pause, while fine dust spiralled upwards into the air. Then came the sound of rocks scraping together once more, rocks cracking with high shrieks and deep groans. Something was pushing up from below. Something else wanted to get out.

As she watched, wisps of dark, shadowy stuff slunk from the cracks between the rocks. They were like plumes of ash, made up of countless particles, gathering together, thickening, moving in the air. But this black substance was not blowing in the night breeze. It was moving independently. As it snaked up from below, it gathered itself into a single cloud which pulsated darkly above the clearing.

Like a murmuration of starlings, Rose thought. She knew, somehow, that the cloud was made up of something that was neither human nor animal, and was not really alive. But as it stretched and contracted there was an answering resonation inside her. A resonation that was deeply uncomfortable. She had a sudden urge to fly as far from this place as possible . . .

Then another upheaval. Something else was coming up now, throwing off rocks and earth as it rose. A huge, rounded lump pushed through, dislodging giant stones then rising and falling gently, as if it were having a breather. Shortly, after another push and more cascading rocks, rose a smaller lump.

A man's back. And the top of a man's head. But huge, too huge – the back as long as a bus – large muscles flexing within it. The giant head was covered in thick, brown, dusty hair.

More stones fell away with a crash, some landing close to Rose's clawed feet. Now the man was crouching amongst the debris, and she could see strong arms and legs, tensed. And then Rose saw the black, shadowy cloud above the clearing dispersing, breaking up into wisps which dissolved in the air so that she could see nothing of it now, even through her sharp, owl eyes.

In one last, great effort, the huge man pulled free from his rocky bed and hauled himself upright, stretching up tall with a clattering of earth and gravel.

Towering over the tops of the trees, his booted feet treading down the rocks beneath him, he opened his mouth to let out a terrible roar . . .

'AAAAARGH!'

Rose awoke in terror, her heart beating fast and hard.

Desperately, she gathered her wits.

She was in a tent. She and Ianto were camping in the clearing in the woods. Ianto had called out, had woken her up. And she had had a dream, a very strange dream, but already she couldn't remember much about it.

'Ianto! Are you OK?' she called.

No answer from Ianto's side. All she could see of him was a dark lump against the slightly lighter outline of the tent. She didn't want to put on her torch and risk waking him. So she tried to still her own gasps of breath and listen carefully.

Now she could just make out the sound of his breathing, which was level and light. He was asleep, despite that loud cry.

As her own heartbeat slowed, she did her best to reassure herself. Everything was all right. It was just a dream; it was just a shout.

Just a dream; just a shout.

Soon she dozed off again, entirely exhausted.

Rose woke gradually, as if she was surfacing from a pool of water. Light and warmth from the sun, and a chorus of bird song – every bird in the wood was singing, surely – poured through the thin walls of the tent as if they didn't exist, filling it with sound and green light.

She turned to look at Ianto. He was lying on his back, very still, eyes closed.

'Ianto, are you awake?' she said gently.

'Hmm!' Ianto jerked upright to a sitting position, as if he were about to sprint off.

Rose found this funny. 'Good morning, Ianto. Do you always wake up like that?'

Ianto turned his head sharply and stared directly at her with wild, wide eyes. But before she could react, his shoulders relaxed, his face settled and his eyes softened as they focused on her.

Then he lay back again with a thump and stared up at the tent's green ceiling, which was patterned with the moving shadows of leaves against the sun.

'Whoa. That was the strangest night's sleep I've ever had. I had a dream, but it was like more than a dream.' He paused.

Then he said, 'You know how in dreams you're usually yourself, doing things?'

'Yes.' Rose had had a dream too, though it was very unclear. Had she been flying?

'Well, in this dream, I was someone else,' continued Ianto. 'Or something else . . . I can't remember. But it felt really real.'

Really real. Yes – her dream had felt real too. She tried to remember it. But the more she chased it, the more it faded away. 'What's the time?' she asked after a bit. Her head felt fuzzy.

'Let's see . . .' Ianto leaned over to check his mobile. 'Eight o'clock! What time's breakfast?' Suddenly he was wide awake.

Mum had promised them a cooked breakfast this morning. Rose was having veggie sausages, mushrooms, eggs and beans, and Ianto was having the works – sausages, bacon, eggs, beans and mushrooms. And as much toast and tea as they could manage.

Memories of dreams melted away like morning mist in sun as they scrambled up and out of the tent. And there were all the trees in their sunlit green; there was the mountain, with its pattern of fields and hedgerows, purple heather bruising the top. White smoke was issuing from the chimney of Mr Williams's cottage and, as ever, it poured as much through the loose stones in the sides as it did from the top.

Stretching up her arms to the sun, Rose felt as if she'd been scrubbed raw. As if the night in the open, in this wild place, had scraped away a layer of skin, made her more alive.

Part of her didn't want to go home, but to stay out here forever.

But breakfast awaited them . . . and that was a good reason to head back. Taking the tent down was much easier than putting it up, though it took a couple of attempts to get it back in the bag.

As they left the clearing and headed into the trees, Ianto turned to Rose with a grin and said, 'Let's come back in the holidays and do more camping. We can bring our own food and cook on a fire. We can collect water from the stream to make tea and stuff.'

'That would be great,' said Rose, smiling and holding out her fist.

Ianto bumped it with his, smiling back.

They took the little path through the trees to the back gate of Rose's garden. Soon her house came into view. The kitchen door was open, and already they could smell frying sausages, hear the radio playing music. Then Rose's mum appeared in the kitchen doorway.

'Hi di hi, campers!' she called. 'Come and get it!'

2

The next day was Monday. When school finished, Rose did as she always did and took the bus back to the village, then walked home up the track. The day had passed in a blur. No chance to speak to Ianto during lessons, and no chance after school either, because tonight he had football practice.

Approaching the bungalow, she was confronted by the sight of something unexpected on their gravelled drive – Mr Williams's quad bike: the little, buzzing vehicle he used to get about on the steep mountainside.

Then she heard voices coming faintly from the back garden.

Stepping past the quad bike she let herself in, heading straight for her bedroom.

Creeping slowly to the edge of her window she lifted the curtain and peeped under it. Mum and Mr Williams were standing in the middle of the lawn – the lawn that was an untidy, lush meadow of long grass.

Mr Williams was a battered-looking man, with an anxious, sun-browned face and bright blue eyes. As ever, he was wearing his grubby, green John Deere cap. Mum had her back to the house and Mr Williams was facing her, with Del, his sheepdog, sitting at his feet. Mum was nodding a lot and seemed to be agreeing, or sympathising, with him.

No one had noticed Rose arrive.

Correction – Del had. She didn't miss a trick, that dog. Her sharp eyes – one blue, one brown – were fixed on her. But Del didn't move or make a sound – she just stared.

What were they talking about? Mr Williams's voice was too quiet to understand. Mum wasn't saying much. Rose felt a sudden stab of panic. Had she done something wrong? Maybe Mr Williams hadn't liked her and Ianto camping in the wood? Because Mr Williams owned the wood, and the fields all about. But Mr Williams didn't look angry – he looked sort of defeated and sad.

Mum was still nodding away, then she put out a hand to lay it comfortingly on Mr Williams's arm. Rose watched Mr Williams flinch away from her, and Mum let her hand drop to her side.

Mum is always so friendly to everyone, thought Rose. Too friendly, sometimes. The same kind of friendly to everyone she meets, regardless of who they are. Rose knew that some people, like Mr Williams, didn't like being touched. But Mum didn't seem to know things like that.

She looked at Del, who was still glaring at her. The sheepdog's intelligent eyes seemed to see right through her.

What's wrong with that dog? Why shouldn't I spy on my mum and my neighbour in my own back garden?

Before she knew what she was doing, Rose was pulling a face at Del – sticking out her tongue and screwing up her nose.

It made no difference. The sheepdog continued to stare, unblinkingly.

Then Rose looked up. To her horror, Mr Williams was looking straight at her. Their eyes locked – hers in shock, his in puzzlement. A second later Rose had ducked down below the window and crawled on all fours to her bed, where she stretched out on her back, heart beating fast. Had Mr Williams seen her pull that stupid face? Would he think it was directed at him? He would. A hot wave swept over Rose's skin, a prickling mixture of fear and embarrassment. She didn't think she'd ever be able to face him again.

Pretty soon the voices trailed off, and the next thing she heard was Mum letting herself in the back door, the crunch of Mr Williams's feet on gravel at the front and then the roar of the quad bike, which steadily receded as it buzzed up the hill.

Rose got up and crept towards the kitchen.

She could hear Mum pulling out cutlery and plates and muttering, 'Oh dear, oh dear, oh dear . . .' to herself. Then Mum turned suddenly, almost dropping the chopping board in her hand.

'Ah!' she gasped, putting her spare hand to her heart. 'You gave me such a turn! When did you get home, love?'

'Oh, just now, really.'

'Did you see Mr Williams?'

'Um, no – I think I must have just missed him. I heard the quad bike . . .'

'Poor Mr Williams,' said Mum, shaking her head and starting to chop an onion.

'Why poor Mr Williams?'

Mum continued to chop very swiftly, making efficient movements to move the onion about the board. She was silent for a moment, head down. Then she abandoned the onion, laid down the knife and turned, suddenly, to Rose.

'Rosie, love – you're not going to like this.'

'What? What do you mean?' Fear prickled in Rose's guts.

'Well, Mr Williams is having a very difficult time at the moment – very difficult.'

'How?'

Mum sat at the table now and faced her. 'He's in terrible trouble financially. Don't tell anyone else this. Ianto will probably know already – but don't tell anyone else. Poor Mr Williams, he hated having to tell me.

'He needs an awful lot of work done on his house. Do you remember, Dad was going to give him a hand, at one point?'

Rose didn't remember that. She was feeling even more panicky at the mention of Dad . . . she clenched her fists and managed not to say anything. If only Mum would get to the point. But at the same time, she was afraid of the point. She didn't want to hear the point.

Mum carried on. 'Well, anyway. The roof's leaking – been leaking for a year or so – and now the joists are rotting. And you can see what a state his chimney's in – that needs completely rebuilding. Then there's dry rot downstairs. The house is falling apart around him, basically. And to fix it all is going to be expensive – *very* expensive, poor guy.'

'But his house has always been like that, and he's happy, isn't he?' said Rose. 'Why can't he just carry on?'

'He's getting on now, love. He's got to be at least seventy, you know? And when you get older, you need a solid, warm place to live in. He's struggling up there. No money in sheep-farming, he says. And he doesn't want to rely on his relatives.

He's a very independent man . . . Do you know, he reminds me of you!'

Mum laughed at this, but Rose didn't find it funny at all.

'So what's going to happen?' she asked, trying to keep her voice as normal as possible.

Mum stopped laughing. She gazed at Rose with frightened eyes and said, 'He's sold the wood.'

Rose thought the news could not get any worse than this. But then it did. Mum went on: 'Some company have bought it so they can . . .' she trailed off, and looked away from Rose. 'So they can build an abattoir there.'

Mum's eyes fixed on Rose again, and they looked wide and lost, as if the truth was just sinking in for her, too.

'Apparently, as well as a big new building complex, they'll be putting in a proper access road to the valley, too. It's a good site, they say – close to the village for workers, and not far from town and the main road. There'll be lots of new jobs for the area, which is good, I suppose . . .'

Rose had passed from panic to disbelief. Mum had got it wrong. Mr Williams had got it wrong too. 'Mum, they can't do that! They just can't. That will mean chopping down all the trees. And getting rid of all the rocks in the middle. It's too much work. There must be much better places to build abattoirs.'

Mum said, hopelessly, 'Thing is, Rose, people don't want abattoirs near them. It's hard to find a place to build one, and to get planning permission. But in this valley, it's just Mr Williams and us. There's not much you and I can do to stop them. Maybe they'll pay us a bit of compensation . . . for spoiling the view.'

Spoiling the view? A whole wood was going to be wiped out, many of its creatures killed, the rest displaced, to build a place of horror – a place where other poor animals would be slaughtered.

Rose stared at Mum, breathing hard. She felt, suddenly, as if she'd run into a brick wall. This horrible situation was immovable, solid – dreamed up by adults, then made a reality by adults. Adults intent on making life miserable for all – and then explaining, so rationally, that this was how it had to be.

The wood was going to be destroyed. The place would be transformed – from a heaven, to a hell.

She had seen abbatoirs before – been past them on buses and in cars. Huge, anonymous places, with a strange smell hanging over them. Big lorries arriving one end and shunting in their cargo of live, frightened creatures; refrigerated lorries departing the other end, full of their remains . . . What horror went on in between?

She had seen abbatoir workers, standing about outside the building in fluorescent jackets, smoking, looking pale and miserable. What kind of a job?

Rose didn't want to tell people how to live, what to eat, or say that people shouldn't have jobs. The world was full of people who ate meat. Ianto ate meat, so did Mum, sometimes – so had Dad. And they were good people. But . . . but . . .

She had never really thought about the phrase 'I can't bear it.' Suddenly, she understood its meaning.

A strangled cry came from her mouth, and she was as surprised as Mum to hear it. She was hazily aware that Mum had come over and was trying to hug her, but she pushed her away, forcefully, so that Mum staggered, almost falling over. Then she rushed out of the back door and down the path, fumbling to open the gate at the bottom of the garden and racing into the wood.

3

It was still light, though the sun was dipping now behind the hill beyond. Plunging into the trees, she pelted forwards over the rutted, leaf-thick ground.

And then her foot hit a root, and she tumbled, face-first, on to the floor of the wood.

Rose's fall was cushioned by leaves – soft, brown, damp – rotting and crumbling together, so that soon they would be a mass of rich, earthy leaf-mould. She lay there, face-down, arms and legs spread out, just as she'd landed. She didn't want to get up. She wished she could just sink into the woodland floor and disappear . . .

A sudden gust of wind caused the leaves above her to rustle, and the light shifted for an instant as the sun peeped through the branches. Then something moved before her eyes. Rose saw a beetle – a tiny creature with a polished, bright green coat like a flat shield on its back. It seemed to glow from within as it busied about its business.

It was a shield bug, Rose knew that. It was walking determinedly on six spindly legs across the leaves and moss, the antennae on its head moving constantly to sense its way, tiny eyes taking everything in from above and the sides. Then it stopped right before her, and moved its antennae in her direction.

Distractedly, Rose moved her hand towards it. The shield

bug's delicate feelers twitched, then it started to climb on to her finger. When all six legs were on board and it stood still, Rose brought the little creature up to her eyes. Now she could see even more. It was perfect. So neat, so symmetrical, so shiny – its segmented green and brown antennae seemed to be made of long, iridescent beads which slowly flexed and curved, taking in this new situation. Its legs, which were green at the top, merging into amber, ended in two tiny claws, which gripped and tickled on her skin.

Tears fell from Rose's eyes as she watched this little creature. So small, so easy to miss, so easy to step on, to crush, to brush off, but just as important as any other being. This little bug, like the rest in the wood, was going to have its home destroyed and changed out of all recognition. The whole wood was waiting here, carrying on as normal, growing, feeding, breeding, foraging, when any day now, in would come the diggers, the earth movers, the builders.

Gently, she lowered her finger to the leaf-mould, and watched as the shield bug disembarked and trundled away, up and over the leaves like a tiny green boat cresting high waves and coming down the other side. A very faint, scratchy sound came to her ears, and she realised, in wonder, that it was the tread of its tiny feet, pulling it forward.

Rose closed her eyes and lay still. Everything was whirling about in her mind like dead, dried leaves – Mum looking at her with frightened eyes; Mr Williams with his falling-down house and defeated expression; the shield bug trundling on its way; Dad . . . Dad. Could Dad have stopped this happening? Dad had always sorted everything out . . .

Let the diggers and earth shifters come, with their tank treads, to clear this place. She would not move from here. They could run her over and mush her up into the dead leaves. Then cart her away with the rest of the topsoil. They probably wouldn't even notice her from up high in their cabs. And then . . . at least she would be with Dad.

She breathed out and slumped into the leaf-mould, and it seemed, in her misery, that she was moving downwards, moving through layer after layer of laid-down leaves, going back centuries, the soil growing darker and richer and more and more ancient as she sank . . .

Then she blinked open her eyes, suddenly. She was in an earth tunnel and in darkness, though she could still see. The tunnel had hard-packed, rounded walls, as if many creatures had been this way for many, many years.

She shrugged her arms – but they were not arms, they were long, thickly feathered wings, pressing against the tunnel walls. She looked down to see two clawed feet beneath her. It had happened again.

Suddenly she was utterly alert. And now she remembered everything from her dream – being an owl, escaping from the stones in the middle of the clearing, flying, seeing the dark stuff and then the giant . . .

Her thoughts were interrupted as her head, which almost touched the tunnel roof, swivelled to catch a faint shushing noise that she knew was the slither of a worm, pushing its way through the earth somewhere behind her.

Then her head snapped forwards again as, from ahead of her, came another sound. The rapid pattering of feet – far off, but getting closer. The tunnel ahead curved around, so she could not yet see what it was. She stood her ground and waited. She was not afraid. Not yet.

The pattering continued, a scratchy scurrying, getting louder and louder until, around the bend, came the maker of the noise.

A long head, darkly furred, with a twitching pink snout and two large hands like clawed spades at the end of powerful arms. A low-slung body, also covered in dark, thick fur.

A mole.

And then she saw its eyes. Unblinking, small, watchful – like little round buttons on a fur coat – but not bright as she would've expected. They were swimming in their sockets in a kind of dark haze, which made them look mat and dull.

Before she knew it, a rush of wild energy passed through Rose, and she felt her feathers ruffling as she stood up tall, making herself as big and as fearsome as she could. Her beak opened and she unleashed a loud screech of alarm.

The tunnel swallowed the sound, the earth deadening the noise, and the mole pulled back a little, cowering down. It was almost as if it was bowing to her. They locked eyes for a moment – the owl's wide, clear and terrible, the mole's opaque and strange. Then it turned on its heel and began to scamper back the way it had come, front feet paddling down the tunnel ahead, back feet pushing.

Rose knew, somehow, that it wanted her to follow it. She hesitated. What was going on?

One thing was for sure. She was not going to follow this creature with its awful eyes. The path ahead, where it scuttled away, sloped gently downwards. She was going back the other way, which rose up slightly – to the surface, she hoped.

With great difficulty, she turned around and began to stumble in the opposite direction. The burrow was so narrow and the ceiling so low that she could not stretch her wings, let alone fly. So she had to walk along it, hobbling on clawed feet. Her short legs were not made for walking.

Soon, she became aware of sounds. Familiar sounds. The rapid scurrying of feet approaching once again. But this time, it was coming from ahead of her. Was it another mole?

The pattering grew louder, whispering down the tunnel. But she continued on her way towards it, doggedly marching upwards until, sure enough, a long, black-furred face appeared around the curve ahead, followed by two front paws splayed out with vicious claws.

Her heart sank as the mole stopped before her. Then, suddenly, the creature opened its mouth to reveal two rows of short, needle-sharp teeth. Rose stepped backwards in alarm. The mole shuffled forward, shortening the distance between them.

And she realised that it was the same mole. The same, dead eyes. The same, awful *feeling*.

How had it come from behind to appear in front of her? Or was this tunnel an endless loop, going round and round, forever . . .

The mole waited, motionless. Instinctively, she jumped, to bring her strong, clawed feet down, upon her prey. But her claws barely left the tunnel floor before her head hit the roof with a jarring thud, bringing her back, painfully, to her feet.

Still the mole did not move; mouth ajar, teeth bared, it waited, blocking the way forward.

Head first, wild with rage, she threw all her weight at the creature, open beak stabbing viciously. But her beak met air. The mole backed up, and Rose's wings fluttered uselessly against her sides as she lost balance and fell forward.

Now she was lying on her front in the tunnel, her beak against the earth floor, and she struggled, scrabbling to stand upright, while she cried out in horror. She could not see it, but she was aware that the mole was very close to her, watching her flap on the ground. Her body felt heavy, her wings disabled, her legs so short and weak . . .

She lay still for a moment. Then, with great effort, she pressed her wings against the tunnel floor and pushed down with them, scrambling painfully with her claws until she was upright once more.

And there was the mole before her.

She was trapped underground. This mole-creature would not let her pass.

Was it all a dream? If it was, she could wake up! She closed her eyes and tried to concentrate – struggling with herself, as she'd done before in dreams, to pull herself up, up and out of this nightmare.

It worked, sometimes. But it didn't work this time.

Because this wasn't a dream. It was real.

4

The mole was staring at her, open-mouthed. Then something happened in her mind. Words spooled through her head, as if a banner had been unrolled.

'The King.'

Then 'This way.'

So. The mole wanted her to meet the king. *What* king?

Suddenly, in the muddle of her frightened mind, the sun broke over the top of the mountain. Because the king . . . the king was Dad. Suddenly it all made sense.

Since he'd died, she'd wanted to see him every hour of her waking life – almost every minute. But she'd never wanted to see him more than at this moment. And so she knew that the king was Dad. And Dad would help her. Dad would make all the bad stuff go away.

A little part of her told her that she was mistaken. That Dad was not the king. That Dad was dead, and could not come back. But she did not want to hear it, and did not listen.

And she turned, awkwardly, and began to shuffle down the tunnel, hating the sound of the mole's pattering feet behind her, hating not being able to see it.

Cramped, confined, she concentrated on putting one clawed foot before the other as the tunnel stretched ahead, gently turning this way and that, but always sloping downwards, very slightly. Going to see Dad . . .

On and on. Further and further. Then, peering forwards in confusion, she saw nothing ahead. No more tunnel. Only blackness. There was a sudden silence behind her, then a subtle tensing sound – a slight shift of fur and feet against earth.

Before she could swivel her head, she felt strong claws ripping painfully into the flesh of her back.

Thrown forward with the impact, dripping blood, she fell out of the tunnel . . . and into air. Instinctively, her wings opened. Flapping weakly, her back and wings shrieking with pain, she circled and looked about her, taking in a large stone cave – perhaps as big as a house. Jagged rocks jutted up from the cave floor and down from the roof. The place was filled with a strange, dim light which came from the far corner of the cave, where the walls curved around, leading downwards to an unseen place.

Rose knew, though she did not know how, that there was another cave there beyond this one. She also knew, though she did not know how, that in that cave something terrible lurked. Something she would do anything to avoid. She veered around painfully in the air, turning back towards the tunnel mouth.

Because now she knew. There was no king. No Dad.

The mole had brought her here to die.

Could she go back again, through the tunnel? The entrance came out halfway up the side of the cave wall, from a seam of earth. In its mouth, Rose saw the mole, its head and front feet hanging lifelessly over the edge. It was very still. She flew closer, ignoring the pain in her back and wings.

What was happening to its eyes? They were two pools of

tiny, writhing black eels which grew to take in the whole of its head, melting the fur and then swirling over its claws and front feet . . . until, within the blink of an eye, it was a soundless mass of swarming dark particles in the shape of a mole.

And then the whole mass collapsed inwards, imploding and spooling out, stretching into a long, dark thread, which snaked its way with lightning speed down the wall and across the cave floor, whipping around the corner into the cave beyond.

Turning back, she saw the entrance to the tunnel sealing itself, filling instantly with hard, packed earth. Now there was no escape from this desolate cave – or from whatever brooded around the corner.

What will happen if I die down here, as an owl? Will I die as a girl too?

She would find out soon enough.

Exhausted, battered and torn, Rose fell to the stony floor, her wings flapping weakly and uselessly. She came to rest on her back in a patch of rubble, looking up. Her legs hung down and her claws curled inwards.

Then she closed her eyes.

5

Rose awoke to a loud thumping from above. Opening her eyes, she saw the ceiling of the cave shaking, vibrating, as shale and larger rocks came crashing down around her.

Too weak to move, she lay there. Now there was an urgent scrabbling above her, as if rocks were being displaced on the surface. More thunderous pounding on the cave roof. At this rate she would be buried by falling rocks, she thought, faintly.

And then, from above, came the loudest, most explosive crack of all. The cave filled with dim, natural light as a fissure snapped open above her, accompanied by a fresh shower of debris. Then there was silence. She saw dust particles filtering in a shaft of late evening sun, spotlighting a strip across the cavern-floor.

New noises now, as a huge piece of wood – in fact a tree trunk – was pushed head-first into the crack from above. Then came a loud roar – a roar she recognised. The tree was wrenched to the side like a lever and, with more crashing rock-fall, the crack widened.

Widened enough that an enormous hand, followed by a long arm, thick with muscle, could reach into the cave and feel its way across the floor.

The hand was gently, blindly searching the cave, feeling its way over stones like a starfish on the sea floor.

It inched towards her. The arm was straining, at the end

of its range, the fingertips reaching out . . . and then it moved on, moved away, along the wall.

Come back! Find me! She struggled to move her wings, her claws, so that she could reach towards the hand, but she was dead on her feet and slumped back down. Nothing was obeying her. Nothing . . . except her voice. Her beak opened, and out came a weak but clear 'Ke-wick!'

The hand stopped dead in its tracks. It backtracked gently, until the tip of one of its huge fingers touched the feathers of her wing. Then swiftly and softly, stretching to reach her, it gathered her up and rolled her into its palm. Rose closed her eyes and lay still as the hand carefully curled its fingers around her. Now she was completely enclosed in its warm, rough grip.

Then she felt herself swiftly lifted up through the cave. The light around her grew and she could feel the cool freshness of the open air of the wood.

But she was not safe yet. Peeping through giant fingers she saw something dark seeping around the corner from the cave beyond the cave, rolling out like a wave and spreading across the floor beneath, then rising up after them like a black fountain.

She closed her eyes as the giant pulled his arm free of the fissure and scrambled to his feet. Now he was up and running, running through the wood. Rose swayed as his arm moved up and down rhythmically. She heard his steady tread and the crunch and smash of vegetation below; sensed the great length of his stride.

Trees whipped past his closed fists, leaves whistling about

Rose's head. She could not make out where they were heading, or what, exactly, they were running from.

All she knew now was that the giant had rescued her, was keeping her safe, would not let her go.

And then, suddenly, she heard a voice – Mum's voice – screaming out, 'ROSE! ROSE!' and the giant seemed to trip, falling forward, hard, and releasing his grip on her. She was thrown through the air and landed, face first, on a carpet of soft, dead leaves. Then she passed out again.

'Rose! Rose, love, can you hear me?' Mum's voice was a shriek of anxiety in her ear, cutting through her head in a zig-zag of pain, leaving a dull ache behind.

She was lying face-down on the floor of the wood, and she was Rose, the girl, again. Mum was kneeling beside her and her arms were wrapped tightly around her. Rose's back hurt terribly and her limbs felt weak and useless. She managed to turn her head and open her eyes.

'Oh, thank God. Thank you, God.' Mum was sobbing now, rocking Rose up and down as she did so.

'It's OK, Mum,' whispered Rose, faintly. 'I'm OK.'

Mum helped Rose to sit up. 'I'm here now, love,' she said. 'I can see you've hurt your back. Don't worry. I'm going to get you home.'

Together, with Mum's arm around her, they managed to stagger along the path through the darkening wood, back to the house.

6

It was the next morning. The sun shone warm and bright behind the thin curtains of Rose's bedroom, and she could hear the twittering conversation of swallows, sitting on the telephone wire outside. She was lying on her back. And there was something between her back and the bedclothes. She reached round, awkwardly, with her hand, and felt bandages.

Her back stung a little, but not too badly. Not as badly as it had. She stretched her legs, testing them. They felt OK. A little tired, but OK. And her arms were a bit sore, as if she'd wrenched them, somehow.

Suddenly she sat bolt upright. What was the time?

Her mobile was sitting on her bedside table. 9.15.

Nine fifteen? She was supposed to be in school! She threw off the duvet and was about to leap from the bed when there was a soft knock on the door, and Mum came in.

'Hello, Rosie love,' said Mum. Then, as if unable to stop herself, she rushed to the bed, pulled the duvet back over Rose and sat down on it, gripping Rose's hands in hers. 'Now,' she said firmly, gently moving Rose's hands as she spoke, to emphasise her words. 'You're not going to school today. I've had a word with Miss Evans and told her you were upset, and fell over in the wood and hurt your back.'

Mum fixed Rose with anxious eyes. 'You're going to have a rest today, love, and I'm going to be here with you.'

'But what about the bakery?' Mum ran the bakery in the village.

'Delyth is managing the bakery today. It's all sorted out.'

Delyth was the lady who helped Mum at busy times.

Rose pulled her hands from Mum's and flopped back against the pillow, breathing out a sigh of relief.

Then memories of last night began to creep into her mind, like snatches of a long nightmare.

'How did you find me?' she asked Mum.

To Rose's horror, she saw Mum's face twist with pain.

'Sorry,' said Rose.

'Sorry? Why are you sorry, love?'

'I don't know. I'm always making you upset.'

'No! No, Rosie, you're not. Listen. When you ran off last night, I thought to myself, I'll leave her to it for a bit. You'd had a terrible shock, and I was very upset too – the thought of what's going to happen to the wood . . .'

For a moment, Rose was confused. What was Mum on about? Then she remembered, with another pain-filled jolt. The wood was going to be sold and an abattoir built.

Mum continued, 'I thought, I'll let her cool down, blow off steam. Then time just . . . went by. I sat at the kitchen table, and stared into space, mostly. I couldn't think straight, I felt so jumpy and exhausted. And then I heard your phone ping from your bedroom – a text – and I came to with a start, because it was nine o'clock, and you'd been gone for nearly four hours!

'I went rushing out into the wood.

'It was still light outside, but under the trees it was very dim, very shadowy. I ran through them, calling out to you. I came out in the clearing – and it was empty. Just the rocky lump in the middle. I sat there for a bit, trying to decide what to do. Then I thought, I'll call Ianto's parents, see if you were there. But stupid me, I'd left my mobile at home. So I couldn't.

'The wood was very still, very silent. Then, suddenly, the most almighty row. Crashing and thumping and screaming, like rocks being split, rocks being shifted, coming from the far edge of the wood, past the stream. It had to be quarrymen, working – but how? No one quarries in the wood. And at that time of night? Without lights? Then came a terrible roaring – must have been machinery, but it sounded like an animal – a huge animal in pain.

'Awful. I was properly frightened now. Were you anywhere near that noise? Were you in danger? So I went running towards the sound. But this time, I lost my sense of direction. I didn't know where I was going any more, in the darkness. And I began to see things. I saw shadowy things, shapes flitting between trees.

'But I kept going. And then the crashing stopped. And there was another sound – the sound of something huge, thundering through the wood – moving towards me, moving really fast. Like, like an elephant stampeding, smashing through the trees. And it was heading for me. And I took to my heels again, running, running to save myself—'

Mum broke off with a sob and covered her face with her hands. Rose leaned forward and put her arms gently around her. Poor Mum.

'Thanks, love,' said Mum, wiping her eyes and managing a smile.

'Next thing I knew I'd tripped – landed face down in the leaves. And then, behind me, a huge thump. Then silence. I lay there, too scared to move. Was the thing waiting to pounce? But nothing happened. So I got up, slowly. And I looked behind me – and there you were. Lying on your front, just a few yards away. You had those awful scratches down your back . . .'

Until now, Rose had been so absorbed in Mum's story that she hadn't thought ahead to what she was going to tell her. Because she knew, without question, that she couldn't tell Mum the truth about last night. The horror of it would be too much for her.

Mum was waiting for Rose to speak. What would she say? She didn't want to tell her a pack of lies.

'Well, I – I heard the same noises, Mum. And I was trying to get away. I think something scratched my back, and then I fell over . . . but I'm OK. I'm absolutely fine.'

It sounded rubbish. Would it do? Mum was watching her, carefully, scanning her face with anxious eyes.

A moment later, it was as if Mum had made up her mind. 'You're here now,' she said, leaning forward to hug her again, tightly. 'And you're all right. The cuts on your back aren't serious. I should think you'll be up and about by this afternoon – I know there's no stopping you!

'I think I let my nerves get the better of me, last night. Woods are always a bit spooky after dark. And we'd had such a shock yesterday, hadn't we?'

Apparently, it would do.

Mum stood up.

Rose surprised herself with what popped out of her mouth next. 'I really wish Dad was here.'

Mum stopped dead in her tracks, then turned back to her. 'So do I, love.'

Neither of them seemed able to say any more, and Rose felt suddenly tired out. Mum left the room, closing the door softly behind her.

Rose fell into a dreamless doze and woke again just before lunchtime. It was hard to believe, at this comfortable moment, what she had been through the night before. She remembered, suddenly, that Mum had mentioned a text. Checking her phone, she saw that it was from Ianto.

I'm really sorry – I didn't know. Talk to you tomorrow.

For a moment she was confused. Why was he sorry, and what didn't he know? The tunnel, the mole, the cave and the giant flitted through her mind.

Then she understood – he was talking about the wood. It was his great uncle, Mr Williams, that had sold it. So he felt sorry. And he hadn't known about it until last night, just like them.

She began to text back, then stopped. What would she tell Ianto? Could she tell him what had happened last night? She felt she would burst if she didn't tell someone. And he was her best friend – who else could she tell? But . . . what if he didn't believe her? That thought was almost too awful to bear.

She couldn't tell him by text, whatever. So, for now, she kept it brief.

Thanks, Ianto. Not feeling well, so at home today. See you tomorrow.

A text pinged back almost immediately.

Look after yourself. 😊

* * *

That evening, as Mum had predicted, Rose was out of bed and making plans. Her back hardly hurt at all now, and when she peeled back Mum's dressing and looked at it in the mirror, she could see that long, thick scabs had formed. She reached around and touched one, gently. It fell away to reveal new, pink skin beneath. She had never seen cuts heal so quickly.

Good. Because she had made up her mind. She was going to stop the building of the abattoir.

As far as she could gather from the internet, you couldn't stop people selling their land. But you could oppose planning applications for new buildings. And this company, the company who were buying the wood from Mr Williams, were going to have to apply for planning permission to build their abattoir.

She was going to oppose it. And she wasn't going to involve Mum, because she knew that Mum wouldn't want to upset Mr Williams. She couldn't tell Ianto, either, because Mr Williams was his great uncle.

Rose felt herself stumble when she thought about Mr Williams – pictured his anxious face, imagined him sitting, as he often did on summer evenings, outside his house, taking the air with Del at his feet. Who was she to muck up his plans?

But then she closed her eyes and clenched her fists. One step at a time, she thought. First I'll oppose the planning application, then I'll sort out Mr Williams's money. I know I can do both . . . somehow or other.

But the whys and wherefores of opposing planning applications were daunting and difficult. Looking at the council's website was starting to make her head spin. It was hard to understand exactly what she needed to do, and who she needed to approach. And would a twelve-year-old be allowed to do it at all?

She was on her own with it – just as she was on her own with the knowledge that she had been an owl, twice; had been trapped in a cave, had almost died there . . .

Then she heard a voice in her mind. '*A problem shared is a problem halved.*'

Miss Evans. Her form teacher. Lovely Miss Evans had said this at the start of the term. Had placed her warm, plump hand on Rose's shoulder, one day after school. Had asked her, '*Wyt ti'n iawn, bach?* Are you all right, bach?'

Rose had been shocked, as she always was, when people asked her if she was all right. Was there something wrong in her face that gave her away? Of course she was all right. Not all right like before Dad died, but all right, as in existing – doing everything she had to do.

She'd turned to Miss Evans and tried to smile, but her eyes had felt hard and glassy. '*Iawn, dw i'n iawn,*' she'd replied. 'I'm fine.' And she'd hitched up her backpack and turned to run from the emptying classroom.

As she rushed out through the door, she heard Miss Evans's kind voice behind her calling, 'Remember, Rose – a problem shared is a problem halved.'

Miss Evans would help her do this.

7

Miss Evans took in a sharp breath. '*Jiw, jiw,*' she gasped, shaking her head, her large, brown eyes wide with shock. '*Dw i ffaelu credu fe!* My goodness. I can't believe it! Mr Williams, selling the wood – and an *abattoir* in its place? Well. I know we need jobs round here . . . but, *jiw, jiw!*'

Rose had cornered Miss Evans the next morning after registration, while the rest of the class trooped off to lessons. She hadn't had a chance to talk to Ianto yet, though he'd waved to her across the form room and mouthed 'You OK?'

Then he'd hesitated at the door, waiting for her, but when he saw her head purposefully towards Miss Evans he'd joined the rest and drifted off to his first lesson.

Now Miss Evans was perching against her desk, plump hands clasped before her, listening carefully while Rose went on to explain that she wanted to oppose the planning application, and would Miss Evans, please, be able to help.

When she'd finished, Miss Evans nodded immediately. 'Of course,' she said, matter of factly. 'This is an excellent opportunity for you to learn about civic responsibility and to exercise your democratic rights – to say nothing of trying to preserve an important piece of woodland. Now then. I'll meet you after school in the computer room, and we'll see what we can do together, all right?'

Rose was speechless with appreciation and thanks. She'd

been prepared for Miss Evans to tell her that it was none of her business, that an abattoir was a necessary thing, everyone had to eat meat, and so on. But Miss Evans had been nothing but supportive and lovely.

She found it hard to concentrate on lessons for the rest of the day, her mind constantly straying to the meeting with Miss Evans, and all they needed to do. Would they have enough time, enough information to make the objection? Had they already missed their chance? Rose didn't know how advanced the planning application was. Perhaps it was all done and dusted already, and the council had approved everything . . .

Lunchtime, and the canteen buzzed and clattered with conversation and cutlery. Rose sat with a tableful of girls from her class, listening while they chattered happily. Luckily, they were used to Rose being quiet these days.

'Hey!' Ianto appeared at the end of the table, pulling up a chair with a scrape.

The girls' conversation came to an abrupt halt. Four pairs of wide eyes watched with fascination as he sat down next to Rose.

'Don't mind me, girls,' called Ianto, with a grin. 'You carry on.'

They giggled and huddled together to resume their gossip, more quietly this time.

'How are you?' Ianto asked Rose in a low voice, serious now.

'Oh, yeah . . . fine – now,' said Rose. So much to tell Ianto! But she didn't know where to start. Could she tell him about the experience underground? About being an owl?

'Look, I'm so sorry about the wood,' Ianto said, saving her from deciding. 'You must have been really upset – I mean, I'm upset, too, but I think you care about that place even more than me, and of course you and your mam will be looking out over the . . . building.'

Ianto didn't want to say the word 'abattoir'. Rose didn't blame him.

'I don't know what to do,' he went on, ruffling his hair in distress. 'Mam and Dad have talked to Uncle Thomas and offered to help him with money – but he won't accept anything. Mamgu was furious when she heard . . .'

Mamgu, Ianto's gran, was *furious*? Since Ianto's grandfather had died, she'd lived with Ianto and his family. She was such a gentle, self-contained person that Rose found it impossible to imagine her being furious. But perhaps she had loved playing in the wood herself, when she was a child. After all, she was Mr Williams's sister, and had grown up in the house where he now lived.

'She kept saying *Doesn't he know what will happen? Doesn't he remember*? And the next thing we knew she'd grabbed her coat and was out the front door. We guessed she was heading up there to speak to him.

'When she came back a couple of hours later, she went straight to her room. I didn't even see her at breakfast this morning. It's so unlike her . . .' Ianto trailed off, and his eyes fell to the floor.

Head down, he said something so quietly that Rose could hardly hear him:

'I've got something else to tell you, too.'

Rose waited, but Ianto didn't enlarge. 'What?' she asked, quietly. *Please, please don't tell me anything else that's awful, Ianto . . .*

'Before I tell you,' Ianto raised his eyes to hers, 'will you look at something for me?'

He bent to fumble in his backpack and pulled out an opaque plastic file. Glancing at the other girls to make sure they weren't watching, he handed it to her, under the table.

'Read it when you get home,' he said. 'Please don't look at it till then. Then phone me, and tell me what you think.'

Then Ianto stood up abruptly, pushing back his chair with a clatter. The girls stopped talking and looked up.

'Catch you later, ladies,' Ianto said to them, tipping his fingers to his head in a corny salute.

But as he turned to leave he caught Rose's eye and smiled nervously and, to her surprise, he seemed . . . vulnerable, exposed.

Not like Ianto.

She slipped the file into her own backpack and turned back to her friends, though she was no longer able to concentrate on a word they said.

When school had finished, Rose fought her way through a tide of fellow pupils to get to the computer room.

When she reached it, she sat for a moment, appreciating the gathering quiet. A few stragglers in the corridor, a few calls and running feet, a last, banging door, and then . . . silence.

Miss Evans appeared in the doorway, big bag over her

shoulder and a steaming mug in each hand.

'*Dyna ni!* There we are – the end of another day,' she said, bustling forwards before passing Rose the mugs and settling gracefully in the chair next to her.

Hot chocolate! Rose was not expecting this treat. She sipped gratefully, enjoying the warmth and sweetness. '*Diolch*. Thank you,' she said. She put as much into the word as she could, because she was saying thanks for much more than just the hot chocolate. Miss Evans was helping her in her spare time. Helping her do something very important.

'Now then, Rose fach,' said Miss Evans, taking a quick sip of her coffee. 'You want to oppose the planning application for the construction of an abattoir on the site of the wood – yes?'

Rose looked at her and nodded emphatically. Yes.

'Well, I'm here to support you, but I'd like you to do as much as you can yourself – is that clear? I know you're a very capable person, so I have a hundred per cent confidence in your ability to do this. Now. How are you going to start?'

'By looking at the council website,' answered Rose, obediently.

'Good. Go for it,' said Miss Evans, sitting back with a smile.

Rose found the website and clicked on 'Planning Applications'. She hadn't got this far last night. She hadn't looked at the actual, actual proposal. It had been too scary.

By entering her own postcode, it was suddenly before her.

Application number: D4/27983
Site Address: Plot adjacent to Fferm Bigfelen, Brynafon.
Description of Proposal: Site preparation works for abattoir

complex, involving re-grading of site, road construction, drainage, street lighting and services, followed by construction of process and production areas, chillers, staff amenities, office, docking bays, package and storage areas and car park.

The words – so sure, so definite, as if the whole thing had already been decided – made her feel unsteady, as if a rug had been pulled from under her feet.

Miss Evans was silent beside her. Suddenly, an urge to run from the room overcame Rose. She couldn't do this, all by herself – without Dad . . .

To her horror, the big, dark hole inside her began to open, and she began to teeter once more at its edge.

'Uh . . .' she mouthed, and turned, wide-eyed, to Miss Evans.

Miss Evans had been sipping her coffee. When she saw Rose's face, she put the mug down.

'What does it say, bach?' she asked, calmly. 'Read it out to me.'

So Rose did. And reading to Miss Evans, who was looking at her attentively, helped to still the beating of her heart, to slow her breathing. She took a step back from the edge. It really was just words, after all.

'OK,' said Miss Evans, slowly. 'That's what this company, the abattoir company, are proposing to do. And that's what the council planning department are going to consider. They will decide whether or not it will happen. Now what do we need to do?'

Rose liked the 'we'. 'We need to oppose it,' she answered, 'to stop it happening.' She cleared her throat and continued, gaining confidence, 'I need to email the planning officer in charge of the application.' She had found this out last night.

Miss Evans nodded. 'There we are. And do you think you might need to check when the council want to receive emails or letters opposing permission?'

'Yes,' Rose said, a little uncertainly. 'I know they give the public three weeks to oppose planning applications,' she went on. But when were those three weeks? There was nothing to tell her on this page. Then she realised she could click on the number. She did so, and more details came up.

She took a deep breath and scanned the page, her eyes slipping about the screen in anxiety. She hated all this – at the edge of panic, befuddled by procedures, unable to think straight . . .

Then she saw the words 'Consultation Period'. Next to them were two dates. One from four weeks ago and one from last week. Her mind felt dull, unfocused. Something was wrong here. But the dates were as clear as day.

They had missed the three-week opportunity to oppose planning permission.

It was all over.

She turned slowly to Miss Evans. 'What's the matter?' she asked, gently.

Wordlessly, Rose turned the laptop towards her and pointed at the screen.

Miss Evans frowned as she read the dates. 'OK . . .' she said thoughtfully. 'Rose, your mam should have received a letter from the council, telling her about the planning application and the consultation period. Do you know if she did?'

Rose shook her head in despair. She pictured the hall at home, and the pile of letters that littered the little shelf beneath the hooks where they hung their coats. When Mum didn't like the look of a letter, or when she didn't know who it was from, she left it, unopened, in that pile. That's where the letter from the council would be.

She didn't want to tell Miss Evans this. But Miss Evans was busy scrolling down the screen, scanning further details. Rose didn't have the heart to look any more. She stared down at her feet, tears forming in her eyes, falling to splash on to the floor . . .

'Right,' said Miss Evans, slowly. Then 'Aha!'

Rose looked up, quickly wiping her eyes on her shirt sleeve. Miss Evans was looking at her with a sudden sparkle in her eyes. 'Well. We've had the bad news – we've missed the consultation period by a week. But you want the good news?'

'Oh. Um, yes,' sniffed Rose. What could possibly be good news now?

'*Two* pieces of good news, actually – touch wood,' said Miss Evans, reaching around for something wooden, then tapping her own head. She seemed to be enjoying herself now. 'The first good news is that there's going to be a meeting, a meeting for the planning application to be considered by a committee of elected councillors. Sometimes members of the public are allowed to go to these meetings to make their case against proposals.'

Rose's head was swimming. It was really awful, swinging from despair to hope like this. Plus, was Miss Evans really expecting her to stand up in a meeting, in front of a committee of council grown-ups, and tell them that they shouldn't allow the abattoir to be built?

'And the second is that the planning officer handling the case is a friend of mine. Siân. She's lovely. Let's see if we can speak to her now.' Miss Evans was already fishing in her bag for her mobile.

She put the phone to her ear.

'Siân? *Shw mae. Sut wyt ti?* Hello – how are you?'

A pause, while Miss Evans smiled and listened.

'Yes, fine, fine . . . No, no – still single!' Miss Evans glanced at Rose and grinned. 'How's your mam?' she went on, changing the subject.

A pause, while Miss Evans pulled sympathetic faces. 'Oh, poor her. So hard, when you're so far away. Do give her my best wishes.'

Another pause, while Miss Evans nodded kindly. Then she got down to business. 'Now then, Siân – I have a pupil with me here.'

Pause, as Siân said something.

'Yes, one of my very brightest . . .' Miss Evans winked at Rose, who couldn't help grinning with pride, despite the nerves that were gnawing at her stomach.

'Now she'd like to come to one of your planning consideration meetings, Siân, to oppose a planning proposal. Case number D4/27983. Do you think you could arrange that?'

Rose gulped. It was all happening so fast . . .

Miss Evans was listening again, and nodding.

'Three minutes? Yes, that should be fine. When's the meeting?'

Miss Evans watched Rose with steady eyes as she listened to the answer.

'OK, I think we can manage that.' She smiled at Rose. 'Lovely, Siân. Thanks ever so much. See you soon, I hope! Ta-ra, ta-ra.'

Miss Evans put her phone back in her bag. Straightening up, she said, 'Well. That's all arranged, Rose. Siân is expecting you at the Town Hall reception on Friday at three thirty . . .'

Friday? Friday was two days away!

But Miss Evans was still talking enthusiastically. 'It really couldn't be better timing – Friday being the last day of term, and everyone having the afternoon off! Now the committee will give you three minutes to make a presentation to them, Rose. Do you think you can do that?'

8

That evening, after supper with Mum, Rose retreated to her bedroom, closing the door behind her then sinking on to her bed with a long sigh. What a day. Her head was still reeling with the idea of the presentation to the council committee. She needed to think about it, to prepare something – but . . . not yet. She didn't have the energy tonight. And she had to do something else first.

Her heart beat suddenly fast as she pulled Ianto's plastic folder, the kind with a little popper on the front, from her backpack. She took a deep breath, trying to still her heart. Why was she so anxious? It was only a few sheets of paper – as far as she could tell. She popped it open, and pulled out the contents.

A handful of A4 pages, each one filled with colour. Ianto's artwork – she would've recognised it anywhere. He had always been great at art. For her sixth birthday, he had made her a card himself, with a beautiful owl on the front. And that had continued, so that on every birthday since – all six of them – he'd made her a special card with a different animal each time – all animals that she loved; all of them from the wood.

She kept these cards in the little wooden box with her other precious things – mostly cards and notes from Dad and old photos of him, her and Mum.

She saw at once that there was not just one picture on the pages, but several, each within its own frame. It was a comic strip, or a graphic novel, told in Welsh. The title, hand drawn, was *Y Cawr* – The Giant.

Then she started to read and she entered another world – a world that was by now familiar.

Y Cawr – The Giant

Pushing up from below, it shifts vast rocKs
CRACK
As if they are made of cardboard.
Imprisoned for centuries, cramped, confined...
Tonight, the giant bursts free of his shacKles.
AAARGH!

Daylight breaks, and the giant sleeps again ...

Until...

Ke-wick.
He is called once more.

A creature of air, she is trapped underground, where her life is ebbing away...

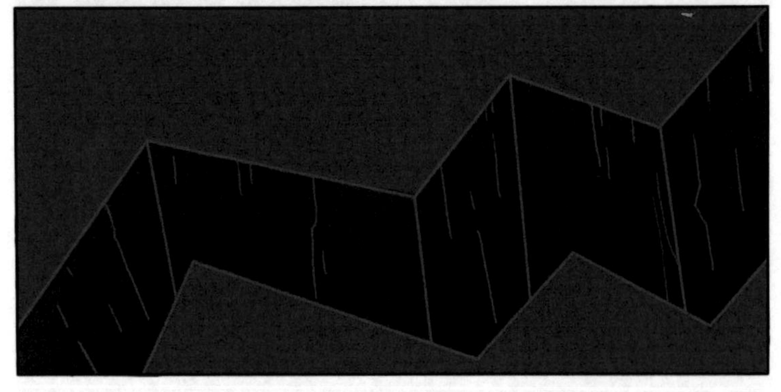

Time is running out...

But he cannot reach her. Until...

Ke-wick!

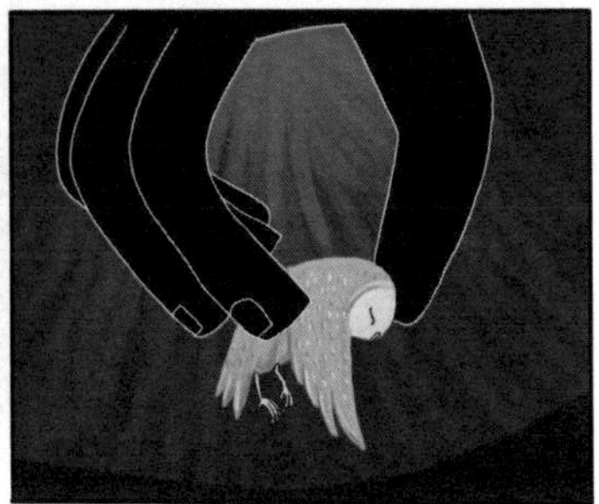

Just in time...

Because other forces are stirring below.
Now he must run with her to safety

but their enemies are closing fast

The giant trips...

And that was it.

Rose was stunned.

So Ianto *knew*? He knew what had happened to her? Alongside her astonishment came another feeling – relief. Relief that she didn't have to tell him about it herself, and risk him not believing her.

But she had to find out how he knew. She put the pages carefully back in the folder and phoned him.

'Ianto?' said Rose.

'What did you think?' he asked, immediately. His voice sounded tight, nervous. As if he'd been waiting all evening for her phone call.

'I think it's brilliant, Ianto. It's like a work of art, and the words are fantastic too. You got everything just right. But – but, Ianto, how did you know?'

Ianto was silent for a moment. Then he said, 'How did I know . . . what?'

Now Rose felt unsure. She wished he was here, so she could see his face and read it, along with his words.

She was going to have to spell it out.

'How did you know about the owl and the giant?'

'Rose,' Ianto said, in a low voice, as if he were afraid that other people might be listening. He hardly ever called her by her name. And when he did, she knew he was being deadly serious. She held her breath as he went on, 'I know about the owl and the giant because,' he swallowed and carried on in a whisper, 'because I *am* the giant.'

Rose's mind spun. Of course. Of course he was the giant!

It was Ianto who'd burst up from the rocks in the clearing, Ianto who'd saved her life!

'And I'm the owl,' she said, simply.

Rose heard Ianto take a deep breath in.

'Yeah,' he said after a bit. 'Yes. I can see that now.'

'You know, Ianto, it's funny,' went on Rose. 'Because I didn't know you were the giant, but now you've told me, I'm not at all surprised. Like I knew, and I didn't know, all at the same time. Does that make any sense?'

'No, none at all,' said Ianto, affectionately. They both laughed.

'I was really nervous about telling you,' he continued. 'But then, last night, when I got home from school – I just felt I had to put it all down on paper. And at first, I didn't think I was going to show it to you, but then it seemed like a good way to tell you. A safe way – because if you'd thought it was rubbish—'

'As if I would ever think it was rubbish!'

'Well, you know, if you'd not believed it, I could've said "Oh, it was just a story idea I had." And then I found myself working on it – working and working, really late, until it was finished. But actually, it's not finished, is it? It kind of ends on a cliff-hanger.'

'Yes,' said Rose, thoughtfully. 'I've got a feeling there's more to it. A lot more to come.'

'Me too,' said Ianto.

A pause, and Rose's mind went to the dark stuff that made up the mole, and the bats. A lot more to come . . .

'So how come you were underground?' asked Ianto.

Rose took a deep breath in and told him what had happened after she'd run from the house. But she left out the mole's words about the king and the way she'd thought it meant Dad. It felt private; it felt sad – and she'd got it all wrong, anyway.

When she'd finished, Ianto let out a breath, as if he'd been holding it.

'You went through all that,' he said.

'Yes,' said Rose, hardly able to believe it herself. 'But thanks to you, I'm OK. We're both OK. Aren't we?'

'Yes. We are – we will be.'

At that moment there was a soft knock. Mum. She didn't open the door, but spoke through it, quietly.

'Rosie? Put away your phone now, love. It's nearly ten. School tomorrow.'

'Yes, Mum,' she called. 'Night!'

'Good night, love,' replied Mum, and Rose heard her flip-flops flipping into her own bedroom.

'Better go now,' she said to Ianto. 'Good night.'

'See you tomorrow,' said Ianto. 'And sleep well.'

She ended the call, switched off the light and lay there, looking up into the darkness.

Ianto was the giant! The thought filled her heart with warmth.

Rose closed her eyes and drifted off to sleep.

9

She awoke with a jump, her eyes open wide. She could see straight through the darkness, see with brilliant precision the four walls of her bedroom and all the familiar objects in it – her old soft toys, the school uniform draped over a chair, the books strewn across her desk. Everything looked a little strange, a little alien.

Flapping powerfully, awkwardly, she half flew, half scrambled to the window and, after a brief battle with the curtains, got behind them and found the inch-wide gap between the frame and the window. She struggled, using claws and wings to ease the window wide, then, flapping hard to get started, she soared up and out, into the night.

Now she was above the wood, wings beating steadily – gliding, then beating, gliding, then beating.

Over the wood, and up the mountainside. Sheep, asleep, huddled beneath her along hedgerows, snagging their wool. She went winging beyond them, over Mr Williams's moonlit house, catching a glimpse down his chimney and, in the farmyard, she saw Del the sheepdog, standing outside the crate where she slept, looking up into the sky – straight at her.

But Rose had already left the farmhouse behind, flying on steady wingbeats. And suddenly she knew why she was here, what she must do. For in front of her on the track to the top of the mountain was the giant. Ianto. He was striding past the ruins of an old, old house that lay encircled by trees, crumbling next to the track. He loomed over the mass of stones then passed them, heading up the mountain with resolute steps. The ground beneath his huge boots resonated with great thumps as he pounded the track, dislodging stones which skittled down behind him. It was as if he was following instructions, obeying something.

Something was wrong. She knew it. Rose beat her wings to reach him, and called out 'Ke-wick!'

The giant paused and turned, so that she saw his large, familiar face. On it was a look of surprise – a little frown. Then his head glanced forward again. And as it did, she saw what was with him.

A tawny owl, just like her.

This owl was hovering urgently in front of him. The giant had stopped dead, his back to Rose, who flapped towards him as fast as she could. He was watching the other owl, his head held very still, and then he started up again as it circled his head and flew onwards. He was following it, stomping ahead towards the very top of the mountain, where the sheared-off edge fell away for metres and metres in a deep, stony drop.

He's obeying the owl, thought Rose, panic growing inside her.

As he thundered onwards the owl circled again, high above him now, climbing higher and still higher in the night sky, until it was just a speck amongst the stars. Then it was gone altogether. Could an owl really fly so high? Rose was too intent on reaching Ianto to watch it further, flying breathlessly towards him. He was now almost at the great, flat stone near the top of the mountain.

'Ke-wick!' she called again, fear filling her.

This time he did not turn, did not waver in his tracks. Now he was striding over the stone, and she was right behind him, calling, calling—

Wham – Rose's cry was severed in mid-air as she was hit with malevolent force by a sledgehammer from the sky. Dislodged from flight, flung down and grounded, two powerful clawed feet hooked into her back and forced her, face-down, into the heather, where she struggled for breath, nauseous.

She sucked in air, then, quick as a flash she used her own claws, her own wings to struggle free – to turn on the ground and face this owl with a scream of rage. Feathers flew as the owl flapped apart from her, and it was screaming now too. Then it came on again, another dive at her, feet first, throwing its body forward, claws reaching out. Beak open, eyes wide – dead eyes.

She would not let it win again. Flapping desperately, she lifted from the ground, her body shocked and shaky. And just in time, the owl missed her by millimetres and tumbled feet-first into a clump of heather.

Now Rose was higher than the false owl, which was already disentangling itself and flapping madly to rise again, turning its head to locate her. She knew she must take this advantage. She must reach Ianto. She swivelled her head to see him stalled, standing at the very edge of the cliff, stars shining through the blackness beyond him.

He was watching the two owls with a confused frown. He took a step forward, away from the edge, towards her.

'Ke-wick!' she called and, forgetting the other owl,

wheeled in the sky to wing to him. If only she could speak to him in a way he could understand! The other owl was an imposter, wanted to hurt him . . . he must come away from the edge.

But the dead-eyed owl had other ideas. Rose felt a whoosh of displaced air as it sped past her, sped past the giant and rose high in the air to hover way above the cliff edge. She could see its large, dark eyes pinning her, and the power in its blunt wings – flapping forward in careful, swift motions.

With a scream of fury, Rose flew upwards at a steep angle and launched herself at it, claws outstretched. The owl responded in a flash, falling backwards, extending its own claws to lock with hers. The impact jarred through her body, then the two of them were tumbling through the air, the owl gripping her feet with strong, sharp talons that dug into her legs and toes like a metal trap.

They spun out over the panoply of bog and fields beyond the mountain, all lit with the silvery light of the moon. Rose saw all of this – sky above, ground below – in turn as she spun dizzily, locked with the other owl in an out-of-control spiral, heading like a rock to the stones at the base of the mountain.

Impossible to break away when she was gripped so hard – impossible to wrench her body forwards to attack with her beak, though she was trying with all her might, flapping desperately.

They plummeted down towards the mountain edge where the giant was standing, looking up at them, an expression of horror on his face.

The next moment they were level with him, and he reached out to them with both hands, trying to catch them – to pull them apart, perhaps – but his fingers closed on air – Rose's head tingling as his skin brushed her feathers – and then, with a great roar, he overbalanced and fell, tumbling over the edge of the mountain past the two owls, his huge body thumping violently against the sheer cliff, dislodging stones and rocks in a great avalanche, arms and legs splaying out until the whole deadly spectacle ceased at the base of the mountain with a great and terrible *crack*.

Now the false owl was loosening its grip. Sensing weakness, Rose lunged forward to sink her beak, viciously, into the owl's head. But her beak closed on . . . nothing. The owl collapsed into a mass of black particles as Rose backed off, her wings flapping forwards in shock and disgust. The turbulence of her beating wings made the owl-shaped cloud break up like smoke dispersed by a fan, spreading around her in a dark mist. Then it re-formed into a ball of black, seething matter which extended into a long ribbon and streamed away in the direction of the wood.

Leaving Rose, hovering, just above the base of the mountain. Just above the giant – Ianto – who was lying sprawled on the ground, face down, his head against a huge rock.

Then Rose saw a dark liquid spreading insidiously, beginning to drip over the edges of the rock.

10

Filled with horror, Rose dropped and landed on the ground next to the giant. The sheer cliff of the mountain towered over the two of them like a skyscraper. There was a sudden quiet in the air, a hush.

He lay motionless on his front, one arm beneath his body, the other wrenched around so that his great hand was facing upwards. His legs stretched out behind him, one foot twisted strangely. She could not see his face. His shaggy hair hung forward to hide it and the stone – the stone that was running with his blood.

She hopped up on to his open palm. His fingers were motionless, half curled. *He can't be dead, he can't be dead!* He couldn't be dead, because she would not survive, if he was.

Part of her mind wondered, as it had before, whether Ianto would die as a human, if he died as a giant. As the thought came, she swayed, unsteady, in his palm. She could not go there. She must pull herself back – pull Ianto back, too.

Hopping on to one of his fingertips, she launched for the edge of the rock, her clawed feet sinking into a slick of sticky, warm blood. Stepping closer to him, she nuzzled her head against his shaggy hair, which was soft and thick against her feathers. She turned her head minutely so that her ear was against the side of his face and listened intently.

A low, shallow vibration. Pause. Then another. Pause. Breath coming in, breath going out – very slight, very weak. But he was still alive.

She must get help. Taking off, she hovered for a moment in the air above Ianto, looking down at his poor, splayed-out body, then she winged away – beating, gliding, beating, gliding, as fast as she could around the mountain, and on, over the bog, past her own house, down the track and into the village.

Soon she was circling Ianto's house in big, looping glides. Round the back. There was his bedroom window – dark, with curtains drawn. Another window, next to it, was his sister, Cerys's, bedroom. Round the front. His mam and dad's bedroom window upstairs – bigger than the others. And next to it the smallest window, the little room that Ianto's baby sister slept in. Downstairs, on the ground floor, was Mamgu's window – his gran. Like Ianto's, all the windows had their curtains drawn, and all were unlit.

Rose flew up and landed, feet outstretched and with a small thump, on the ridge of Ianto's roof.

And then she began to screech and call for all she was worth.

Despite the racket she was making, her keen ears soon picked up sounds from below her, from within the building. The light thumping of feet down stairs, sleepy voices. Soon the front door opened and light from the hall poured out in front of her on to the path. Still calling wildly, she flapped from the roof to land on the arching arm of the streetlight in front of the house.

Ianto's dad was standing on the path in red pyjamas. His bare feet were long, white and uncomfortable-looking on the rough surface of the paving slabs.

He looked up at her, squinting against the glow of the streetlight. Then the light snapped on behind their bedroom curtain and, soon after, Ianto's mam opened the front door and stood just inside, wrapped in a fluffy, purple dressing gown.

Ianto's mam and dad were talking now – in loud whispers, so as not to wake the neighbours.

'*Beth sy'n bod arno fe?* What's wrong with it? Is it injured?'

'It looks OK.'

'Then why's it making so much noise? The whole estate will be awake in a minute!'

Rose was getting tired now. She couldn't keep the screeching up. Ending with a loud *ke-wick*, she pushed off from the streetlight and flew down to circle, swooping above Ianto's dad's head, making him duck suddenly, shocked. Ianto's mam gave a little cry, eyes wide above the hand that had risen to cover her mouth. Then came more sounds from within the house and the patter of feet down stairs.

Cerys, Ianto's seven-year-old sister, burst past her mam and out on to the path. She was wearing red pyjamas too. Standing next to her dad, fairly squirming with excitement, she began a barrage of questions in a loud voice.

'*Beth sy'n bod?* What's happening? What was making that noise?'

Then, 'Oh, look, Dadi! It's an owl! An owl! Look! Look, Mami!' Cerys was jumping up and down in excitement and pointing, her small finger following Rose.

'Yes, darling, it's an owl. Shush now – we don't want to wake the neighbours.'

'What's it doing? Why is it flying round and round?' she asked, doing her best to talk quietly now. It was obviously hard for her.

Now Rose gave a final swoop and, screeching meaningfully, turned her back on them and winged away, off in the direction of the mountain. This was the point where, according to films and books, the humans would follow her to find and help the injured person.

But it wasn't working like that here. They weren't following her. They were heading back indoors – the adults, at any rate.

'OK, show's over now,' she heard Ianto's dad tell Cerys.

Then came another sound from within – a high cry. It was Siriol, Ianto's littlest sister. She must have woken up, and found herself alone. Rose swivelled her head to see that Ianto's mam had gone inside, and that Ianto's dad was following her. But Cerys stayed, resolute, on the path, looking up at her in wonder.

'It's stopped! In the air! It's turned around and it's hovering, Dadi! It's watching us – look! Look!'

'Come on now, bach. School tomorrow,' Dad said from the front door.

'But it wants us to follow it . . .' said Cerys, trailing off, eyes still fixed on Rose's.

Good girl! thought Rose, hovering frantically. Then she had another thought. Surely they would wonder where Ianto was, with all this kerfuffle going on. Surely they would know that he wouldn't sleep through all this. Surely they would go and check on him. And then they would find the empty bed and organise a search party . . .

Cerys's eyes grew big. She had had an idea. 'I'm going to get Ianto,' she whispered to Rose, speaking slowly and clearly so the owl would understand. 'He will follow you with me. Wait here.' And she tore her eyes from Rose's and rushed inside.

Rose flapped around to the back of the house and perched in a tree to watch Ianto's window, which was still dark, curtains drawn. She could hear sounds within the house, pattering of small feet up stairs, murmurs of adult voices.

Then Ianto's bedroom light snapped on. Voices again – louder, anxious. Cerys's high voice joining them, raised in what sounded like fear. Siriol was crying again, even more loudly.

Had they found the empty bed?

She waited. She waited for ages, anxiously watching the back-lit curtain of Ianto's bedroom, listening to indistinct voices and sounds from within, which were quietening down now, even Cerys's. Siriol had stopped crying. Then the light in Ianto's bedroom went out.

Immediately, Rose flew round to the front of the house and perched on the streetlight once more. Soon Ianto's parents were going to burst from the front door, fully dressed, and leap into their car, heading out to search for Ianto.

The light in their bedroom was still on. But there was no sign of them coming downstairs. *Come on! Hurry up! Ianto is out there – terribly injured . . . Help him! Help him!*

Then the light in their bedroom went out. No one came

out of the front door. All sound ceased from within the house. All movement ceased.

Hang on. Not all movement. Her head swivelled slightly and leaned forward minutely, her sharp eyes focusing on the little window at the front, on the ground floor. A curtain had twitched open. Open just enough for a small, pale face to peer out at her from a darkened room. It was Mamgu. Mamgu's pretty, kindly face was watching her with an expression that Rose found hard to fathom. Something between fear, and hope, and sympathy. They held each other's eyes for a long moment, and then the curtain twitched closed again, and Mamgu was gone.

Now she was alone.

Not knowing what else to do, Rose took off and flapped, wearily, back over the sleeping village, up the track, past her house and on around the great bog, where starlight glinted wetly on peat.

Around the side of the mountain to where the base of the cliff was littered with fallen rocks, lying together in a grey jumble.

The great stone, dark with blood, stood up from the rest like a sacrificial altar. But it was empty. The giant – that is, Ianto – had gone.

The nervous energy, the fear and the anxiety, which had kept her running for so long could take her no further. She fell to the ground before the bloodied stone to rest, unconscious, in a crumpled heap at its side.

After some time strode a figure from the other side of the mountain. Tall, strong, he clambered swiftly over the rocks towards the owl, dislodging small stones as he came. On his head a battle-helmet, banded with gold, which gave off a shining light from within. At his side a sheathed sword with a golden handle. When he reached Rose he tenderly picked her up, a scrap of feathers in his hands. Then he carried her around the mountain and up the hillside to her house.

11

Sunlight streaming in through thin curtains . . . Rose was coming round, still half asleep, the bedclothes warm against her body. She did not want to wake up. There was something awful that she didn't want to remember.

Wisps of thoughts drifted into her mind as she came to. Where was she coming to? *What* was she? Girl or owl?

Slowly everything became solid. She was Rose, the girl, again. She was in her bedroom, and now she was sitting up in her bed. It was morning – it was school today, Thursday. What time was it?

Seven-thirty. And from the silence in the house, the stillness, she knew that Mum wasn't here. She had already left for work.

Rose threw her head back on to the pillow. She felt exhausted, wiped out. Could she even go to school today? She felt too tired and shaky to do anything. And then came the night's happenings, a series of scenes, fast-forwarding through her mind. The horror of it. Ianto's blood . . .

Ianto! Reaching out, she grabbed her phone and dialled. It clicked straight to answer phone. 'Ianto, I . . .' she began, but she couldn't go on, and she ended the call.

She couldn't give anything away on voicemail. If he was badly hurt, or, or . . . worse, then other people might listen to it – like Ianto's parents. She knew she would have to tell them, eventually, if he was badly hurt, or . . . but not yet.

He had to be OK. He had to. With shaky fingers, she texted: *Ianto, are you OK? Let me know.*

Then she sank back against the pillow again.

How did I get home last night? Her last memory was of collapsing against the stone at the base of the mountain. Had Mum brought her home, like before? No. If she had, she wouldn't have gone to work today. So how had she got home? Had she made her own way as an owl, or as a girl, and just, somehow, forgotten it?

Then another thought dawned, and she was filled with sudden, desperate hope. If she had got home in one piece, then perhaps Ianto had, too. Maybe that's why his parents hadn't rushed out of the house to search for him. Maybe he was back in his own bed. Maybe he was all right.

But what about his terrible injuries? When the mole had ripped into her back she had had real injuries, injuries that had stayed with her as a human. And they had really hurt. Although they'd healed very fast . . . Perhaps he will be OK. Please be OK, Ianto! Text me back, please!

Registration. Miss Evans was reading out names to a restless class. It was the day before the last day of term, and everyone was itching to finish school, to leave it all behind for six whole weeks. Rose had arrived early in the form room, her heart in her mouth. One by one, every member of her class had trooped and straggled through the door – every one, but Ianto.

When she came to the Ls, Miss Evans announced, '*Mae*

Ianto bant heddiw – Ianto's off today. Apparently, he hit himself on the head.'

She immediately regretted her choice of words, grimacing, because the class – all except Rose – burst into loud laughter, and one of the boys, Ianto's friend Aled, shouted out '*Roedd rhywun yn gorfod gwneud!* Someone had to!'

More laughter. And even Miss Evans smiled. There was a real end-of-term buzz in the room now – although Rose wasn't feeling part of it. She felt anxious and light headed. She hadn't had any breakfast – too nervous to eat.

Miss Evans went on, 'I asked for that. All right, Aled, settle down now. From what his mother says it's not serious and he should be fine to come to school tomorrow.'

That was good. That sounded very good. But Ianto hadn't replied to her text yet. Was he really OK?

While the rest of the class streamed untidily out of the door, Rose hovered about to speak to Miss Evans.

Miss Evans had sat down at her table and was gathering papers together. She looked up and smiled when she saw Rose. 'Rose, bach. You all right?'

'Yes . . . yes, I'm fine,' she said, stumbling on, 'Miss Evans, is Ianto OK?'

Miss Evans's kind eyes studied her face, and her plump hands stopped their paper-gathering. 'As far as I know, yes. His mam wasn't too worried. From what I can gather, he fell out of bed and hit his head on his bedside table, and has quite a nasty bump. But they don't think it's serious enough to go to the doctors. He's staying at home as a precaution, really. Don't worry, bach. He'll be fine.'

Miss Evans stood then, and bustled gracefully around the desk to her. Putting her hand on Rose's shoulder, she asked, 'Are you sure you're all right? You're looking very pale.'

'No – I mean, yes, I'm fine. I'm fine. Thank you, Miss Evans. Got to go now . . .' and Rose began backing away, grabbing her bag and displacing Miss Evans's hand.

'I know you're worried,' continued Miss Evans.

Rose froze. How did Miss Evans know?

She continued, 'I know that the idea of addressing a room full of adults is difficult.'

Phew! She was talking about the council meeting. Not about last night.

'But I have full confidence in you,' she went on, smiling. 'How's the presentation going? All done and dusted?'

Rose stared, blankly, at Miss Evans. She had done nothing to prepare for the presentation. Her mind slipped about in panic as she tried to think about it – then, defeated, she turned and ran from the room.

Lunchtime. Rose was sitting on a low wall in the sunshine, alone, opening the foil wrapping on her sandwich. She hadn't been able to face the canteen. Not today.

An impromptu game of five-a-side football was taking place on the yard in front of her, and boys and girls were scuffing about, shouting, as the ball thumped and skidded between them. She watched, uncomprehending. She had sleepwalked through this morning's lessons, unable to speak. She felt as if she were looking at everything and everyone through frosted glass. How could people behave so normally, be so carefree? She felt a stab of loneliness and fear that made her slightly dizzy.

Then, *Ping*. A text. Fumbling in the bag at her feet, she pulled out her mobile. It was from Ianto!

Sorry, was asleep! I'm fine, don't worry. Come and see me after school.

Tears sprang to her eyes – tears of relief, tears of joy. He was fine. Not just 'all right' or 'OK' but fine!

She wiped her eyes on her sleeve and sniffed. The text had put new heart into her, and so did her sandwich, which she bit into with sudden enthusiasm. It was delicious – peanut butter and avocado. She hadn't realised how hungry she was!

Then she replied to Ianto. *So glad you're fine!! See you after school.*

She wanted to add an *x*, as she would with girl friends, or with Mum, but in the end she didn't. She and Ianto never put *x*s on their texts, and it would be awkward to start now. So instead she imagined giving him a kiss, just on his cheek, to say how glad she was that he was OK, that he was still with her. And to her surprise, she found her own cheeks glowing warmly at the thought, and she couldn't help the smile that spread across her face – the first time she had smiled all day.

12

At last the long school day ended. Now she was turning off the main road to enter Ianto's estate. How very strange that she'd been here just last night, as an owl. There was the streetlight where she'd perched, calling desperately to Ianto's family. Where she'd seen Mamgu peeping apprehensively through the curtains.

Now she was walking up the path and ringing the doorbell. A little tune rang out, just audible from outside the house. Then a small figure approached through the frosted glass of the door. It opened and there stood Ianto's Mamgu.

Rose smiled at the sight of her. Mamgu was simply the neatest, prettiest old lady Rose had ever seen – her skin soft and smooth and slightly tanned, her wide eyes as blue as the summer sky. She was also very small, so small that when she sat on the Lewis's big sofa her feet didn't touch the carpet.

It was always hard to believe that this immaculate lady was scruffy Mr Williams's sister. And today there was no sign of the strange, fearful expression she'd worn last night – or the anger that Ianto had mentioned – as she smiled warmly back.

'*Helô, Rose fach. Dere mewn,*' said Mamgu. 'Hello, Rose love. Come in.

'You're here to visit the patient, I expect?' she went on, as Rose stepped inside. 'He'll be glad to see you. He had a nasty knock on his head last night, you see, so we thought it best to keep him off school.'

'*Ydy e'n iawn?* Is he all right, Mrs Lewis?' Rose tried to sound as normal as she could, but she couldn't help a pang of worry, again, as an image of Ianto, immobile against the bloodied stone, flashed into her mind. She was following Mamgu along the hallway now, resisting the urge to dash straight upstairs to see him – Mamgu seemed to expect her to come into the kitchen first.

'Oh, yes, I think he'll live!' Mamgu turned to her with a smile, then she moved gracefully about, opening cupboards, pulling out a tray and pouring Ribena into two glasses.

On a high chair at the kitchen table sat Siriol, Ianto's littlest sister – the one who had cried last night. She was only one and a half. In front of her was half a banana, peeled, which for the moment she ignored as she stared in awe at the visitor.

'*Helô Siriol! Sut wyt ti?* Hello, Siriol! How are you?' asked Rose, trying to sound bright and cheerful.

Instead of answering, Siriol leaned to one side and looked up at Rose, smiling.

'We're going to pick Cerys up from choir practice in a minute, aren't we darling?' said Mamgu, as she placed two flowery plates on the tray.

'Cerys!' said Siriol, ecstatically. Her little face became alert with joy.

'Yes – Cerys! You love your big sister, don't you?'

But Siriol wouldn't be drawn into conversation again. She smiled once more, mysteriously, and looked down at her banana.

Rose and Mamgu shared a smile, over her head.

At last Mamgu handed the tray, loaded with Ribena and a plate of biscuits, to Rose, who grabbed it and thanked her, adding to Siriol, 'See you later, Siriol,' giving her a little wave as she backed out of the kitchen.

Siriol ignored her – only interested in the banana now, which her small hands were carefully pulling in half.

Slowly and mindfully, so as not to spill the drinks, Rose carried the tray upstairs.

Ianto's bedroom door was half open. Rose began to feel nervous, remembering the crumpled body, the blood . . .

She took a deep breath and pushed open the door.

There was Ianto. Brown hair, brown eyes that smiled together with his mouth, sitting up in bed in a long-sleeved T-shirt. He looked normal. He looked OK. He put down the book he'd been reading.

Rose sat at the end of the bed and placed the tray between them. She was hugely relieved to see him. To see him smiling, alive . . .

To her horror, tears began to fall from her eyes, and she was unable to stifle a gulping sob.

'Hey!' Ianto's smile faded and he reached over and put his hand on her arm. His voice was full of concern and confusion. 'What's the matter?'

'Sorry – sorry. I didn't want to cry! I just . . . I've been so worried about you – after last night and everything. It's been such an awful day. I thought you were really badly injured, or even worse, and I didn't know how I'd cope . . .' Rose sobbed again. She couldn't believe she was saying these things to

Ianto, crying like this in front of him. But the tears were pouring out of her.

Ianto's hand was still on her arm, squeezing it gently. She rubbed her eyes and took a deep breath, managing to look him properly in the face. And then she saw – not just his kind, dark eyes, which were already twinkling with humour again – but the lump on his forehead. It was sticking out of his head like half a hen's egg, with a dark red gash, a big scab, through the middle of it. Her tears stopped as she stared at it in fascination. She'd never seen anything like it, except perhaps in comics or cartoons.

'Impressive, eh?' Ianto touched it lightly with his fingertips. 'Would you believe it was even bigger this morning?'

Rose passed him a glass of Ribena and he took one of the biscuits – a Hobnob. 'Does it hurt?' she asked.

'Not so much now,' he said, finishing the biscuit in two bites. 'But these do.' He pulled up one of his sleeves, then the other.

Rose gasped. His arms were covered in bruises – dark red, purple, black – and cuts, which had stopped bleeding but looked raw and painful.

'My legs are the same – maybe even worse,' he went on. 'I haven't shown anyone else. Don't tell them, will you? They all think I fell out of bed and hit my head – I don't want people worrying about me . . . or asking awkward questions.'

'I won't, Ianto. But are you really OK? Shouldn't we go to the hospital or something?'

'No, really, I'm fine. These are just bruises – I'm used to them from football. They won't last. Nothing's broken. And

Dad knows about concussion and stuff, being a policeman. He says I'll be fine. He said that when a lump sticks out of your head, you're OK. It's when you can't see it, and it's sticking *into* your head – into your, like, brain – that you need to worry.'

That was good to hear. Rose felt able to sip her Ribena now and bite into a Custard Cream.

'So,' she said, simply. 'What happened?'

Ianto grabbed a chocolate digestive and munched on it. Swallowing, he began. 'After we spoke last night, I fell asleep almost straight away. I was so glad that you were the owl, that we were together in this thing, whatever it is . . .'

'Me too,' said Rose, nodding eagerly. She was feasting her eyes on Ianto, drinking him in. He was all right. He looked wonderful to her.

'I fell asleep,' he went on, 'and the next thing I knew, I was in the wood, on top of the rocks in the clearing. I was straight there. And I was a giant again. But this time, I knew about you. And I was looking out for you – you, as an owl. And then you appeared in the air in front of me, hovering. You circled my head—'

'Ianto! That wasn't me! It wasn't me.'

Ianto nodded, slowly. 'So you were the other owl. I didn't know which was which, when the other one arrived . . .'

Then he whistled. 'Wow. It really attacked you, didn't it? But you gave as good as you got.' He looked at her, shaking his head and smiling. Then he went on, 'It was obvious that it wanted me to follow it. And because I thought it was you, I did. I thought there was something important you needed to show me, or that you were in trouble – I didn't know.

'I tramped up the track. Amazing how quickly you cover ground, as a giant. Past Uncle Thomas's, past the flag, up to the ruined place . . .'

'That's where I caught you up!'

'Yes. I heard you call out behind me. I turned around, and there was another owl. But I still thought that the first owl – the one I was following – was you, and that this one was – well, I didn't know. Some other owl. But then the first owl spoke to me. It wasn't like speaking, really. It was like . . .' Ianto broke off and screwed up his face, in thought.

'Was it like a string of letters which you can't read, but you know the meaning of, running through your head?'

'Yes,' said Ianto, in surprise. 'Just like that. I knew exactly what it was saying, however it did it. It said – *The king. This way*. It seemed really important. So I carried on, following the owl up the mountain, towards the king, I thought. Then the owl attacked you.'

'Ianto,' said Rose, her heart beating fast. '*The king. This way*. That's what the mole said to me in the tunnel. Then it trapped me underground.'

Ianto whistled again and his eyes, locked on Rose's, were suddenly anxious. Then he went on, 'It led me to the top of the cliff, and I fell off . . .' He trailed off, closing his eyes tightly. And as he did, Rose saw his face drain of colour, the jagged scar standing out, dark scarlet, against his pale skin.

When he opened them, for a flash he looked afraid, defeated. He shook his head, as if to clear it, then he stared down at his lap. Rose reached over and squeezed his hand –

gently, so as not to hurt the bruises there. It was her turn to comfort him.

After a bit, Ianto spoke again. 'I was trying to separate the two of you,' he said, quietly, looking up at her now. 'By this time, I couldn't tell which owl was which – you were both spinning through the air in front of me, your claws locked together. I knew that one had to be you, and I was afraid you would be badly hurt. I reached out to you . . . and I fell . . .

'The next thing I knew, I was on the floor, in here, and Cerys was shouting in my ear. My head hurt so much I thought it would burst. My whole body hurt like crazy, but my head was the worst.' He touched the lump gently, with fingers that, Rose noticed, shook just a little. She wanted to hug him, but held back. They never hugged each other. 'Everyone came crowding in. And when I finally managed to talk, I said the first thing that came into my head, which was I'd fallen out of bed and hit my head on the table here.' He motioned to the bedside table and chuckled a little.

'Actually,' he said, and he fixed Rose with a look that was suddenly determined and full of spirit, 'it's been really handy staying home today. I've been dying to show you this. Look what Mamgu gave me to read.'

He lifted the book he'd been holding when she came in. It was an old book, bound in thin brown leather with gold lettering across the front and on the spine: *Chwedlau Cymru* – Welsh Myths. The author's name was also spelled out in gold, in smaller letters – Thomas Williams.

'Thomas Williams,' said Rose. 'Is that your ancestor? The poet who won the Eisteddfod Chair?'

'No, this Thomas Williams was a historian and a writer. It was his grandson, Thomas Williams, who was the poet.'

It was a great source of pride and happiness to Ianto's family – and to the whole village – that Ianto's great, great grandfather had won the Eisteddfod Chair, back in 1961. The highest honour that Wales could give to a poet – or, indeed, to anyone, at that time. For a poem, written in a special, formal style.

So. This Thomas Williams, the writer of the book, was the poet Thomas Williams's grandfather.

'It'd be much simpler if all your ancestors weren't called Thomas Williams,' said Rose.

Ianto smiled at her. Then, 'Look,' he went on, flipping open the book. 'Here he is.' And there was a black and white photo of Thomas Williams, historian and writer. Ianto turned the book her way, so she could see him clearly.

An elderly man, with wild-looking grey hair and a big, untidy moustache looked right into her eyes. He wore a dark waistcoat and jacket and a high, stiff-looking collar, bright white, which held up his head. He was seated before an out-of-focus painted background, showing mountains, and in his hands he clasped an open book and a poised pen. He looked a little uncomfortable, Rose thought. Perhaps he preferred the real outdoors, and soft, well-worn clothes to these – the Sunday best that seemed to imprison him.

But a sparkle of intelligence twinkled out from his eyes and sprang from the page, making him very alive. Rose could see at once that here was someone who told the truth, who was strong for the truth. Funny how you could tell all these things from a photograph – a very, very old photograph. For, glancing at the title page, Rose saw that the book had been published in 1901.

‘1901! It’s a hundred and twenty years old!’

‘Yes, it’s pretty old. But look.’ Ianto grabbed the book and flipped through to the last few pages, then he thrust it back into her hands. A chapter title in big, old-fashioned type, leapt out at her – *Dychweliad y Brenhinoedd* – The Return of the Kings.

‘Read it,’ said Ianto.

So she did. It was all in Welsh, and a literary kind of Welsh, but she understood every word.

13

Dychweliad y Brenhinoedd – The Return of the Kings

There was once a king who had two sons. The kingdom he ruled stretched from the edge of the sea, over the mountains and into the plains, at the time, centuries ago, when Cymru was made up of many kingdoms.

This king had built a great court in the middle of his kingdom, in a valley beneath a mountain. It was a site well-defensible and strong – with hills either side and a great marsh spreading out to the north. And in the centre of this court, as was the custom of the time, a magnificent, timbered feasting hall had been built from the felled trunks of ten broad oak trees.

Time passed, and the king's eldest child, Berwyn, turned twelve. The king gave Berwyn a gift of a young kestrel, so that the prince might learn to hunt with it.

Berwyn loved his kestrel, and soon had her trained to take small prey from the air and bring it back to him. Instead of keeping her blinkered, tied to a post, Berwyn set her free. But although she could fly wherever she chose, she always came back to him.

One day, Bleddyn, the younger prince, was wandering in the woods. He saw his brother's kestrel flying swiftly over the tops of the trees, heading back to Berwyn.

Bleddyn lifted his bow and took an arrow from the

quiver on his back. Aiming into the sky, he pulled back his arm and sent the shivering arrow towards the bird.

The arrow rose into the sky in an arc. It came down, nose first, and sank its barbed head into the kestrel's neck, killing her instantly.

She fell to the ground with a small, soft thump.

Bleddyn was astonished. He had never killed an animal with an arrow, though he had tried. Even large, slow creatures, like wood pigeons, had been beyond him. But now he had slain his brother's kestrel, who was small and swift.

It had been as if, when he'd pulled back the bowstring, he had been guided by another hand.

Part of him was afraid of what he had done; part of him was glad – for he was envious of his brother.

He did not want to look at the dead kestrel, and so he ran away to a cave in that wood, and he thought about what he had done.

The next day, Berwyn searched and called for his kestrel. The king sent out servants, ordering them to comb the woods, the fields and the marshes, until they found the bird.

Soon one of them returned with a small, feathered body of shining browns and greys, an arrow through her neck.

The king knew from the fletching on the arrow that this was his son Bleddyn's doing.

'Take out the arrow,' he told the servant. 'Give the body to Berwyn, and tell him an eagle killed her.'

Time passed. The princes grew to be men, and the great king died. Now Berwyn was king. And he proved to be a ruler in the mould of his father. Ready to take a hand at the plough if need be, or else to lead his men into battle, riding at the front of his troops, sword in hand and on his head the shining symbol of his rank – a gold-banded battle-helmet.

And Bleddyn? Bleddyn had developed in other ways. He had sought out seers, soothsayers, sorcerers and shape-shifters, and had learned all he could of their art.

He was adept – a willing student, drinking in dark magic. Highest amongst his skills was the ability to transform himself – and others – into forms of animals . . . and into creatures that were neither animal nor human.

One day the king, Berwyn, rode out with a troop of warriors to oversee his southern borders. Word had reached him that a neighbouring ruler was on the march there, threatening war. The men set out with horses caparisoned, banners billowing, at a gallop through the woods, hooves kicking up earth behind them. When they returned some days later, victorious, Berwyn ordered a feast to take place in the great hall.

The hall was filled to its wide, high rafters with wood-smoke, the smell of roasting meats, loud laughter, singing and poetry – for the king held a lively court, and kept about him many wise and gifted bards, counsellors and musicians.

Late into the night, while the huge fire blazed brightly

in the centre of the hall and the carousing continued, unabated, two children – a boy and a girl – crept into the place, unnoticed by the king and his men. They were cold and hungry and had been attracted like moths towards the bright, warm fire, the smell of roasting meat and the boisterous merrymaking of the adults.

Crouching under a long table, they snatched at scraps of food, revelling in the heat of the flames and hugging each other with delight at their own daring.

But there was a curse on the great hall, enacted by Bleddyn – a curse designed to remain in perpetuity. Uninvited guests would be transformed, each according to their nature, into dumb creatures. Berwyn, the king, had approved this curse, knowing that should an enemy enter the hall where all the highest in the land are gathered, unarmed, oftentimes incapacitated by drink . . . Well, such an attack could spell the end of a kingdom. He had heard tales of such things from other lands.

Morning came, and sunlight crept across the floor through the great doors of the hall. Amongst the slumped and snoring bodies, overturned benches and ashes of the fire, there was no sign of the two children. Instead, hunched on a beam, high in the ceiling, was a tawny owl. And below her, stretched out between tables, a giant.

An owl for the girl, because she was clever, fierce and loyal. A giant for the boy, because he was brave, strong and kind.

The owl and the giant were captured – the owl in a net and the giant in thick ropes – and swiftly borne to

Berwyn. The giant was possessed of great strength, but was too confused by the change in his body to break the rope. He and the owl huddled closely together and, despite their bonds, bowed deeply before their king.

Berwyn saw at once that these dumb creatures were innocent. He ordered his men to free them, and he took the giant and the owl into his court. For their part, they remained loyal and loving subjects. For his part, the king recognised their worth.

The giant proved a formidable warrior in the king's service. A special coat of mail was forged for him, weighing near a ton. Striding behind the cavalry, thrusting at the enemy with a great spear and club, he was among the bravest and most loyal of all the king's men.

And when the king went out to hunt, he would take the owl with him, riding upon his wrist. Her sharp eyes and ears, her clear intelligence, served him well.

Soon the whole court, indeed all the people of that land, looked upon the owl and the giant as lucky talismans, given as gifts from their gods.

But what of Bleddyn?

Soon, the time came for him to take his chance.

Bleddyn laid a trap – thus:

He lured the owl to him with a scrap of meat, then threw a sack over her and tied the top. While she screeched in fury and terror, he rushed with the sack to an open place, deep in the wood. In this place was a cromlech, a structure made of vast blocks of stone that was ancient and mysterious, even then. For centuries people of the past had worshipped the spirits of their ancestors there, and it was full of strong magic.

He left the bag inside the cromlech, weighed down by a stone, then he hid behind a tree. The owl ripped at the sack with her beak and claws, flapped her wings wildly and screamed with rage, but it was an enchanted bag and could not be torn.

Alerted by her calls, and with a great roar of his own, the giant came crashing through the trees. He ducked his head to enter the cromlech and grabbed the sack, ripping at it to free his friend.

Bleddyn acted swiftly. He raised his yew-wood staff and spoke an enchantment. At once the cromlech collapsed, entombing the giant and the owl beneath it.

Then there was silence in the clearing in the wood.

Now Bleddyn hastened back to court.

'I have seen your owl and your giant,' he told Berwyn. "They were fleeing the kingdom to offer their services to the ruler of the southern lands. This I know. I looked into their minds and I saw what was writ there.'

Berwyn did not doubt his brother's word. He mounted his horse and set off after them – alone.

Presently Bleddyn shrank to the size of a small bird. His skin became smooth, darkly feathered. His feet shrivelled to tiny and useless – but his arms spread to become splendid, scimitar wings. He had transformed into a swift. He shot through the air before his brother to hide once more behind a tree, turning back to human form.

Then he heard the sound of approaching hooves. When the king and his horse were upon him, Bleddyn stepped from the tree, raised his staff and spoke words infused with hatred, words which flew like a poisoned arrow, sinking its barbed head into his brother's flesh.

Berwyn fell lifeless from his horse, landing on the damp, dead leaves of the wood. His horse, wide-eyed, raced onwards through the trees at full pelt.

Bleddyn was astonished. He had never killed a human with this curse. But now he had slain his brother, the king, who was brave and strong. And who had always been a friend to him.

It had been as if, when he'd intoned the curse, he had spoken in another voice, a voice even more deadly than his own.

Part of him was afraid of what he had done; part of him was glad – for now he was king.

He did not want to look at his dead brother, but he had to. He dragged Berwyn's body to the cave, and sat there for a while to think about what he had done.

When he left, he used magic to cover the cave entrance with earth.

And all the things that should accompany a great ruler on his journey to the Otherworld – the weeping hordes, the burial mound, the wooden chariot – had been denied to Berwyn.

Late that evening, there was great clamour in court. Where was the king?

Bleddyn stepped forward. Now was his time. He had seen his brother riding out to hunt with the giant and the owl, he announced. Perhaps, he went on, Berwyn had been killed by a boar, or a wolf; or had fallen from his horse and hit his head on a stone.

But then, where were the giant and the owl? It may be, Bleddyn said, that they murdered the king and fled. Otherwise, surely they would have returned to tell the tale?

King Berwyn's soldiers and servants searched the kingdom for weeks after: the beaches, the woods, the fields, the marshy places, even the lakes; but they found nothing of any of them – king, horse, giant or owl.

And all the people of that land lamented for long months after, mourning deeply a king that had died so young, that had been brave and good.

Because, of course, Bleddyn was king now. And he came to realise that people feared him, distrusted him; that he had not a friend in the kingdom. Some muttered that he had murdered Berwyn, the owl and the giant. That he had used dark magic to become king; that he was not the true king.

And all the things that should accompany a great ruler during his time on the throne – the love of his people, the loyalty of warriors, the respect of neighbouring kings – were denied to Bleddyn.

Then began a terrible time in the history of that land. One by one, the worthy men and women who'd surrounded King Berwyn like planets that orbit the sun, disappeared from the great court. Some were murdered.

Some fled. Many sought refuge in neighbouring kingdoms, where they plotted to take their country back.

And indeed, the surrounding countries, sensing instability, invaded, and Bleddyn, with his dwindling band of soldiers-for-hire, was besieged on all fronts, losing territory at a great pace. And he learned something: no enchantment could make people stand by him, make them loyal to him, make them fight for him of their own free will.

One day, he awoke to find himself entirely alone in the great hall. The last of his mercenary retainers had fled in the night, and they had stolen what they could before sweeping from the place. Weapons, gold pieces – all hard-won, now all gone.

Bleddyn heard the advance of enemy warriors into the valley now, the thunder of hooves, the shouts of men, the hollow call of the war-horn . . .

Rather than die by the sword or the spear like a common man – like a brave man – he crept from the court into the wood. Passing a clump of water hemlock, he pulled it from the earth, roots and all. Then he came to the place of the cave. He raised his staff and the ground opened to reveal its dark interior. He slipped inside and closed it behind him.

Lying near to his brother, he ate the whole of the deadly plant – leaves, stem and roots. Immediately, his body shuddered with sickness and seizures. An hour later, he was dead.

* * *

But what of the giant and the owl?

The death of Bleddyn released them from all enchantment. With a great, rasping groan, the fallen stones of the cromlech shifted apart, allowing a young man and a young woman to crawl from beneath them. Years had passed since those two children had hidden in the great hall, so that they were now full grown.

They straightaway ran, in some alarm, to hide amongst the trees of the wood, as all around them swarmed enemy warriors, intent on capturing the court, and on slaughtering anyone in their path.

Then a roar arose as the feasting hall was put to the torch, throwing great clouds of smoke and ash into the sky, and the two young people fled the wood to the safety of the rocky mountain above the valley.

It is said that the man and the woman married, and built for themselves a stone house on the side of the mountain, and that they had children of their own, and grandchildren . . .

14

Rose turned the page eagerly, but it was blank – the very last page of the whole book. The end of the story.

She looked at Ianto. He looked back. For once, her mind refused to focus. Then she opened her mouth and said the first thing that came into her head. 'It doesn't feel like the end of the story.'

'No, it doesn't. Because we're the giant and the owl now,' said Ianto, eagerly. 'Maybe,' he went on, 'that means we have to decide what happens next.'

They were both silent for a while, trying to digest this, to digest everything.

'Where the story takes place – it has to be the wood,' he went on.

'Yes. What does he say?' Rose took the book and flipped through it. 'Here it is. ". . . *a valley beneath a mountain. It was a site well-defensible and strong – with hills either side and a great marsh spreading out to the north.*" That's the wood. Then he talks about the two children – the owl and the giant – being human again and growing up and living on the side of the mountain in a stone house. And then having children and grandchildren. Do you think . . .' Rose didn't quite dare to say it.

'Yes, I do think. I think that they were my family's ancestors.'

'And they built Mr Williams's house, did they?'

'The ruined house further up, probably. Mamgu says that her great great great grandparents lived there. Uncle Thomas's house is newer – I mean, it's really old, but it's newer than the other one.'

'Your mamgu's great great great grandparents. That's like, this Thomas Williams's – the one who wrote the book's – mam and dad, is it?' It was hard to keep up.

'I think so.'

'Wow.'

'And maybe that's why I keep becoming a giant now,' said Ianto.

'So then, how come I keep becoming an owl – is that because I'm your friend? Is it because we camped for the night in the wood – like the kids in the story, in the great hall?'

'Maybe.' Ianto nodded, a little uncertainly this time.

Rose took up the book again, and flipped through to find the contents page. The other chapters were Welsh stories, or myths, that she knew already – tales from the Mabinogion, stories about Taliesin, about the Lady in the Lake, about King Arthur.

'It's funny,' she said. 'We know all the other stories in the book, but I've never seen this one before. Have you?'

'Never before now,' agreed Ianto.

Rose went on, 'The book's called *Chwedlau Cymru* – a chwedl is a myth. No one knows if myths are true or not, do they? Maybe Thomas Williams just made it up – as a joke, or something?' As soon as she said this, Rose didn't believe it. She turned the page to have another look at him. The clear, blue eyes. The serious expression. This wasn't someone who would have a joke.

Ianto wasn't convinced either. 'He wrote lots of books about real history – you know, like about Owain Glyndŵr and Hywel Dda and stuff. He was famous at the time, and people thought a lot of him. He wouldn't mess about. If he was writing a book about myths they'd be real ones, not ones he'd made up. Plus, if he did make it up, how does that explain what's happening to us now? There must be some truth to it.'

Ianto's face was clouded with thought. Then it brightened. 'Hey!' he said. 'Maybe he knew the story because it had been passed down to him through the generations of our family. Like it's been passed down to me, I guess, just now, by Mamgu . . .' Ianto trailed off, frowning a little.

'Whatever,' said Rose. 'What would be *really* handy, though, is to know how to stop it happening.'

Ianto cracked a smile. He pulled the book towards him and held it up, so that he and the photo of his ancestor were face to face, locking eyes. 'Hey, Great Great Great Great Great Grandfather,' he said. 'Help us. Tell us what to do!'

Old Thomas Williams stared back at him, uncomfortable in his collar. If he knew any more than was in the story, he wasn't telling.

'Do you think . . .' Rose hesitated. She wasn't sure about this. 'Do you think we should tell your mamgu? Or tell your parents?'

'No.' Ianto's answer was definite. 'Mam and Dad wouldn't believe us. I know they wouldn't. They'd be really worried about us getting hurt, but they'd never believe we turn into an owl and a giant. They'd probably think someone real was hurting us, or that we'd gone mad . . . They'd get social services involved, or something, and we'd never sort it out for ourselves. And Mamgu – I don't know. I think she knows more than she's letting on. Otherwise, why give me the book to read, now? But I don't want to worry her either. She's been so upset already about the wood-selling stuff and Uncle Thomas. Anyway, if she does know something that might help us, she can tell us herself, can't she?'

Rose nodded. She imagined telling her mum, then discarded the idea at once. Unlike Ianto's parents, Rose thought Mum might believe two children could turn into an owl and a giant. But, oh, how she would worry about them. If she knew that something wanted to hurt them – wanted to kill them – she would go out of her mind.

Rose and Ianto looked at each other, and nodded, together. Then they laughed, realising how funny they must look.

Good. This whole puzzle was for them to sort out.

'Why is it called *The Return of the Kings?*' asked Rose, suddenly. 'They don't return. They're dead.'

'I hadn't thought of that,' said Ianto. 'You're right. But – perhaps they *have* returned. Or – one of them, at least.'

They stared at each other, in unspoken horror. Yes. He meant Bleddyn. The dark stuff. The stuff that made itself into animals, then dissolved.

Then Rose's heart seemed to stop beating for a moment. 'Remember the cave, under the ground? The place I was trapped in,' she said, her voice shaking a little as the dark, hopeless place flashed into her mind. 'I was in an empty stone chamber, but there was more to it than the bit I was in. There was something around the corner, where the dark stuff went when the mole dissolved. And something was glowing in there, just a little bit of light – I could see it coming round the corner. Do you think it was the cave where Berwyn and Bleddyn . . .?'

She felt numb with horror at the idea of being so close to – to what? Skeletons? Ghosts? The dark, shadowy stuff . . .

Ianto was nodding his head. 'Yes,' he said. 'I think you were in part of that same cave. That's why the dark matter slipped around the corner, like you say. It was going back to its source, back to Bleddyn.'

'It's Bleddyn who is attacking us,' said Rose, almost to herself.

'The question is,' went on Ianto, 'how do we stop him?'

How could they fight such a foe? She closed her eyes to think.

Suddenly, unexpectedly, a picture of Dad popped into her head. He was standing up straight and tall. His arms were crossed in front of him, his legs were a little apart, and he looked as if he'd been carved out of granite – solid and indestructible. On his head was his yellow builder's hard hat, the one that he used to wear for work. He meant business.

Rose opened her eyes again.

'This is what we do,' she said. 'We go back to the cave. And we get Bleddyn before he gets us again.'

'*Get* Bleddyn?'

'Yes,' she said, determinedly. 'We destroy him.'

Then she added, less sure of herself, 'Somehow.'

Ianto's face broke into a grin. His eyes twinkled, and Rose had never felt so glad to have him on her side.

Him and Dad.

'*Let's do this thing,*' Ianto said in an American accent, and he held out his fist, wincing a little from his bruises as he did so.

Rose smiled back and bumped his fist. Gently, so as not to hurt him.

Then they became aware of excited children's voices in the hall below, mingled with the calm tones of Mamgu. Soon came the sound of small feet racing upstairs, and Cerys burst into the room.

'*Shw mae, Rose.* Hi Rose,' she said breathlessly, leaping straight on to the bed to hug Ianto, who grimaced with pain as she scrambled over his bruised legs.

Cerys buried herself in her big brother's chest then lifted her head to address him. 'Are you all right? Does it still hurt?'

She looked at the lump on his head then down to the bedside table with awe – as if she couldn't believe that an ordinary piece of furniture could do such a thing.

She's not stupid, thought Rose.

'Oh, not so bad. I think I'll pull through,' said Ianto, winking over her head at Rose.

Then Siriol tottered into the room; it had taken her a while to climb the stairs. She headed determinedly for the bed and grasped at the duvet with her little hands. She wasn't quite big enough to pull herself up.

Ianto disentangled from Cerys to lean down and lift her up, and she giggled with joy as he held her upright on his lap, bouncing at her knees. Then she stopped laughing and reached out a hand to gently touch the bump on his head.

'I think it's bigger than it was this morning,' Cerys said, crowding close to Ianto again. 'It looks like something's growing inside it. Maybe a chick will hatch out of it! Or something even bigger, like – like—'

'Elephant!' said Siriol, delightedly.

Everyone laughed, and Siriol looked about with surprise.

Then Cerys said, 'Hey, Ianto! Have you told Rose about the owl?'

'Er . . .' Ianto grinned up at Rose. 'You tell her, Cerys. I wasn't lucky enough to see it, remember?'

Cerys turned to Rose, her face full of excitement and importance.

'Well,' she began, swallowing dramatically. 'Last night I was woken up with a big shock. Something outside was screeching – just like a person, screaming! I woke up and I ran downstairs and out into the garden – and guess what it was?'

'An owl?' said Rose.

'Yes! And it was flying round and round above my head! It was like it was trying to tell me something. I thought it wanted us to follow it. And I wanted to follow it. But Mam and Dad said we had to go back to bed. But before we did, I stayed outside and watched it. And you know what?'

'What?' asked Rose, smiling.

'It hovered in the air. And it was watching me with its big, black eyes. I felt like I knew it, like it was a friend. And then I thought, if Ianto was here, he would want to follow the owl, like me. And I told that to the owl. I told it to wait there until I got Ianto. And it was like the owl understood. And so I went to Ianto's room. And,' she turned back to Ianto and threw her arms around him, 'poor Ianto had fallen out of bed and hit his head!'

She buried her head in his chest again and Siriol, getting the idea, struggled against her to do the same. Smiling, Ianto wrapped his arms around them both.

Then Mamgu appeared in the doorway. 'Rose, bach – I don't want to rush you, but you know it's coming up to six o'clock?'

Six o'clock? Mum would be wondering where she was.

'Thank you, Mrs Lewis. I'd better go.' Rose stood up and mouthed to Ianto, over the girls' heads, '*I'll text you.*'

Ianto nodded. His brown eyes were serious now.

Mamgu followed Rose down the stairs to the front door.

'Goodbye, bach. Remember me to your mami,' she said, as she always did. Then as Rose turned to walk down the path, she went on, 'Rose – you and Ianto are good children. Nothing really bad can ever happen to either of you.'

This was so unexpected that Rose spun around to look at her.

But it was as if the words had not been spoken. Rose saw the same sweet lady, standing on the doorstep in a neatly-pressed brown and cream trousersuit, like a little wren in the entrance to its nest.

Mamgu gave a wave and disappeared inside the house again, shutting the door.

15

Rose opened the front door of her house, and had hardly put down her bag before Mum came rushing from the kitchen and almost bowled her over, grabbing Rose and squeezing her tightly against her. But it wasn't a happy kind of hug – it was the frightened, clinging kind.

'Mum! What's the matter?' Rose pushed herself away to get a proper look at her.

Mum's face was drawn and tight, and her eyes were red from crying. Rose's heart sank. What now?

'I'm sorry I'm late, Mum.' Perhaps she'd been worried about her? 'I had to go round to Ianto's – he's hurt his head and was off school.'

'Hurt his head?' This seemed to bring Mum back to normal, just a little. Now she looked alert, worried. 'How?'

'Um, he hit it on his bedside table, I think, last night.'

'Is he badly hurt? Has he seen a doctor?'

'No. His dad had a look, and he thought he'd be OK. And he is OK – just a bit of a lump, really. He's fine.'

'Oh, thank goodness for that. Rose, love, oh! I don't know what's going on at the moment. It feels like everything's gone mad.'

The two of them were in the kitchen now, Rose having steered her that way, thinking that whatever Mum had to say would be better if they could sit down, and maybe have a cup of tea.

Mum was still talking. 'First this awful news about the wood, then you falling and hurting your back in there and me getting chased by my imaginary monster,' Mum caught Rose's eye and they exchanged a little grin, despite themselves, 'and now Ianto banging his head . . . it feels as if something – something out of control is going on.

'Anyway,' Mum sat down now, and so did Rose, slumping warily into the chair opposite, 'what I really wanted to say was, I'm so sorry.'

Mum reached into her apron pocket and, hesitantly, pulled out a folded letter, passing it across the table to Rose.

Rose unfolded it. But she had already guessed what it was.

Yes. It was from the council. It was about the proposal to build the abattoir, and it asked them if they wanted to oppose the planning application. The letter was over a month old, and it gave the date last week as the deadline. Mum must have found it in the pile on the shelf in the hall.

'We could have done something, love. We could have opposed it. We could have said, never mind Mr Williams, we don't want an abattoir on our doorstep, we don't want the new road, the lorries, the traffic, the noise and the lights, and all those poor animals . . . the animals in the wood and the animals in the abattoir, being killed. I'm so sorry. It's all my fault. I didn't open the letter – it's addressed to me and I didn't open it. It's too late now.'

Then Mum slumped forward, putting her forehead on the table, her arms stretched out in front of her. 'It's too late now . . .' she repeated, her voice muffled by the table.

It was time to put her out of her misery.

'Mum, it's OK.'

Mum raised her head to look at her, arms still outstretched.

'I'm going to a meeting at the town hall tomorrow. It's a meeting of elected councillors. I'm going to make a three-minute presentation – and I'm going to oppose the planning application.'

Mum was staring at her, taking this in. Then a smile grew, her eyes softened and she started to cry again, but in a different way. A better way. Swiping away the tears with the hem of her apron, she straightened up and hurried around the table to hug Rose once more. This time it was a good hug, a warm hug, and Rose hugged her back.

'You're a wonder, do you know that?' said Mum, pulling away to put on oven-gloves and grab two fat baked potatoes from the oven, plonking them on plates. 'How did you arrange all that?'

Over a tea of chickpea salad and baked potatoes with cheese and butter, Rose told her how she and Miss Evans had found out about the meeting and organised that Rose should go. She didn't mention that she hadn't done any preparation for it, and that she had no idea, yet, what she was going to say.

Meanwhile Mum was shaking her head with admiration – her baked potato, forgotten for the moment, steaming before her.

'You – are – a – wonder,' she repeated, emphasising each word. Then, 'Oh Rose, I thought you were going to hate me so much for not opening that letter. I was dreading you coming home. I thought you might run away again, and get hurt again . . .

but that this time you wouldn't come back to me. I don't think I've ever been so worried, or hated myself so much.'

Rose didn't know what to say. It had been stupid of Mum not to open letters. But she would never leave Mum, ever, whatever Mum did. Because she knew Mum, and she knew that Mum had a heart of hundred-carat gold, was her one-and-only wonderful Mum, even if she was sometimes a bit . . . what? What *was* Mum? *Emotional*, thought Rose.

Bonkers, came another thought, unbidden, and Rose felt ashamed of it.

'Mum, please just open letters from now on. We don't get many. We can deal with them together, maybe,' she said.

'I will. I'm sorry, love. Sorry, again. You know . . .' Mum trailed off and looked down at her plate.

'What?'

'I'm pretty useless at the moment, Rosie,' Mum said in a low voice. 'I know I can run the bakery, I'm good at doing that, but . . . I can't seem to do much else. Not since Dad . . . I haven't been a good mum—'

'Hey! Yes you have. You're great!' exclaimed Rose. And before she knew it, she'd continued, 'I haven't been a good daughter. I'm always angry and irritable. I'm not like that to anyone else. You don't deserve it. I'm sorry.'

Rose surprised herself with these words. But it was a relief to say them. And to hear Mum's.

Mum gave a little chuckle. She was looking up now into Rose's eyes, and she said, 'You're a wonderful daughter. And I think, actually, maybe, we're both doing very well, all things considered.'

They exchanged a warm grin as they tucked into the last of their potatoes.

After tea, Rose rushed to her room. She sat at her desk, took a deep breath in and got on to the council website. She had to get this dreaded presentation sorted out. It felt like the worst, most stressful homework in the world, almost impossible to do and then, if she failed at it, the worst possible outcome – the abbatoir would be built. The pressure was almost unbearable.

What on earth was she going to say? With shaky fingers, she clicked on '*What matters can be taken into account when opposing planning permission*'. She saw at once that it was against the law to build on 'sites of special scientific interest' and 'conservation areas'. If only the wood were one of these things!

She knew that 'sites of special scientific interest' meant having rare newts or bats and things. And the wood, though bursting with all kinds of life, didn't have any very rare creatures, as far as she knew. Neither was it a 'conservation area' – which meant having a listed building, or a structure of historical importance on it. In fact, as far as she was aware, there were no man-made buildings there at all.

So in the end, nervily, haltingly, she jotted down notes about disturbance from the noise of the traffic right by their house – all those lorries, toing and froing; about the scale of the place: a small, wooded valley, transformed into a huge great building complex; about the big security lights, lights that would be on twenty-four hours – meaning no more star-gazing in the valley.

And all the way through, she felt unsure that what she

was doing was right, unsure that it was enough – enough to stop them building the abbatoir.

In the end she was too tired to think straight, and when she went over her notes they no longer made sense – her tired, untidy writing jumbling together on the page. She finished up, switching off her computer and crawling into bed. She fell asleep within seconds.

And that night, nothing happened. No transformation. A sound night's sleep – until there came a dream, that played out in Rose's mind very early in the morning, just as it was beginning to get light.

She was being bundled, manhandled, by something that was so swift and strong that she didn't stand a chance. Not a chance, as she was stuffed into a strong sack that was dark, airless, terrifying. A scrap of sky above her was snuffed out the instant later as the bag was tied shut and she was plunged into utter darkness.

Then she felt herself lifted, jostled up and down so that she was tumbling feet over head, flapping desperately. The sound of breathing, exertion, from outside, as if her captor was running fast. She was fighting to escape – beak, claws ripping, wings flapping, crying out in rage. But the material of the bag was impossible to get a grip on. She could not tear it. Could not escape.

Then she was suddenly still, and below her she could feel a cool hard surface through the material of the bag, which had settled about her. She scrambled to get to her feet and half managed it, until she was pulled up short – the bag was weighed down at the end, too tightly for her to stand.

New sounds from outside. A series of crashing noises approaching her at speed. A great bellow: '*Aaargh!*' And she was taken up again, thrown about within the bag. She knew it was not the evil one this time. It was her friend, the giant, and he was struggling with the bag, pulling at the material to open it, to release her. She tried to help from within, renewing her efforts with beak and claws, flapping desperately in its dark confines—

And then, an almighty crash. Heavy, vast and dense was the pressure above her, was the silence, the darkness. Then heavy immobility, suspension. Not owl, not girl.

Just mind. Trapped mind. Waiting. Waiting, with the presence, next to her, of another mind. Waiting to be set free . . .

Rose awoke with a jump, and the connection was broken. The thread of the dream went spooling away.

But as it drifted off, Rose held on to one thing. She had been entombed underground, under large rocks, in profound darkness.

And she knew where it had been. It was under the rocks in the clearing. Being trapped within it felt just the same as it had before, when she'd emerged from its stones that first night.

And then she made a connection.

In his story, Thomas Williams had written about a cromlech, a cromlech in the middle of the wood that Bleddyn had made to collapse, to trap the owl and the giant.

Rose knew about cromlechs. They'd been to see one on a school trip, with their history teacher. It stood in a sheep-grazed field not far from the sea, not far from here.

Five huge, long stones had been arranged together to form four upright supports and a roof, leaving a space within, where you could stand more or less upright.

The place had a feeling to it – a strong sea-breeze blew through it, yet it did not feel desolate. It felt alive and timeless, full of strange, strong magic. *A place that was ancient and mysterious, even then.*

The rocky patch in the clearing in the wood was the collapsed cromlech from the story.

And suddenly Rose knew exactly what she was going to say at the council meeting.

She grabbed her phone and texted Ianto.

Then she showered, put on her school uniform, and went into the kitchen. Taking her bowl of porridge from the stove, she sat down to eat.

Before her on the table was a note, from Mum.

Rose
This is just to say a big GOOD LUCK for the council presentation today. I am sorry I won't be there to support you, but I'll be thinking of you at 3.30 and wishing you well – wishing us well! I know you'll be brilliant.

Also, Rose, I know that Dad would be VERY VERY PROUD of what you are doing.

Love always, Mum

16

'Here they are.' Ianto handed her a shopping bag.

They were standing outside the form room, having just finished registration.

'Thanks, Ianto,' said Rose, taking it and putting it carefully into her backpack. 'I promise I'll look after them, and I'll give them back tomorrow.'

'Why do you want them, anyway?' Ianto asked curiously. He was looking much more himself today – tall and sparky. The egg-shaped bump on his forehead had miraculously disappeared, and all that was left was a yellowish bruise with a thin red scar through it.

She said, 'You know, you look just like Harry Potter, with your scar, and your hair. All you need is some round specs.'

She didn't want to lie to him, but she didn't want to tell him about the council meeting either. *I'll tell him afterwards,* she thought. *When we know the outcome.*

'Ha ha.' Ianto grinned. Then he lowered his voice, looking about to check no one was listening. 'So. When are we going to get Bleddyn?'

The question threw Rose. She'd talked big, yesterday, about finding the cave and 'getting' Bleddyn. But then, and now, she was hazy about how and when. She just hadn't had time to give it any thought.

It seemed that Ianto had. 'Look. Let's meet this afternoon. School finishes at lunchtime. We could head straight for the wood. I was thinking – we should bring spades and stuff. We might have to dig to get into the cave. We might even have to shift some rocks—'

'*Hei, Ianto! Ti'n barod i* . . . Hey, Ianto! You ready to . . .'

Aled was standing in front of them, performing a strange action with his arms raised, as if he were swinging a hula-hoop round his hips.

Ianto looked perplexed. '*Beth*? What?'

Aled, grinning, repeated, '*Ti'n barod i* . . . You ready to . . .' and did his dance again, nodding encouragingly, '*Paaardaay!*'

'Aled,' said Ianto, 'I literally have no idea what you're on about.'

Aled, only a little deflated, went on. 'End of term celebrations with the boys! Starting this afternoon! *Fast and Furious Nine* at the Cineworld! Pizza afterwards!'

'Oh – yeah,' said Ianto, glancing at Rose with a helpless expression. 'I forgot.'

Aled stopped his gyrating and whistled. 'You *forgot*? Only the most exciting thing to happen all year – and you forgot?'

Ianto looked at Rose again, as if for guidance, and Aled glanced from one to the other, a slow smile spreading across his face. 'Ah, I see,' he said, theatrically. 'Now you have other plans . . .'

'No—' Rose and Ianto spoke together, then they met each other's eye and grinned. Ianto's cheeks were flushed pink, Rose noticed.

'That's OK,' said Aled, who never let anything dampen his

enthusiasm. 'Rose, why don't you come too? It should be a real laugh.'

'Thanks, Aled,' said Rose, and she meant it. It was pretty big of him to invite her to an all-boys' outing, 'but I've got other plans this afternoon.'

Ianto turned to her, a puzzled crease in his brow. But there was no time for any more explanations, because the buzzer was sounding for their first lesson, and the three of them had to run down the corridor to get there on time.

17

At last school wound to an end, and hordes of pupils streamed out of the school gates to freedom – or, at least, freedom for a little while. As everyone kissed and hugged and laughed around her, Rose felt numb – unable to join in. No one seemed to notice, which made her feel even more alone.

All she could think about was the council presentation and the encounter, which was surely to come, with Bleddyn. What chance did she or Ianto have of succeeding, in either case?

Ianto had been herded away by his friends for their big afternoon, and he and Rose hadn't had a chance to speak again. She would text him when the meeting was over.

Rose wandered into town, by herself. She had a couple of hours before the meeting at the Town Hall, so she headed for the park – where she hoped to go over her presentation.

It was peaceful in the park. She was the only one sitting on the grass. Parents and grandparents watched their kids playing in the little fenced-off playground, pushing swings, helping toddlers up ladders and down slides.

Rose remembered Dad pushing her on the swings – pushing her so strongly that, at the very highest point of the ride, the chains went slack and the seat seemed to buckle beneath her, and she was breathless, and thought she was going to tumble off, and fly. But Dad was looking after her, and he would catch her. So she could giggle raucously, and call for him to push her harder, make her go higher, and higher . . .

Pain twisted inside her. This was a fresh memory, which had bubbled up past her defences and burst, leaving behind a smudge of loss and misery. Tears pricked her eyes.

Stop it, stop it, she said to herself, blinking rapidly to prevent the tears from falling. She stood up, turned around and sat down again, so that she was looking at the stone fountain in the middle of the park, and the roses – big, blown flowers of pink, yellow, white – planted in curving beds around it.

Roses. Dad's favourite flowers. That was why Mum and Dad had called her Rose. He had planted roses in their back garden and had lovingly fed and tended them – but now they had become so overgrown with long grass and brambles that you could no longer see them at all.

Now the tears were falling from her eyes, unstoppable. Wherever she turned, there was Dad, insisting that she remember him.

I want to remember you, Dad, but it's so difficult for me. It's too difficult – too painful. Please understand.

A sob escaped her throat. She didn't have a tissue, so she used her shirt sleeve to wipe her eyes. She wanted to blow her nose too – but she couldn't do that on her shirt sleeve. She couldn't turn up to the council meeting with snot on her sleeve. At this thought, a little burst of laughter escaped her, despite the tears, and she stood up to go to the park toilets and grab some loo-paper.

* * *

At last, it was 3.15. Feeling very nervous now, rather as if she were in a dream, and repeating to herself, over and over, what she was going to say, Rose made her way through the park to the Town Hall.

The Town Hall was a grand building with large wide steps, which she climbed, then took a deep breath before pushing through its big double doors.

Just inside, a lady was sitting at a reception desk, and she smiled at Rose. '*Prynhawn da,*' she said. 'Good afternoon. Can I help you?'

Encouraged by her welcome, Rose swallowed and replied, '*Dw i yma i weld Siân Peters.* I'm here to see Siân Peters. I'm making a presentation at a planning meeting, at three thirty.'

The lady eyed her screen. 'Rose Morris, is it? Sit down over there – Siân will be with you soon.'

Rose had hardly sat down before – '*Rose! Helô, braf cwrdd â ti. Siân dw i.* Good to meet you. I'm Siân.' Another smiling lady, dressed in a smart suit, had appeared before her, holding out her hand.

Rose shook it, awkwardly. Siân's hand was warm, and it squeezed hers supportively.

'You all set for the meeting?' she asked.

'Yes,' said Rose, the nerves starting up again inside her, making her throat feel dry and her heart beat fast.

Siân turned and Rose followed her out of the reception and down a long corridor.

Glancing sidelong at Siân, Rose saw that she was wearing

beautiful golden earrings which were shaped like owls, and which dangled and turned and caught the light in a delightful way. Not safe, cartoon owls, but real-looking ones, fierce and dignified. Rose was dazzled by them.

Before she knew it, she blurted out, 'I like your earrings.'

Siân stopped in the corridor, looking pleased. 'Oh, thank you, bach,' she replied, smiling and touching one of them lightly, making it quiver and sparkle. 'I made them myself.'

Rose was amazed – this council lady had actually made these beautiful objects?

'To tell you the truth,' Siân continued, in a lower voice, 'I'm hoping to give up this job and open a shop, to sell my jewellery. I've worked for the council for over twenty years now, and I'm ready for something new. Time for a change, you know?'

Rose was surprised that Siân wanted to tell her her plans – she wasn't used to adults confiding in her. And she felt glad that Siân was going to follow her heart and do something she enjoyed. But she did hope that she would do her job today, would concentrate on listening to her and making sure that the wood was safe.

The next thing she knew, she was in a large room full of people seated in chairs before a desk with a screen behind it – mostly men in suits, but a few women too. And every head, as she entered the room with Siân, turned to look at her.

'*Dyma Rose Morris*,' said Siân, as she and Rose headed towards the desk. 'This is Rose Morris. And she'd like to make a three-minute presentation, opposing planning permission for this application.'

Then Rose and Siân fiddled about with her laptop. Rose was pleased that Siân was so efficient and that they were soon good to go, because she felt all fingers and thumbs and was horribly aware of all the faces turned her way.

Then Siân sat down in an empty seat in the front row and smiled encouragingly at her.

It was time to start.

'*Rose Morris dw i,*' she said. '*Dw i'n byw yn*— I'm Rose Morris. I live in—'

And then she stopped. For the first time, Rose looked out, properly, at the adults ranged before her. They looked back, and in their faces she got nothing – no encouragement, no interest.

One man, in particular, looked put out. Arms crossed over his chest, he was regarding her with a frown. Then he looked down at his watch.

It was obvious they weren't going to make concessions for her being young. *And quite right*, she thought, desperately, *I do want them to take me seriously, but, but . . .*

The dreadful silence stretched on. Standing, suddenly hot, her mind entirely blank, Rose glanced in panic at the doors at the back of the room. Just get away from here—

Dad was sitting on a chair at the back of the hall. He was wearing his work boots, and he was leaning back. He looked just as he did when he used to come in from work and sit in front of the stove, holding a cup of tea and reading the newspaper, his tired legs stretched before him.

He looked exactly as he used to, except that he was still wearing his bright yellow hard hat. Because when he finished work, he always left his hat in the back of the car – where, when she was little, Rose would enjoy trying it on and playing with it.

His hat glowed golden-yellow, and seemed to brighten the whole room.

Now Dad crossed his arms. He was watching her with bright, warm eyes. He was smiling. He nodded, encouragingly. Then he gave her a thumbs-up.

Without thinking, Rose responded with a thumbs-up of her own, and her face broke into a smile.

Dad had come to support her.

The panic passed as if it had never been there.

And, with a start, she remembered where she was. The councillors in front of her were looking at her in amazement now.

They think I've gone bonkers, she thought. *First sputtering out like that, and now grinning and making thumbs-ups.*

Taking a deep breath, she collected herself and began again, with new heart.

'I live in the bungalow on the track up to Fferm Bigfelen, Mr Williams's farm,' she said, hearing her own voice with surprise, sounding strong and sure across the room. She took in a breath. 'I would like to oppose the planning application for building an abattoir complex in the wood which backs on to our house.'

Now she clicked her laptop, and brought up a section of Ianto's Ordnance Survey map on the screen behind her, showing the whole valley with the wood at its centre and, in the very middle of the wood, a treeless clearing filled with small, round shapes.

'This map shows the site,' she went on. 'In the very centre of it there is a large, stone structure, mostly covered by earth and grass, which is marked on the map by these round shapes, which mean boulders.'

Then she brought up one of her own photos of the rocks in the clearing in the wood, which she'd taken at a wide angle so that you could see the whole of its length, and much of the wood encircling it.

Everyone was looking at the screen. She had their attention now, she realised. They were all wondering where this was going.

'The boulders stick up out of the earth in a way that suggests they have been placed there, rather than being a natural phenomenon,' she said.

Then, holding her head up straight, she took a deep breath and said, 'The basis for my objection is this. I have good reason to believe that this collection of rocks is of extreme historical importance.'

She could see the people in the room glancing at each other. There were a few mutterings, and one woman jotted on the file in front of her.

Siân was smiling up at her.

Perhaps Siân doesn't want the abattoir to be built, either, thought Rose, suddenly. She'd assumed that because she worked for the council, she wanted it to happen. But maybe she didn't.

Pause. Now was the time to sock it to them.

'I believe that it is in fact the remains of a cromlech – that is, a megalithic monument made by prehistoric people. The very size of the rocks in an otherwise flat and stoneless part of the wood suggests this, but I also have written evidence here.'

And she reached for old Thomas Williams's book, which she'd placed on the desk in front of her.

Now they were all really listening. Every eye was on her. The grumpy man was staring, still frowning, as if to say '*Prove it!*'

She held up the book. 'This book was published in 1901, and was written by a local man, Thomas Williams. In his time, he was a well-respected authority on Welsh history, and had many volumes published.

'In the book, Thomas Williams describes the valley in question exactly, and states that it is the site of a prehistoric cromlech, which collapsed at a later point in history.

'And if it is, then it will be a monument of great importance, not just for our area, but for Cymru, for Wales. And what is more, the site will almost certainly become a conservation area. And the council's planning rules state that conservation areas must not be built upon.

'I would like to ask the council to take my evidence into consideration and to carry out a proper, archaeological exploration of the site, to confirm whether or not the stone structure is a prehistoric cromlech, and to put on hold any plans to develop the site until the results of this survey are published.'

Taking a deep breath after this galloping sentence, she glanced down at her laptop and saw that she had fifteen seconds left.

She carried on, rushing a little now, 'The book also states that the valley was the centre of one of Wales's ancient kingdoms, possibly from Celtic times. It may be that there are other important archaeological finds to be made there.'

And, because she just had to, she said, quickly,

'The wood is a beautiful place. It's home to so many species – a really special habitat. And local children have enjoyed playing there throughout the ages, and adults like to walk there too, with their dogs . . . It would be a terrible blow to the village to lose it.'

And now the seconds on her laptop clicked from 59 to 00 and her time was up. The faces were still on her, though they looked a little stunned now, she thought. The woman who had made notes looked up at her and smiled, as if to say thanks. The grumpy man was still frowning, but in a confused kind of way now, leaning across to his neighbour to hold a whispered conversation.

She clicked her laptop and the photo of the stony clearing disappeared behind her, like magic.

Siân stood up. 'Thank you, Rose,' she said, helping Rose unplug the laptop and gather her things. Then she walked from the room with her, leaving the rest of them inside. Obviously, the meeting was going to continue now.

Just outside the room, Siân put her hand on her shoulder.

'Well done, bach!' she whispered. 'I didn't know what to expect, but I certainly wasn't expecting that. An excellent presentation – and, though I can't make any promises about outcomes, I can tell you that we'll be looking into your claims.'

Now that she'd said her piece, Rose didn't have any words left. *I have done all I can to save the wood,* she thought. *I can't do any more.*

Oh no. She wasn't going to cry *again*, was she? No, she wasn't. She pulled herself together, and managed to smile shakily at Siân.

'The meeting's resolutions will be posted on the council website – tomorrow, or Monday at the latest,' Siân continued.

Then, after glancing about to make sure they were alone, Siân bent towards her and quickly whispered in her ear, 'You may have made an old lady very, very happy, bach. Thank you.' Then she slipped back through the doors and into the meeting.

Rose wandered down the corridor, dazed. What on earth did she mean by that?

Then she stopped in her tracks, and whipped around. Dad! She had forgotten Dad! Back at the doors, she heard the rumble of a male voice from within. The meeting was continuing, and she couldn't go inside again. But there were two small windows, one in each of the swing doors. She peeped through the right-hand one at an angle, and was just able to see the back of the room.

There was the chair, the chair where Dad had been sitting.

It was empty.

18

Over an evening meal of vegetable moussaka and trifle for afters, and as dusk began to fall outside the kitchen window, Rose filled Mum in on the planning meeting.

Mum listened, agog, alternately nodding then shaking her head in admiration or disbelief, the woods dark through the window behind her.

'So it looks as if we're living next door to a prehistoric monument?' Mum turned around to look at the wood. She gave a little shiver, Rose noticed. 'Wow. And we always thought it was just a funny, rocky lump in the middle of the trees. Fingers crossed, Rosie, fingers crossed. When will we know?'

'Tomorrow, or Monday at the latest, we'll know what they decided at the meeting.' Rose spooned up another scoop of trifle and let it melt in her mouth, enjoying the flavours and different textures – jelly, cream, sponge . . .

When, *ping* – a text. Ianto.

Meet you at midnight in the middle of the wood. Bring a torch and a spade.

She gulped and the trifle went down the wrong way, making her cough and splutter. Mum jumped up and came round to give her a gentle thump on the back as Rose slid her phone back into her pocket to hide the message.

* * *

It was nine thirty, and Rose was lying in bed. The alarm on her mobile was set for eleven forty-five. Outside, by the back door, stood one of Dad's spades. By her bed, a torch.

She needed to get some sleep, so she'd be fresh for the night's adventure. But sleep wasn't coming. Instead, a vision of Dad this afternoon, sitting there at the back of the room, supporting her. And it filled her with a strong, calm feeling – a feeling that he was still with her. Not in the way he had been before, of course, but still there, somewhere, somehow.

And then something began to happen, in her mind. Memories, impressions, pictures – of Dad, everything she knew about Dad – came flooding through, like a film on fast-forward, at first, which gradually slowed down, as her body relaxed. And she was powerless to stop the film, anyway, she realised, so, in the end, she stopped trying. She *wanted* to think about him. She wanted to remember him. She didn't care any more if she was frightened.

She closed her eyes and imagined holding on to Dad's hand, and allowed all the pictures, all the stories, to come.

Dad was a builder, but he hadn't always been a builder. He had been born, and grew up in a big town in Wales, south of here, next to the sea, where they made steel. Dad's first job was in a steel mill. His dad had worked in the steel mills there, too. And so had his grandad, and his great grandad before that . . . in fact, Dad reckoned his ancestors had been making steel or iron in Wales for as long as anyone could remember.

But Dad had been made redundant from the steel mill when he was still quite young. So he'd started work as a builder. He'd left his home-town and gone all over the place, to find work.

One job had taken him to Bristol, where he and a gang of workmates were building a housing estate. In a layby nearby was a burger van with the words 'Snappy Snacks' and a picture of a crocodile eating a burger painted on the side of it. Inside the burger van, behind the propped-up window, was a pretty, lively young woman in a big apron, who stood in front of a hot griddle.

Dad and his workmates went there to get their lunches, and for cups of tea and coffee. The young lady behind the griddle noticed that Dad had a lot of tea breaks – in fact, he got through more cups of tea and burgers and chips and slices of cake than anyone she knew – and he liked to stop and have a chat too. He enjoyed telling jokes, and he soon found that this young lady would laugh at them all, however rubbish they were – which was nice. He found her especially pretty when she laughed. And then he plucked up the courage to ask her out, to the cinema.

He was over the moon when she said 'Yes!'

And then they had got married, and Dad and his mates finished building the housing estate. She sold the Snappy Snacks van, and Dad brought her back to Wales with him. Not to the town he came from originally – but to this part of Wales instead. He found a job with a building firm, and he bought this small plot of land from Mr Williams and built this bungalow in his spare time, and made its garden. And then Rose was born, and the three of them lived happily together – but not happily ever after.

Happily, for a short time. So short a time.

Rose took a deep breath in. Tears were starting to flow from her closed eyes, so she opened them, and let the salty liquid trickle down her cheeks and into her hair, on to her pillow. This story, the story of Mum and Dad, was a story that Rose had loved to tell herself – before Dad died, that is. It had always been strange to think of Mum and Dad at a time when they were young and carefree – Mum so pretty and Dad so handsome – before Rose had been around. It was like a romantic film, or a book, but then it was also about the two people she knew best in the world. Funny. It almost made her feel shy of them.

She sniffed, and continued, closing her eyes again and making herself push forward, squeezing Dad's hand as memories flooded in again.

Dad had liked to reach round from the front seat of the car and squeeze her knee – then meet her eye in the mirror, and wink at her.

He had read to her every night from when she was very little. She would get into her pyjamas and they would snuggle into his and Mum's bed – always a treat – and she would nestle up to his arm, and listen, enchanted, to his voice. Every so often she'd look up at his face, too, and watch him. Then back at the book. Enjoying the pictures.

They were still doing this, even when she was old enough to read things for herself, and probably too old for such things. The last book he read to her was *The Borrowers*, and they had both loved it. They hadn't finished it, though. She wasn't sure that she would ever be able to.

Dad had not spoken Welsh. He had not spoken Welsh, but actually he understood it very well. His grandmother had been a Welsh speaker, and she had spoken to him when he was little. So it had gone in, somehow. But it hadn't come out. It was as if his Welsh was locked inside him, and he had lost the key – for now, at any rate. He had been very proud of Rose going to a Welsh-speaking school and learning the language so well – he was always telling people how good she was at it.

Rose thought, now, with heavy sadness, that if he'd lived they could have spoken Welsh together. Maybe he could have taken some evening classes, just to bring it back. And she could have helped him. Together they could have spoken it again, and Mum could have learned to speak Welsh too . . .

Dad's family. Rose knew that his mam and dad had died before she was born. But had Dad had brothers and sisters, and cousins and uncles and aunties? He must have done. There must be some relatives out there, somewhere. Why didn't they ever see them? Where were the photos of them? Why hadn't she asked him about them, when she had the chance?

Then Rose sat up with a start. She had just remembered something. She got up and padded over to the little wooden box where she kept precious things, like photos and Ianto's cards. She opened it and reached under the contents to pull something out. It was a little roll of off-white stuff that was like rubbery, thin leather. *Vellum*, Rose was sure it was called. Made from a calf's hide. What people long, long ago used to write on, before paper.

It was tied with a piece of string.

Rose took it back to bed and put on the bedside lamp.

Then she undid the bow in the string and carefully unrolled the vellum, which stayed a little stiff, a little curved.

Small, black ink lettering, strange and antique, but each letter clearly depicted, spelled out Welsh words, arranged on four lines. It was an englyn – a traditional Welsh poem that expressed a truth.

Dad had given this strange object to Rose. He said his grandmother, the Welsh-speaking one, had given it to him before she died. Dad had not been able to make head nor tail of the words, he'd said. So he'd given it to Rose, knowing that one day her Welsh would be good enough to understand it. Up till now, Rose had found it too difficult to read. In fact, she hadn't looked at it for years, certainly not since Dad had died.

But now, the words jumped out at her with clarity, as if the black letters were speaking, urgently, to her, relieved to be out of the box, unrolled, insisting on their strange message. She realised that her Welsh had improved vastly in a couple of years, because she understood every word. And as she read it, she felt a shiver run down her spine, leaving a tingle behind.

The poem had a title: *Y Drydedd Dylluan ar Ddeg ar Hugain.* The Thirty-Third Owl.

Impossible to translate an englyn into English, properly, because they're full of ingenious rhymes and repetitions, but it went something like this:

The Thirty-Third Owl
Cave-coffined, two kings under earth – the bad and good –
Sound Celt-crafted instruments of iron and wood.

Kin wakes kings. Iron breaks wood – for second birth.
King takes king; iron makes good – to end the curse.

It was a riddle – it hid the truth and it revealed the truth, all at the same time.

And, Rose saw at once, it was about Bleddyn and Berwyn – the two kings; one bad, one good, lying underground.

It had to be them! But what were the instruments? And all the stuff about iron, and wood? The best line was the last one, about ending the curse. Yes! That's what she and Ianto were going to do.

Then she thought of the title. The Thirty-Third Owl. How did the owl come into the story? And . . . could it be *her*?

She frowned. She was too tired to think about it now. She had to get some sleep.

When she released the edges of the vellum it curled itself back into a roll, so that she only had to tighten it a little, retying the string and placing it carefully back in the little wooden box.

Then she got under the covers and put out her light.

'Goodnight, Dad,' she said, as she closed her eyes. His face appeared in her mind. He looked strong and serious, but he did not speak.

She wasn't expecting to fall asleep before the alarm went off, but she did.

19

Midnight. And the stony mound in the middle of the wood crouched beside Rose as she watched the dark trees in front of her, ears pricked for sounds, waiting for Ianto.

The night sky was peppered with stars and a bright crescent moon. They gave just enough light to see without a torch, out here in the open. Under the trees was another matter. It was dark under there. And no lights came from her house or, she saw, glancing up the mountainside behind her, from Mr Williams's.

A rustling, cracks of twigs and snagging ferns. A light was approaching through the shadows of trees and shrubs, bouncing along the path that came from the village.

It was Ianto. Or was it? The light came closer and closer, until a figure – tall, determined – broke through the dark foliage and emerged into the clearing, switching off the torch and pocketing it as he approached. Yes. It was Ianto.

'Hi,' she said, in a low voice.

'Hey,' he replied. His dark eyes sparkled with moonlight. He was carrying a spade, slung over his shoulder like one of the seven dwarfs.

She picked up her own spade which had been lying beside her.

'All set?' said Ianto.

'Yes. I think so,' she said.

Then she remembered the little piece of vellum. 'Ianto,' she said, in a low voice. 'I've found something, that might help us – like Thomas Williams's book helped. I'll show it to you tomorrow.'

Ianto looked curious. 'Is this something to do with what you did this afternoon? Why you needed the book, and the map?'

'Um, no – that was something else. I'll tell you about that tomorrow, too.'

'OK . . .' said Ianto, still watching her, his mouth twisting into a half-smile.

'Hey, how was the big afternoon out?' she asked, changing the subject.

'Oh, yeah. It was good, I guess. Except I couldn't concentrate on anything – all through the film, I was just thinking about tonight.' Ianto paused. 'Good pizza, though,' he added.

'I didn't know if we'd be me and you, or owl and giant,' Rose went on. They were standing there, chatting, as if they weren't quite sure what to do next.

'Me neither,' said Ianto. 'I had no idea what would happen. What *will* happen. I'm not even sure where the cave is. Are you?'

Rose was thrown by this. She'd assumed that Ianto remembered its location. 'No,' she admitted. 'I walked for ages underground to get there, but I don't know where I went.'

'I'm fairly sure it was over that way somewhere.' Ianto pointed westwards, the trees stretching darkly beyond his hand.

Then Rose recalled, 'Yes. Mum said the noises came from the far edge of the wood, past the stream.'

'Past the stream,' Ianto repeated, nodding. 'Right. Let's go.' And he held out his fist.

Rose grinned and they touched knuckles. Then they turned and plunged into the darkness of the wood, scrambling through undergrowth towards the stream. It was hard to hold a torch in one hand and a spade in the other. And her spade was surprisingly heavy. In the end she balanced it on her shoulder like Ianto, supporting the handle with a steadying hand.

There was no clear path here, so they walked single file, Rose leading. Sometimes the way was blocked by a tangle of brambles, or fallen branches and trees. Then they clambered over and around the obstacles – difficult with two hands full, and with torchlight bobbing all over the place.

Then suddenly, the sky opened out above them and the stars twinkled down again. Before them, curving through a gap in the trees, flowed the wide streambed, shining water trickling musically in moonlight.

The stream was low tonight – low enough to jump from half-submerged stone to half-submerged stone. So they splashed across. And then they headed on, pitching into the darkness of the trees before them.

Presently they emerged from cover again. They were at the far edge of the wood, where it met with the foot-stones of the hill that rose gently beyond it. Bracken covered this lower slope and a dry-stone wall, crumbling now and reinforced with barbed wire, marked the wood's boundary with one of Mr Williams's many fields. This one looked little used – full of long grasses, bracken and nettles.

Ianto stopped and switched off his torch. Rose did the same. Sudden silence, now that they weren't moving. Only the wind in the trees. Then that stopped too. The wood was still, as if it was watching them intently.

'I think it's around here, somewhere,' whispered Ianto.

Rose nodded, putting down her spade. Although, if she was honest with herself, she had no real idea where the cave had been.

Ianto, as a giant, had dug through the ceiling of the cave. They had both assumed that the cave had been hidden once more, that they would need to dig to get to it again. Why had they assumed that? But, yes, this area looked untouched – bracken shoots glinted glossily in moonlight from ground that was unbroken – mossy, grassy. No bare, overturned earth, no displaced rocks. If this was the right place, that is. How could they know?

She wondered if Ianto had any such doubts. As if he could read her mind, he turned to her.

'What do you—'

'*Hoo hoo-hoo hoooo,*' came a quavery answer. But it didn't come from Rose. It came from high above them.

Looking up, hearts beating fast, they saw a dark shape – squat, oval, solid – sitting at the very top of a tall larch tree.

Message delivered, the owl pushed off from his perch and launched into the air, flapping and then turning to take himself away, skimming low over the wood canopy, then off out of sight.

'Well,' said Rose, grinning at Ianto. Ianto grinned back, and his teeth shone white in the starlight. 'I take that as a sign. Come on – what are we waiting for?'

And with sudden, mad enthusiasm, she grabbed her spade and began to dig, slicing the blade down through the bracken, then using her foot to force it into the turf, in the way Dad used to. Then she shovelled the earth behind her. It was heavy work. And she soon found she was hitting stones, and having to scrabble them out of the way by hand. But, like the tramping through the wood, it was good to be doing something, doing *anything*, rather than waiting, and thinking . . .

Ianto worked beside her. Soon, between them, they had dug a hole that was about a metre deep and a metre wide, and the only way to work now was to get inside it and dig within the hole. And with their next plunge of the spade, they both fell forwards, fell downwards as their spades connected with thin air and the ground beneath them gave way.

20

'Aah—!' The shock of it forced a cry from Rose, which she smothered instantly with her hand.

They'd landed in a tangle of limbs and spades on a packed-earth floor. Scrambling upright, they saw that they were in a cavern, an earth cave with no roof. The Milky Way glowed brightly above them, marking out the edges of the hole they'd dug.

Back to back, Ianto and Rose shone their torches at the cavern walls. And saw that it was not a cave but a tunnel, which stretched before them in both directions. They had broken through its roof and fallen to its floor.

'Which way?' Rose whispered. Westwards, under the hill which loomed above; or eastwards, back towards the middle of the wood?

Ianto considered. 'Everything always starts in the wood,' he whispered back. 'So I think we should head back this way.'

He waved his torch and the beam danced against the dark earth walls. The light wasn't powerful enough to reach the end of the tunnel and after a few yards it petered out, defeated by the darkness ahead.

Rose nodded agreement, taking a deep breath. And so they left the square of Milky Way behind them and walked down the tunnel, shining their torches ahead into the pitch darkness, clasping their spades like battle-axes and heading back the way they'd come, but underground this time.

Rose thought, hefting it in her hand, *This is Dad's spade.* It was solid and strong. A worn, wooden handle and a polished steel blade. It made her feel safe. Or safer, perhaps.

Ianto went first this time and Rose walked behind.

This couldn't be the same tunnel she'd stumbled down as an owl. The ceiling was too high – about a foot higher than Ianto's head. Who knew where that other tunnel was – if it still existed, that is.

The tunnel seemed to eat sound. So that their tread, their breathing, the rustle of their clothes – all was smothered, as if they were in an aeroplane and they needed to swallow, to make their ears pop. The lack of normal sound made Rose feel alone, despite the sight of Ianto striding ahead, within touching distance. And the idea of the darkness behind her was disturbing. Every so often she would turn and shine her torch back the way they'd come. There was never anything there – the light fading out after a few yards – and no sound.

Soon Rose lost her sense of direction. The tunnel twisted and turned, never dramatically, but enough to make her unsure, after a bit, which way they were heading. Nothing to navigate by, no sight, no sound . . . suddenly Rose couldn't bear this endless tramp any more. Her heart was beating fast – faster . . .

And then Ianto stopped dead in front of her. He was shining his torch at the tunnel wall to his left. She edged closer and pointed her own beam to join his. There was another tunnel, coming off this one at a T-junction and heading away into the darkness beyond their torchlight. This tunnel was not cut into earth, however, but into stone – roughly hewn, craggy rock, once more a little higher than Ianto's head. The floor looked smoother, as if countless heavy boots had marched over it for centuries, but it was still rutted with ledges and cracks. Ianto turned to face Rose, and raised his eyebrows.

She nodded in answer, swallowing her panic, and the two of them turned off the earth tunnel into the stone one.

The sound was different in here. Although they tried their best to move quietly, every footstep, every breath they took sounded loudly and echoed sharply about the solid, jagged stone that surrounded them.

Then, with a loud, bright *clang*, the steel of Rose's spade struck an outcrop of rock. They froze in horror as the sound ricocheted about the length of the tunnel, tolling like a bell in summons, only gradually growing fainter and fainter until, with one last, tiny chime, it petered out completely.

Rose and Ianto stood, motionless, ears straining for a reaction – but only deep silence echoed back at them.

Warily, they continued, stepping as soundlessly as they could. Rose gripped her spade to her chest now, which was awkward and made it hard to hold the torch steady.

And then, they heard something. Something that was not the rustle of their own breathing and footsteps. A gentle, irregular drumbeat on stone that barrelled, whispering, around the walls of the tunnel, indistinct, distant at first, but getting louder and louder as it approached. And it was approaching at speed.

By this time, both of them had turned and were running

back the way they'd come, arms flailing, torchlight throwing crazy beams all around, spades heavy in their hands. Their feet clattered on the stone floor, spades clanging the walls as they pelted down the tunnel chased by the sound behind them which had loudened into a mad clattering, like heavy hooves on paved ground.

No time to think. At the mouth of the stone tunnel, Rose turned left, heading towards the heart of the wood. As she sped down the earth tunnel, some part of her mind, full of fight or flight, was amazed at her own speed. At *their* speed, because she could hear Ianto's strong footsteps behind her. Or could she? Was that slapping just part of the mad galloping thing that pursued them?

Then, to her astonishment, she found herself bursting through a curtain of greenery – ferns, bracken, twigs and branches – and into the wood. She did not stop, did not break stride and did not look back. Clutching her spade, legs snagged by brambles, she sprinted crazily, half falling and pulling herself upright again until, suddenly, she knew where she was.

In front of her was an oak tree that she knew and loved, its broad trunk covered in rough, knarly bark. It loomed up before her – solid, spreading, opening its arms wide. Without thinking, Rose threw down her spade and, grabbing one of the lower branches, hoisted herself up, grazing hands and arms, scrabbling with her feet. She didn't stop until she'd climbed to its very heart, then sat, panting with exertion, mind spinning, in the fork of one of the great oak's sheltering branches.

Only then did she realise – Ianto was not with her. He had not followed her out of the tunnel.

From her perch, she could just make out the way she'd come. Through the darkness she could see a low bank, covered in trees and brush – she must have come out of there. But she knew the wood so well. Why hadn't she noticed the tunnel entrance before?

But that was not important, not now. Where was Ianto? The floor of the wood glistened dimly in the starlight which filtered through the canopy. Nothing moved. The horror was hitting her again. The horror of losing him. What had happened? When had he stopped chasing after her? *Why* had he?

And all the time, the thundering was approaching through the tunnel, getting louder and louder, until something huge, dark and strong, as if fired from a giant bow, burst through the dark foliage on the bank.

It was a wild boar – wide, barrel-chested body coated in dark, bristly fur and a mane that stood up stiffly along the ridge of its back. All its weight, its strength, was concentrated at the front, in its massive shoulders, the immense neck.

And its head. Small, dark eyes. Large, curved fangs pushed back blood-red lips, opening to roar as it leapt forward into the wood—

And the next moment, another movement – a springing-up beside the tunnel entrance. A figure, raising his weapon above his head – iron, glinting in moonlight – to bring it down, with a great roar of his own, hard, brutal, on to the boar's head.

The blade sliced deep into the animal's thick hide, just behind the ears. But the weight of the boar's momentum, the speed it had been travelling, pushed it forward despite the attack and it hurtled on, pulling the weapon from the warrior's hands, leaving the blade impaled in its neck, the handle waving crazily as the animal bellowed and wheeled to turn on its attacker.

A shaft of moonlight illuminated his adversary. It was Ianto. Ianto had sunk his spade into the wild boar's thick neck. And it was Ianto who now faced the enraged, injured creature, with no means of defending himself. He stood, weaponless, at the entrance to the tunnel, legs tensed, bouncing slightly, arms out at either side, ready to react, ready to run, eyes fixed on the boar.

At once, Rose scrambled down from the tree. The boar was several yards away, eyeing Ianto and bellowing in rage. Picking up her own spade – *Dad's spade* – she raised it above her head and advanced quickly, soundlessly, behind the injured boar.

The closer she got to it, the more certain Rose was. This was not a real boar. No blood gushed from its wound. Instead, a trickle of darkness, light, floating off in the night air, flowed from the animal's neck.

It was Bleddyn.

All the easier to kill it, then, she thought.

And the moment the boar tensed to spring forward, Ianto's spade handle rocking in its neck, she mustered all her strength and brought her own spade, edge first, spinning down through the air and slicing, with a strange, swishing noise, deep into its back.

21

The impact of the spade cutting through the boar's tough hide vibrated up her arms and her fingers sprang open, letting go the handle and leaving the blade sunk halfway into the animal's back. With a scream of pain and surprise, the creature spun to face her, two wooden handles waving in the air now, both stuck deeply into its body.

But Rose had turned and was already sprinting back to the safety of the oak. Behind her came the thump and thunder of hooves, the sound of a thick body pushing through undergrowth, getting closer and closer, until she could hear the animal's breathing – hard, painful snorts – right behind her, almost upon her now, ready to impale her on those fearsome tusks . . .

But here was the oak. Gasping for breath, Rose ducked under a branch that dipped from high up to almost touch the ground. And from behind her, more bellowing. No time to look around. She was at the tree trunk now. Reaching to grab a branch, she hauled herself up with a strength that astonished her. No scrabbling this time. She climbed higher and higher, until she was back in the heart of the oak, sitting, panting with exertion, in the crook between the two branches.

Only then did she look down through the dim light and the foliage beneath her.

To see the boar, felled now, sprawling on its side beneath

the low-hanging branch. Two spades lay on the ground beside it, glistening darkly in the moonlight. All at once, she understood what had happened. When the boar had charged towards the tree, the spades had slapped into the branch and the impact had wrenched them, one after the other, from its back, deeply gouging the thickly-muscled flesh. The body was lying still now, soundless.

It was dead. Together, she and Ianto had killed it.

Then she heard a rustling, from lower down the tree. Leaves were shaking, moving; twigs and small branches snapping. The disturbance was working its way up towards her . . . until a head popped out of the leaves just in front of her. A head topped with brown, ruffled hair, a face with twinkling eyes and a grin.

'Well, that was a bit of a boar,' he said.

She groaned at the joke, but she couldn't help the answering grin at the sight of Ianto, safe and sound.

He pulled himself up to sit next to her and, together, they watched the body of the boar below them.

Black matter, like thick smoke, was pouring from the two huge wounds on its back and neck. But the dark substance didn't disperse into the air and disappear. To their horror, they saw that it was gathering together in mid-air beneath their feet. Soon the body on the ground collapsed entirely, as if the large, spinning ball of dark matter above it were sucking it dry. Then its outline simply disappeared.

Now they saw the pulsating, smoky sphere rise higher in the air. They shrank back, holding their breath as it passed through the foliage around them then broke through the tree canopy above their heads. Looking up, they could see it pulling itself about in the sky, a solid, dark mass, stretching out then massing again, outlined sharply by the sparkling light of the stars. It reminded Rose of a lump of dough being kneaded and knocked about by Mum's strong hands.

Rose turned to Ianto. 'What now?'

'It hasn't re-formed yet,' he said, still looking up at it. 'Let's grab the chance and head back down the tunnel.'

Rose swallowed. 'Good plan,' she whispered, trying to sound as brave and light-hearted as him. Actually, she couldn't think of anything she less wanted to do. But they had to. They had to go back into that stone tunnel, and follow it down until it reached the cave. Then they had to face whatever was there, and fight it – again.

So they scrambled down the tree, dropping into the soft, dead leaves beneath.

Rose reached out and put her fingers to the oak's broad, rough trunk. '*Diolch*,' she whispered. 'Thank you.'

Oak leaves rustled gently in the breeze. '*Diolch i TI*,' it seemed to reply. 'Thank YOU.'

They grabbed their spades from the ground. Rose gratefully hugged hers to her chest, noticing that both their blades were clean and bright.

Then Ianto leapt through the overhanging ferns into the earth-tunnel entrance. Rose, following at a run, was astonished to plough into his back, then the two of them sprawled against the bank, spades clattering in a jumble of limbs and tools for the second time that night. What had happened? They scrambled to their feet and scrabbled at the foliage to find the tunnel entrance. But it wasn't there. Nothing but ferns, brambles, earth. A quick, torchlit examination of the rest of the bank showed that it had disappeared completely.

They turned to face each other, unsmiling this time. Rose had no brilliant ideas left. She'd had enough for one night. Now all she wanted was to get home, go to sleep, try to recover from all this, before . . . before whatever happened next. The thick canopy above meant they could see nothing of the dark matter that was kneading itself in the sky. Kneading itself into something new . . .

'Let's go home,' she whispered. 'Come back to mine, it's nearer.'

Ianto stared at her for a moment, a stare that contained the old bravado, but which softened then, as if admitting defeat. 'OK,' he whispered back. 'We can try again tomorrow.'

So they plunged once more into the undergrowth, dodging through trees, to get on to the path that led to Rose's back garden.

And presently Rose's house appeared through the wood at the end of the path. After such a strange and frightful night, it looked impossibly normal, impossibly everyday, standing low in the overgrown, moonlit garden, the back door and two windows either side so familiar, like a friendly face. But there was something not quite right about it, at the same time. What was it?

As she hurried down the path behind Ianto, desperate now to get out of the wood, she saw what was wrong. Squatting darkly on the ridge of the roof – just as she had the other night, on Ianto's house – was a huge, majestic bird.

She reached forward to grab Ianto's shirt and pull him back.

'Whaa—' he whispered, loudly, and Rose slapped her hand over his mouth to shut him up as the bird twitched its head towards the sound.

A massive presence; over a metre high. Huge wings folded neatly at its sides, full of hidden strength. Feathered legs reached down to large, powerfully clawed feet.

A fierce, curved beak revealed itself in profile as eyes that frowned blankly beneath straight brows penetrated the trees and pinpointed their location.

It was a full-grown, golden eagle, lit up by the light of the crescent moon.

As they cowered back and stepped, as quietly as possible, behind a tree, Rose's only thought was Mum. Mum was inside the house, asleep. Right beneath the eagle.

The thought was unbearable. And then she realised something. She would rather the eagle – or Bleddyn, or whatever it was – attacked her, than attacked Mum. The strength of this truth made her brave. She would not allow Mum to be harmed.

Before she knew what she was doing, she sprang out from behind the tree. Ianto grabbed at her arm, but he wasn't quick enough and she pulled away easily, running up the path to the back gate. She had the eagle's full attention now. It was facing her from its perch on the roof, sleek head held high, looking down at her with eyes that, though sharp, had no depth.

Looking into them, she felt a surge of pure, strong anger.

'Get away from our house, you evil creature!' she shouted,

waving her spade in the air. Her voice came out loud and hoarse, echoing strangely in her head after all the night's whispering. 'You don't scare us! We know who you are; we know what you've done. And you won't win – we will defeat you. However long it takes – we'll get you in the end.'

A sense of dizzy unreality was hitting Rose. Her words were so brave, so sure. Perhaps they really could defeat Bleddyn! Why not? They had made it this far, after all. But first, she had to get him away from Mum. Make him follow them, instead.

The huge bird sat for a moment with its head very slightly on one side, as if it had been listening carefully. And then it leaned forward to a crouch, its long back straight, head thrust forward – before springing powerfully from the roof, spreading its huge wings – fully two metres in width – and diving straight at her with deadly speed.

Rose was already backing rapidly into the trees, facing the bird, seeing the claws grow huge before her eyes as it pounced; but she was amongst the thick, protective branches when, with a great *smash*, the eagle collided with the foliage at the level of her head, exactly where she'd been a second ago.

Now she turned and dived into the depths of the wood, followed by a dazed-looking Ianto. They ran stumbling through the trees, not bothering with torches now. A great, crashing kerfuffle was going on behind them as the huge bird struggled to untangle itself from the undergrowth, to pull its massive body up, up into the air once more.

They ran, branches and brambles whipping their faces and bodies, away from the house to the part of the wood where the trees were thickest, with thin trunks, packed close together, stretching upwards to reach the sun.

Airborne now, the eagle climbed high into the sky and then soared in long, slow circles above the wood, pinpointing them easily with its sharp ears as they scrambled through the undergrowth.

What goes in must come out and, when it did, the eagle would strike.

22

They were crouching in the shelter provided by an upturned tree. Long ago, it had blown over in the wind, pulling up its own roots and a huge piece of earth to boot, making a cave-like canopy in the floor of the wood. Tall trees and bushy shrubs surrounded them.

The eagle was made for open ground; for vast, deserted spaces, big skies. It couldn't come through this thick canopy – it wouldn't be able to fly properly, it would damage its wings. Or so they hoped. They couldn't see through the leaves to check where it was, or what it was doing. But they guessed it was circling the wood, waiting for them to emerge. *As long as it's away from the house*, thought Rose. *As long as it's away from Mum.*

Suddenly she felt cold and tired.

As if he could sense her feelings, Ianto reached out and held her hand. His hand was warm. He gave a little squeeze, and she turned to share a smile.

'All right?' he asked, keeping his voice low.

'Yes.' She nodded, determinedly. But she had run out of ideas, again.

And so had Ianto, because he asked, 'What now?'

Rose thought about it. She said, 'We can't hide here all night. We have to come out and face him. Keep fighting him, I guess, keep going. Put an end to all this.'

'But we need to keep him away from your house, away from your mam,' said Ianto.

Rose looked up at him, at his warm brown eyes. Now it was her turn to squeeze his hand.

'How about we lure him out on to the mountain?' he continued.

'That would mean breaking cover, being exposed, to run up the track. No shelter on the mountain either.'

'I know. But can you think of a better plan? And we've got our trusty weapons.' Ianto reached for his spade and brandished it, blade up, grinning.

Rose grinned back. Grimly. 'OK. You're on. Let's go and kill Bleddyn . . . again.'

Ianto snorted with laughter, then covered his mouth to stop the noise. 'And again,' he spluttered, in a low voice, 'and again and again . . .'

'Wonder how many animals he can turn into?' whispered Rose, giggling too. They were both light-headed. 'Hey, wouldn't it be nice if he turned into something sweet and cuddly – like a koala? Then we could take him home, and keep him as a pet.'

'No. He'd be an evil koala. He even managed to make a mole sinister, remember?'

Their smothered giggles died away.

'It'd be good if we were the giant and the owl again now, wouldn't it?' said Rose, looking up at the dark canopy of leaves, which were swaying, noisily, in a sudden gust of wind. 'We'd stand a better chance.'

Ianto had opened his mouth to reply but was drowned

out by a small explosion of sound from above. Rain, falling suddenly and sharply on leaves. The forest floor became even darker as rainclouds rolled overhead, and soon large drops were cascading their way through the foliage and dripping on to them. The earth gave up a damp, warm smell as the water came down.

'Come on!' said Rose, leaping to her feet. 'The sound of rain will drown our footsteps. Let's head for the mountain.'

So they stood, grabbed their spades and picked their way through the densest parts of the wood, moving uphill towards the mountain as quietly and as quickly as possible, through the darkness, the trees, and the rain.

Soon they were at the very edge of the wood, the corner where it met the track that led up the mountain.

They shared a determined stare – and then, together, they stepped out from under the trees.

And looked up. Raindrops hit their faces, soaked into their hair. The sky was even darker now, thick with clouds, though the moon still glowed through a misty veil, its edges fuzzed.

They could not see the bird. But that didn't mean it wasn't there. Circling high up, in this darkened sky, with raindrops falling thickly, how would they see it? Rose wished she had her owl's night-vision, her owl's senses. Instead of being earthbound, big and clumsy, stumbling about in the dark.

At the side of the track was a thick hawthorn hedge, above the ditch where the stream ran. The stream, enlivened by this unexpected downpour, rushed thickly down the mountainside.

No need for discussion. Ducking down so their heads

were below the level of the hedgerow they crept, feet splashing through the stream, up the mountain; one behind the other, Ianto in the lead.

Now they were at the junction with Mr Williams's drive. And there was the flag pole on the corner. They had to leave the shelter of the hedge to cross over to it, the stream gurgling underneath through a pipe. Ianto ran at a crouch to the other side then stood up straight in defiance. He was looking up at the moonlit dragon on the flag, which flapped darkly and snapped wetly in the rain and wind.

The red dragon, brave and fierce, its front leg raised with claws extended, gave them new heart. Rose joined him and they shared a smile. Then they continued up the wet track, leaving the flag and Mr Williams's unlit stone house behind them. Heading upwards, on to the clear, wide mountainside.

Soon the hedgerow thinned to a few old and windswept survivors, more knarly wood than leafy shrub. No more cover.

And then the rain stopped. As suddenly as it had come. The stream continued to chuckle, but otherwise there was silence. Across the path was the ancient, ruined house, sheltered in its collection of stunted trees.

Where is the eagle?

Rose paused to look up at the sky, clutching her spade. It couldn't be this easy. It had to have seen them – had to be watching them. And they had to be prepared for it. The clouds were rolling away to the east now, revealing the moon's sharp edges and the panoply of stars. The sky was lighter, brighter again. But it seemed empty of birds, empty of movement.

Then a thought struck her, with sudden, awful certainty.

It let us come up here. It wanted us to come up here. It's waiting for us.

She screwed up her eyes, her heart beating fast, and looked, more sharply this time, at the ruined house amongst the trees.

There, clinging to the top of the tumbledown chimney, sat a huge, hunched shape, powerful claws gripping stone. The rain had given the shiny feathers on its head a punky, gelled look. But the bird was far from comical. It looked even more dangerous, in this untidy state.

And it was watching the two of them with an unblinking stare.

'Ianto!' hissed Rose. Ianto, who was striding ahead, turned and hurried down to her. Wordlessly, she pointed at the bird, which was sitting up straighter now, tensed.

There was nowhere to run. Nowhere to hide. They were out in the open, the sky above, low grass and heather below. The eagle had taken the only shelter on the mountain.

And then it struck. Crouching first, as before, zeroing in on them – it punched out from its perch on the chimney. Flying low, bolting towards them at lightning speed, curved beak thrust out then, at the last moment, the talons whipping forwards and stretching out in front.

There had been no plan. No time to run. No time to do anything but duck, huddle together and protect their heads with their arms. At the last moment – pure instinct – Rose turned her back on the bird and, holding the stem of her spade, thrust it upwards.

Then she found the handle wrenching in her grip, and the

world went dark for a moment as the eagle's huge wings blocked out the moon and stars. A scrabbling, as strong claws hit and grappled metal, then Rose was swept forwards, the toes of her trainers trailing helplessly along the ground, still grasping the spade handle with all her strength. *It won't get Dad's spade. I won't let it.*

She felt Ianto's arms grabbing her feet in a rugby tackle and heard his shouts, but the eagle was too fast, too strong, and his reaction came too late. He lost his grip, fell, then scrambled to his feet to run beneath her, yelling helplessly as she was pulled into the air by the golden eagle.

Wind whipped past her face and the world wheeled beneath her swinging legs as the great bird carried her onwards and upwards, on the end of her dad's spade.

Carrying her over the edge of the mountain . . . and suddenly, the long, long drop gaped below. Now it was too late to let go. The fall would kill her, no doubt about that. She had to hold on, had to let it take her where it wanted.

If only she could turn into the owl, right now, then she could simply let go and fly away. She closed her eyes, desperately, to concentrate on becoming an owl. To empty her mind, despite the pain in her arms, which felt as if they were being pulled from their sockets; despite the abyss beneath her dangling feet, filling her with horror . . . Her eyes sprung open in panic.

What she had to do now was . . . what she had to do . . . *Think, Rose!* But she couldn't think. Her mind was blank with terror.

The eagle was riding the thermals now, wings outstretched, soaring in long, wide circles over the great bog and the fields below, gaining height with each turn. The ground below seemed impossibly far down, like a sky-diver's view before opening their parachute.

If only she had a parachute! She knew that she could not hang on for much longer. The pain in her arms and shoulders was intense, and her hands were hurting too – despite herself, her fingers were beginning to loosen; she could not grip the wood for much longer . . .

Then came a sound from the ground – intermittent and faint at first, but growing stronger and louder. A familiar sound. A buzzing sound, getting closer and closer.

Rose looked down. The eagle had come full circle and she was facing the mountain again. And a quad bike was speeding up the rough mountain track towards her, headlights blazing. Mr Williams gripped the handle bars, and he and Del were straining forwards in the front seat, as if to make it go even faster.

Now she could see Ianto too, running up the mountain towards the vehicle, waving his arms. The sound of his shouts were carried to her on the gusting wind. Then the buzzing cut out abruptly as the quad bike stopped at the top of the mountain and Mr Williams and Del leaped off.

Suddenly, Rose felt the eagle hesitate in the air, wings pulling forward to hover slightly so that her feet hung down straight, but only for a moment. Because then the great bird began to dive, dive for the group around the quad bike, with Rose hanging helplessly beneath. The bird and the girl rushed through the sky, high and fast, back over the lip of the mountain.

Now Del was bounding towards them, leaping into the air and twisting with fury, barking and snarling. Now Mr Williams was reaching into the back of the quad bike and pulling out something long and thin. *A stick?* With both hands he put it to his shoulder, head cocked to one side to hold it in place. *A gun.* He lifted the barrels, pointed them straight at her, swivelled smoothly to track her progress, then pulled the trigger.

Rose screwed her eyes tight, gripping the spade handle for dear life. The gunshot exploded like a crack of thunder in her ears, and a shudder vibrated down through the wood of the spade. Then she felt herself splattered with something that was cool and wet and horrible. But before she could process any of this, she was falling from the sky, still holding the spade, as if it would help her to fly, like a magic broomstick . . .

Two seconds later, she landed on something that gave slightly. Something firm and embracing, that made a noise like 'Ooomph'.

It was Mr Williams.

The impact knocked the air from Rose's lungs and she collapsed, falling forwards from Mr Williams's arms and sprawling amongst the heather, gasping for breath.

In the meantime Ianto had reached them, grabbing her shoulders and pulling her to a sitting position. Although he was right next to her, he was still shouting, in panic. '*Rose – wyt ti'n iawn?* Rose – are you OK?'

She lifted her head to look at him, feeling as if she might be sick. Bringing dazed eyes to focus on his face, which was white with shock, she drew in a long, gasping breath, then nodded, exhaling. '*Iawn. Dw i'n iawn,*' she croaked. 'OK. I'm OK.'

They were speaking Welsh together. And she was back on the ground, on the wonderful, solid ground. She touched her face to see if the horrible, wet stuff was still there. It wasn't. She looked up. Nothing to see in the sky. Mr Williams had blasted the bird to smithereens.

Mr Williams! She turned around and there he was, on all fours amongst the heather, coughing and choking to get his own breath back. He had been winded too – winded by her. Del was gently licking his cheek, wagging the very tip of her lowered tail. She had been frightened.

Mr Williams sat up and pushed her away. '*Cer o 'ma, bach,*' he said to his dog. 'Get away, lass.'

Then he pulled himself to his feet and strode back to the quad bike. 'Come on, you two,' he called over his shoulder to Ianto and Rose. 'Get on. We need to make plans.'

Wordlessly, Rose struggled upright. She and Ianto placed their spades into the back of the vehicle, next to Mr Williams's gun. Then they squashed together on the seat next to him.

The buzzing quad bike flew down the hill, bumping wildly over stones, with Del running alongside, keeping up easily, ears blowing backwards, tongue lolling determinedly from her mouth.

23

They were inside Mr Williams's house. In his large, front room. As he bolted the door behind them, Rose stepped down on to a flagged stone floor and looked about, fascinated.

The ceiling was low and beamed. To the right was a big fireplace filled with an old-fashioned stove. A kettle was steaming and whistling faintly on one of its hot plates. Above it, on the chimney breast, were framed photographs of people – old and new. Rose spotted one of Ianto, as a toddler, smiling at the camera and holding his dad's hand.

Before the stove was a long, wide wooden table, almost completely covered with newspapers. Four wooden chairs stood around the table and, apart from one, they were also stacked with newspapers and other papers.

Against the wall, opposite the front door, was a big old wooden seld, or Welsh dresser. It was full of coloured plates and jugs and cups, and many more things besides – painted eggs, plastic daffodils, postcards, trinkets and ornaments.

The other half of the room contained a large, comfy-looking sofa, and a little bed. On the bed, was a guitar. As if Mr Williams had just been playing it, before he'd come rushing out to help them. And all three walls around the bed were covered in bookcases, bursting with books, some of them two-deep on shelves: some titles in Welsh, some in English. Stairs, against the far wall near the bed, led up into darkness.

A round, orange lampshade hung low over the table, and the lit bulb within it gave the whole room a homely glow.

Rose surprised herself by blurting out, '*Dw i'n hoffi eich tŷ*. I like your house.'

Mr Williams was pulling closed the curtain on the little window above the sink in the corner. He turned to her.

'*Roedd rhaid i fi ddod â'r gwely lawr llawr*,' he said. 'Had to bring the bed downstairs. Can't sleep up there any more, with the rain coming through the roof.'

Then he lifted the piles of newspaper from two chairs and stood with them stacked in his arms, looking about. In the end he put them down in the corner, by the sink.

Sitting down at the table, his face suddenly lit by the orange glow of the lamp – bright blue eyes, anxious expression – he gestured to Ianto and Rose to sit opposite him in the two vacated chairs.

They sat. Ianto was very quiet. Rose glanced sideways at him, and saw that his face was white and drawn.

As if he'd just noticed the state they were in, Mr Williams jumped up and went through a little door behind them to another room – the bathroom? – coming back with two towels and two pairs of thick, woolly socks, which he threw towards them. 'Here,' he said.

Gratefully, they rubbed at their hair and faces with the towels, which were warm and rough. Rose bent down to take off her soaking trainers and socks, and Ianto did the same. Mr Williams grabbed newspaper from one of his piles and stuffed balls of it inside the shoes, then left them in front of the stove. He draped their wet socks over the stove's bar. They dried their damp, white feet and put on the socks.

That felt a hundred times better. Fascinated, Rose realised that steam was wisping from her and Ianto's still-damp heads.

Del gave a little whine. She was pacing back and forth, back and forth, in front of the door.

'She's not used to being inside,' said Mr Williams, watching her. 'But I'm not letting her out. I might have blasted that thing to kingdom come for now, but it'll be back. As I expect you two know, by now.'

He looked at them across the table, eyebrows raised, arms crossed.

Ianto and Rose glanced at each other in amazement.

'You know?' said Ianto. 'You know what's been happening to us?'

Mr Williams's blue eyes screwed up and his shoulders began to jiggle up and down. Then, 'Heh, heh, heh, heh,' he went, convulsively.

Rose was alarmed – until she realised that he was, in fact, laughing.

'Oh, I know all right,' he said, once his shoulders had stopped jiggling. 'But the first thing I need to do is apologise. Apologise to you both.'

Ianto and Rose looked at each other again. Why on earth would Mr Williams need to apologise?

'I've done it all wrong,' he went on, and there was suddenly not a trace of laughter in his voice. He fixed his eyes on Ianto. 'Ianto, bach, I should have told you about it – about the curse. On your twelfth birthday. I didn't. I didn't know it would happen to you. To tell the truth, I'd almost forgotten about it myself, what with everything. Being alone . . .'

What *was* he on about?

Ianto echoed her thought. 'Uncle – what are you on about?'

Then Mr Williams sprang up again and headed for his bookshelves. He scanned along the spines with a finger, muttering to himself. Then he pulled out several volumes in a block, to look at the ones stacked behind them.

'It should be here, somewhere . . . It *was* here, I know it.'

'Uncle, you wouldn't by any chance be looking for *Chwedlau Cymru* by old Thomas Williams, would you?' called Ianto, winking at Rose.

Rose grinned back, glad to see that Ianto's spirits had returned.

Mr Williams whipped round, a book from the pile in his arms falling to the floor with a bump. He bundled the books on to the sofa and rushed back to the table.

'You've seen it? You've read it?'

'Oh yes, we're familiar with it,' said Ianto, casually. '*The Return of the Kings*, and so on.'

Ianto was enjoying himself now.

'Where did you get it?' Mr Williams lowered himself back into his chair.

'Mamgu gave it to me, when I was off school this week.'

'Mary gave it to you?' Then Mr Williams's shoulders started to jiggle again. 'Heh, heh, heh, heh,' he went.

'It would be her,' he continued, shaking his head now. 'My little sister. Always one step ahead. Always sneaking about and finding things out, listening at doors, poking her beak in. Always nicking my books, too.'

'Hey! That's not fair. Mamgu was doing us a big favour, Uncle. That story helped us understand what's going on.'

Mr Williams was silent again now, watching them both. Then he nodded. 'Fair play,' he said. Then, 'So you both know what happened all those years ago. A couple of thousand years ago, I'd say.

'Now you need to know what's happened in between. Because old Thomas Williams didn't want every Tom, Dick and Harry knowing our family business. He left a lot out, as you might have noticed. The story didn't end there.

'But before I start . . . how about a cup of tea, and something to eat? You two look like you need sustenance.'

Rose realised that she was absolutely starving. So did Ianto, because they were both nodding eagerly at this suggestion.

When they'd all finished cheese and pickle sandwiches made from thick slices of white, crusty bread and their hands were clasped around steaming mugs of sugary tea; when Del had settled with a sigh in front of the door, head on paws, eyes – the blue and the brown – fixed on her master, Mr Williams began.

24

'I better tell you my own story, first,' he said. 'That's the one I know best.

'On my twelfth birthday – this is sixty years ago now – Mam and Dad gave me a bike. It wasn't new, and it wasn't a kids' bike – in those days kids rode adults' bikes and bolted blocks of wood to the pedals if their feet didn't reach them. It was a big old bone-rattler. But anyway, I was over the moon with it. And I was soon bumping down the track on it to the village, to show it to Gwenllian. Gwenllian was . . . my best friend. Best friend in the world.'

Mr Williams paused. Then he seemed to wake up, as if from a short dream.

'No. I better go back further. Tell you about Tadcu, and Gelert. Tadcu – Grandad – lived with us here. It was me, Mary, Mam, Dad and Tadcu. Mamgu passed away when I was a baby.

'Wish you'd known Tadcu, Ianto. First class boy. Top drawer. Used to talk to me like I was a proper human being, not just a kid. I could tell him anything.'

'He was the poet,' said Ianto.

'That's right. The poet, who was the Chaired Bard at the Eisteddfod. You know what that is, Rose?'

'I do.' Rose nodded. She made a mental note – *I must ask Ianto to show me his poem, the one that won.*

‘Well, one evening, a few years before I was born, Tadcu was down in the pub. It was a cold night, early spring, and he was enjoying a quiet pint in front of the fire. And then a man came in, a stranger. He was holding a cardboard box. He gathered everyone about him, then he opened the box. Inside, cowering in the corner, was a small, white ball of downy feather, its little curved beak open in fear and anger, its fierce eyes looking up at the men’s faces.

‘It was a *gwyddwalch bach* – a baby goshawk.’

‘Wow,’ said Rose. Goshawks were very rare. And very beautiful. But she was also outraged. ‘That’s against the law – goshawks are a protected species.’

‘I know, bach. But things were a bit different, back in those days.

‘All Tadcu knew was this little creature was afraid, and far from home. So he gave the stranger all the money he had in his pocket, and he took the bird home with him. He called him Gelert. He fed him on tiny scraps of meat, and kept him in his and Mamgu’s bedroom. And Gelert grew. Soon he was flapping his wings, jumping about. He wanted to fly. *Gek, gek, gek*, he’d go. He started pulling things apart. Wrecked their quilt – attacked it and plucked it like a chicken, throwing the stuffing all about. Practising. Mamgu put her foot down, then.

‘So Tadcu made Gelert a roosting box and put it up in the barn. Before long he’d lost his baby down, and was flying around in there. Then he developed his adult coat of feathers: smooth, brown wings above; brown barred white and soft as clouds underneath. Pale white stripe over his sharp, amber eyes. Started making sorties over the wood, finding his own prey. But he always came back to Tadcu. Used to streak down from the sky and land, thump, on his wrist.

'Well, at the end of that summer, and with a heavy heart, Tadcu took a backpack and went away, on foot. Gelert followed him – flying above him during the day, roosting in a tree at night while Tadcu bivouacked below. Tadcu walked all the way into the middle of the mountains, the mountains north and east of here. The mountains where, surely, Gelert's egg was laid. Where not many people live – now or then.

'When they reached the mountains, Gelert went winging away to explore, calling *Pi-aaah, pi-aaah* – and the sound came echoing over the dark conifers that coated the mountainsides. When he disappeared from view, Tadcu turned and walked home again beneath the trees. And when he got back here he went straight up to his room. Didn't want to talk to anyone. He was missing Gelert already, terribly. But he knew he'd done the right thing.'

Mr Williams cleared his throat.

'Anyway, that was Gelert. Back to my birthday. My twelfth birthday. That evening, after I'd struggled back up the track on my bike, I helped Tadcu put old Bes, our carthorse, to bed in her corner of the hay-barn. Bes was a treasure – and a character, too. She used to poke her head through the front door every morning and neigh till Mam gave her a cup of tea, poured into a saucer. She lived to a good old age – forty or so – and we buried her in the corner of the lower field there, where the larches grow.

'So I was mixing up a bran mash – with a dollop of sweet molasses – in a tin bucket. She liked that at the end of the day. It was haymaking time – early August – and she'd been working hard, pulling the hay cart from the high field.'

'Didn't you have a tractor in those days?' asked Ianto.

'We did, boy. Heh! It's sitting outside in the yard – hasn't moved for forty years. But tractors couldn't cope with the high field. Too steep, you see. So Bes helped us, instead.

'That night, while Bes was eating her chow, Tadcu said he had a present for me. And he gave me *Chwedlau Cymru* by old Thomas Williams.

'Now old Thomas Williams, as you probably know, was Tadcu's tadcu. And old Thomas Williams had given that same book to Tadcu, when he was twelve, too.

'And he seemed to want me to read it, then and there. So I sat down on the soft, tickly hay, and I read the last story. *The Return of the Kings.* Just like you two did. Then I looked up at Tadcu. It was all right, I thought, but it wasn't a real story. It didn't end properly. *What happened next?* I asked. And did Bleddyn really just lie down and die, after all that he'd done?

'Then Tadcu told me some things. Things I'll tell you two . . . soon. Time's getting on, and I need to tell my story, first. Anyway, what Tadcu told me didn't make any sense to me, at the time. *Tadcu's spent too long scything in the sun,* I thought. *He's gone soft in the head.* And he *was* getting on a bit, I reckoned. Seventy-two – same age as I am now!'

This thought tickled Mr Williams, and his shoulders began to heave up and down again. 'Heh, heh, heh, heh . . .' he began.

Rose and Ianto waited for him to recover, rapt with attention.

When his laughter died away, his face grew serious again. 'The next night,' he went on, 'Gwenllian and me made a plan. We were going to take Dad's bell tent, the one he brought back from the war, and camp down in the wood.'

Aha! thought Rose, and she and Ianto shared a quick glance.

'So that's what we did. We put the tent up in the middle of the wood, next to the rocks there.

'We made a little fire and boiled a kettle for tea. Gwenllian had brought some apples. Best cup of tea I've ever had, before or since. Best apples, too. Of course, Gwenllian had to sneak out that night to meet me. Her parents didn't like her hanging around with me, you see. Didn't want her getting involved with the lot who scraped a living on the side of the mountain. Thought they were a cut above. Hah!' Mr Williams snorted the last word, with sudden anger.

'We watched the stars,' he went on, calming down, 'and then we fell asleep. And, well, I think you two know what happened next.'

'You woke to find that you were a giant and she was an owl and you were breaking out of the rocks?' supplied Ianto.

'Exactly that. And dark smoky stuff – Bleddyn, of course – rose up from the stones too. It swarmed together, then it came apart as a huge flock of starlings, coming after us, screaming and stabbing, before we could even adjust to our new shapes. Gwenllian didn't stand a chance. She hardly flapped her wings before she was mobbed by shrieking birds, attacking her viciously with their beaks.

'I fought them off best I could with my arms and I grabbed her out of the air. Then I held her in my hands like this.' He demonstrated, putting his curled hands together as if he was holding a quantity of marbles. 'She didn't like it. She was screeching like crazy and jumping up and down inside, trying to flap her wings. She wanted to be free, to fight the starlings, but I knew that the flock would tear her apart. They were doing enough damage to me – covering me like a hiveful of angry bees, stabbing at my face, my neck, my arms, making a diabolical din with their whistling and screaming. I had to keep my eyes tight closed, or they'd've had them out in an instant. And they were swarming around my hands, trying to get at Gwenllian, trying to make me drop her.

'I could feel the blood streaming, warm, down my face. Blindly, I stumbled through the wood and fell, head over heels, down the hill just behind where your house is now, Rose. I was making an unholy row – uprooting trees, knocking out rocks, sending them thundering down the hill to take out more trees as they went. But still, I kept Gwenllian safe in my hands. And still, the cloud of starlings came after us, stuck with us, never letting up with their stabbing and clawing.

'I knew where I was heading, but I couldn't stop myself tumbling faster and faster now – my hands and arms were useless, holding on to Gwenllian for dear life, as I rolled and crashed down the hill, thumping my head, my body, almost knocking myself out . . . Then, of course, I stopped falling. I'd hit the bottom. I slithered feet-first into something soft. Something cold and wet and thick, that gave way and sucked me in, deeper and deeper.

'The bog. And, of course, in those days there were no

wooden walkways across it. Just acres of sopping wet peat, ready to suck you in and drown you. Now I knew for certain that I was done for. That *we* were done for. A huge great lump of a giant in that bog . . . and you know how heavy those giant's boots are, don't you, boy?'

Mr Williams looked at Ianto, who nodded, eyes wide.

'Those boots soon filled with mud, and though I tried, I couldn't pull them out, couldn't pull them off my feet. And, of course, the more I struggled, the deeper I sank. And I knew I couldn't be far from the edge – but how to get to it? How to pull myself out? Impossible while I held Gwenllian in my hands. With my eyes tight shut. And now that we were held captive by the bog, those starlings were attacking us again in earnest.'

Mr Williams took a slurp of his tea, shaking his head.

'By this time I was almost up to my armpits in it – exhausted, in great pain, and sinking lower every second. I held Gwenllian up, safe in her finger-cage – and I thought to myself, *There's nothing more I can do now. We're going to die – and we're only twelve!* Then, from inside me, came out a huge roar of anguish, pain and anger. So loud was it, so deep and desperate, I could hear it echoing all across the bog. So loud that even the starlings let up their mobbing for an instant.

'The echo of my shout faded to a murmur, but the screeching of the starlings started up again. And their attack. And then – Gwenllian bit my thumb, hard, with her sharp, powerful beak. Drew blood. I was so shocked, I opened my hands – which was what she wanted, of course. I felt her burst off my palm, like a feathered arrow from a bow. The starlings were in my face, so I couldn't see what was happening, couldn't open my eyes. I prayed that she'd taken them by surprise and escaped. And I had a feeling, a feeling that she'd got away. I reckoned, see, that when Bleddyn makes himself into more than one creature, they can't move far from each other. You know – can't be in two places at once.

'But no time to think about that. Because then I heard another sound. The thundering of hooves, coming closer and closer. And shouting, indistinct at first, then louder, clearer.

'It was Tadcu. He was galloping to the rescue on old Bes.

'Tadcu was shouting: "Don't struggle! Don't move! I'm going to get you out. Thomas, listen – don't fear those starlings. They can't hurt you."

'Bes had stopped galloping by now. And judging from Tadcu's voice, he had to be at the very edge of the bog. "They aren't real starlings, bach," he went on. "They're substanceless, unreal – remnants of an old, old spell, which cannot persist. Think of good things, Thomas, boy, think of good things. Think of God and all the gifts he has given you. Think of your parents and how they love you. Think of our family, stretching back through the ages, doing our best. Think of Gwenllian, your dear friend, and how she wants to protect you, though she's small. Think of the love that you have for our home, for Cymru!"'

Mr Williams paused to take a breather and a sip of tea, after this stirring speech.

'Wow,' said Ianto. 'Did that work?'

Mr Williams chuckled, shoulders heaving. 'No!' he splurted. 'Mind you, he was asking me to think – and you try thinking, when you're being pecked to death by demented starlings.'

‘So what happened?’ asked Rose. ‘Did your tadcu have a gun?’

‘No, he didn’t. See, Tadcu was a pacifist. Conscientious objector during the First World War – and took a lot of stick for it. Spent time in Wormwood Scrubs, at His Majesty’s Pleasure. That’s where he started writing poetry. Time on his hands, you know?

‘So, no. He didn’t have a gun.

‘And then things took a turn for the worse. Because the starlings – Bleddyn, I should say – didn’t like what he’d just said. Didn’t like to hear about good things, and hope, and such like. The whole swarm of them lifted from me with a great, chattering screech, up into the air. I opened my eyes. I saw the dark flock turn in the starlit sky, change shape and dive, like a long spear. Dive down on Tadcu, and on Bes.

‘And soon Tadcu had been driven to the ground, arms over his head, and Bes was screaming, a sound I’d never heard before – and never did again, thankfully. She was rearing up in panic – shaking her heavy head and stamping her hooves to be rid of the deadly birds, which fluttered about her like mosquitoes. I reckon she could have galloped to safety. But that wouldn’t have been Bes’s style. She wouldn’t leave Tadcu, and she was doing her best to fight back.

‘But the worst thing about this, the absolute worst thing, was that I could do nothing. Stuck as I was in the bog, still sinking.

‘And, to my horror, under the savage blanket of birds, Tadcu’s body had stopped struggling.

‘I roared again – a cry of despair and fury. It came echoing back to me from across the wide bog.

'Then, well, you won't believe this.'

'Try us,' said Ianto, grinning and glancing at Rose.

They knew that Tadcu must have survived, because he went on to win the Eisteddfod Chair. And that Bes had lived to a ripe old age. But it was hard to see how they'd got out of this fix.

Mr Williams took another slurp of tea. Then he continued.

'From far away, from over the hills to the north and the east, from the other side of the shimmering, moonlit bog, two specks came speeding towards us. They grew in size and their shapes became defined as they approached. Then one overtook the other. And I realised what it was, what they were. The first was a powerful goshawk, full grown, majestic. Deep, quick wingbeats propelling him forward. And behind him, flapping determinedly, flying faster than I'd ever seen an owl fly, was Gwenllian.

'Somehow, she had fetched Gelert from his mountain fastness.

'And, well, a starling is no match for a goshawk.'

'But it was a flock of starlings,' said Ianto.

'Ha!' said Mr Williams. 'Well, that night we learned a handy lesson. It goes like this. When Bleddyn makes himself into more than one animal – like a flock of starlings – you take one out, you take them all out. Remember that, now.

'His wings stretched out wide, his tail straight and long, Gelert sped straight towards Tadcu. I felt a whoosh of air as he cleared my head, and glancing up I saw the soft, barred underside of his magnificent wings. And then he swooped at speed, talons out, and snatched one of the starlings as it was lifting its head to stab Tadcu. Instantly, the whole lot of them burst, like dark bubbles, and particles of black stuff fell gently towards the ground. Then they gathered together into a dark mass and sped away, back to the wood.

'Sudden silence, now. Tadcu on the ground, Bes looking about in confusion.

'Then, slowly, Tadcu moved. Struggled to his feet and stood, shakily, hands on knees. Blood was pouring from his head and his arms. But he was alive.

'Gelert wheeled above him, head swivelling, sharp eyes fixed on Tadcu. Making sure he was all right. Then, with a great, echoing cry of *Pi-aaah*, he turned in the night sky and sped back the way he'd come. Home, to the forests of the inner mountains.

'Gelert had repaid his debt; he had saved his saviour.'

Mr Williams paused, eyeing the two of them. Letting this sink in.

Then he began again. 'Gwenllian flapped to my shoulder, with a *ke-wick*. She gently nipped my ear. To say sorry for the peck on the thumb. In the meantime, Tadcu had been busying about. He was hitching a harness to Bes and tying a thick rope to it. "Here," he shouted, throwing me the other end. "Tie it under your arms."

'I caught the rope and did as he told me. And not before time, for I was still sinking into the bog – almost up to my neck now. I kept my arms out in front, holding on to the rope.

'Then "Hyaaar!" called Tadcu, smacking Bes's haunch.

'Bes pulled at the harness. She sweated and strained with

the effort, eyes rolling. Tadcu was at her head, speaking urgently into her ear. Gwenllian took off and glided over to hover in front of her, too, crying out to spur her on.

'At first, nothing. Bes, head down, front legs driving forwards, hooves stumbling, unable to get a grip. Then, suddenly, a shift. Slowly, slowly, with a great sucking, smacking sound, the mud began to release its grip on me. I could see the effort was taking its toll on poor Bes. White sweat lathered her sides and she was snorting and crying out with exhaustion, but she carried on – pulling, soldiering on, with Tadcu and Gwenllian calling encouragement.

'And then I was out of the mud altogether, on top of it – as if the bog had given birth to me. And what a labour it had been! I could help Bes now, by swimming forwards on the surface. Until, head to toe in mud, I beached up with the rest of them.

'Poor Bes was in a bad way. I helped Tadcu unhitch her. Head down, legs shaking, she could scarcely stand. Tadcu had a bottle of water on him, and he lifted it to her lips. She sipped, and she steadied, but we all knew there was no way she'd make it home up the steep track.

'So I bent and gathered her into my arms – just as I'd carry a lost sheep, stuck in a snow drift, to safety. And Tadcu and me and Bes climbed the mountain for home.

'Gwenllian rose into the sky and headed back to the village, to her own home. And that . . .' Mr Williams paused, and then he closed his eyes, tight. When he opened them, he looked suddenly lost.

'That was the last time I saw her.'

Rose felt stunned. She glanced at Ianto. He was staring at his great uncle with a puzzled frown.

'How come?' asked Ianto.

'Aah,' said Mr Williams, putting his head down and pinching his eyes with his thumb and forefinger.

And Rose knew, suddenly, that Mr Williams was acquainted with the same kind of grief that she was.

Poor Mr Williams.

He looked up, suddenly. His blue eyes were bright and shiny.

'She got caught coming in. She'd turned back into a girl, and was climbing through her bedroom window. Her parents were in her room, waiting for her, wanting to know where she'd been. She told them the truth – well, part of the truth – that she'd been with me, camping in the wood.

'They went *ballistic*,' said Mr Williams, using the English word. 'That's the word you use now, isn't it – you kids?' He gave a brief snort of mirthless laughter. 'And the next day – *the very next day* – they packed her off to London on the train. To stay with some aunt or other, just for the holidays, they said. But they were lying. Because a month or so later, they moved to London, too. Her dad had got a job down there. Some fancy job. And they never came back. None of them.'

'But . . . but didn't you stay in touch with her?' Rose was still in shock. The story was almost unbearable.

'Aaah . . . Listen. It wasn't like it is now. We didn't have mobiles. We didn't even have a landline up here till the seventies. If we needed to make a phone call, we'd walk down to the phone box in the village. And a phone call was a big deal. You did it in emergencies, not to have a chat . . .' he trailed off.

'But didn't you write to her?' asked Ianto.

'I . . . no.' Mr Williams looked up defiantly, as if they were accusing him. 'I was never one for writing letters. She wrote a couple to me but I never replied, and then she stopped. *What's the point?* I thought. She'll never come back here. She'll meet a fancy London boy, and that'll be it. I'll never see her again.

'It seemed easier that way.'

There was silence in the room. Then Del, asleep on the flagstone floor, gave a little groan. They turned to look at her. Her paws twitched and clenched.

'What happened next, Uncle?' asked Ianto, turning back to him. 'When you got back here, that night?'

'Well, I'd just put Bes down beside the hay-barn and *ping*, I was back to being a boy. Good job, because if it'd happened while I was carrying her, I don't think I'd have lived to tell the tale!'

Mr Williams was trying to be lighthearted now, trying to smile. But his eyes were still bright with unshed tears.

'Was Bes OK?' asked Rose.

'What? Oh, yes. We rubbed her down and threw a couple of blankets over her. Gave her a bucket of bran mash, more water. And next morning, she was poking her head through the open door there, neighing for her saucer of tea. Right as rain.

'Tadcu and I weren't so good, though. We were covered in cuts and bruises. How to explain that? So Tadcu said we'd been out for a spot of night-fishing, and we'd fallen into brambles on the way back, in the dark. Mam and Dad seemed to believe us – it was such a busy time of year, perhaps they were too tired to pay attention.'

'So. When did you meet Bleddyn again?' asked Ianto, after a brief pause.

'I didn't. Not till tonight.'

Rose and Ianto looked at each other in surprise.

'What – you only had that one adventure?' said Ianto.

'Yes. Just the one.'

Mr Williams placed his elbows on the table and leaned forward, his eyes moving between the two of them. 'And that brings me to the other things you need to know, about this whole business. How it works. What Tadcu told me in the hay-barn, that night. And why I need to apologise to you both, again.'

Rose wasn't sure she could take much more drama tonight. It had to be nearly morning now – Saturday morning. Surreptitiously, she pulled her mobile from her pocket. 4:32 a.m. No wonder she was tired! She must make sure she got home before Mum was up and about, heading for the bakery. Mum didn't always look in on her before she left, but Rose didn't want to take any chances.

She looked up and caught Mr Williams's eye. She saw a mixture of anxiety and determination there.

'Don't worry, bach. I'll get you both home safe and sound. Just hear me out a little longer, then we'll call it a night.

'The three of us need to get some sleep because, soon, we're all going after Bleddyn. We surely are. And we're going to break his curse – once and for all.'

25

Rose came round, gradually, from a profound, dreamless sleep. Warm sunshine was streaming through the curtains on to her bed.

Her head felt heavy and numb, and there was a hollow feeling in her stomach, which, along with the bright sunlight, told her it was late – late in the morning, or even into the afternoon.

It was the beginning of the summer holidays. But it felt nothing like a holiday. No lightness of spirit, no sense of freedom. Just the knowledge that the wood was in danger and that she and Ianto (and Mr Williams?) were going to have to fight Bleddyn again. And win. Somehow. Before he killed them.

By the time Mr Williams had finished the story about the bog and Gwenllian, she and Ianto had been tired out. Could scarcely keep themselves from falling off their chairs. But they'd woken up all right, at what he'd told them next.

'Well,' he'd announced. 'I said before that Tadcu told me some other things that night in the hay-barn, about this whole business.'

Ianto and Rose had nodded, dazed with fatigue.

'Told you I thought he'd gone doolally in the sun, and was talking nonsense?'

They nodded again.

'Thing was, he hadn't gone doolally,' he went on, shaking his head. 'He was all there. What he said was the truth.

'Anyway, here it is, as far as I recall. Listen carefully, you two. It's very important. It's what I should have told you, Ianto, when you turned twelve. But I didn't. I'm sorry.' Mr Williams looked down at the table top.

'Why didn't you?' asked Ianto, his voice flat and tired.

'I thought . . .' Mr Williams tailed off and picked at a newspaper with his fingers, pulling it towards him then shoving it back. He looked up and started again. 'I thought that because I didn't marry Gwenllian, didn't have children or grandchildren, that it wouldn't happen this time. Not that I thought much about it at all. No one to talk to about it, you see. Up here on my own. Was beginning to think I'd imagined the whole thing, made it up, made up the adventure at the bog, even – or that Tadcu had imagined it all and told me the story. You know?'

Ianto didn't respond, but continued to regard his uncle with sharp, brown eyes.

'Anyway,' Mr Williams concluded, 'I didn't know it would happen to my nephew – great nephew – whatever you are, boy.'

'Thanks, *Uncle*,' said Ianto, sarcastically. Rose glanced sideways at him. He wasn't joking. The beginnings of a frown were creasing his forehead.

Mr Williams didn't seem to notice, frowning himself now in concentration. He cleared his throat. Then he went on, 'Turns out that the same thing – the giant and the owl thing – happened to Tadcu and his best friend, another twelve-year-old girl, sixty years before it happened to me. And to *his* tadcu, the writer of the book, sixty years before that. And to his tadcu, and to his, and so on, and so on, and so on.'

What? Wordlessly, Rose and Ianto turned and stared at each other. They were part of a continual process, going back hundreds of years through history. How? Why?

They looked back at Mr Williams, who had closed his eyes and was frowning. Where his story about the bog had flowed delightfully, like a summer stream, this one was turning into a stuttering, stop-start affair. Like being stuck in a bog.

He opened his eyes. '*Ahem.* See – since the time of that first giant and owl, all those years ago – and I reckon about two thousand, myself, in Celtic times – there have been many other owls and giants. They spend the night in the wood, as kids, then they come out of the rocks as giant and owl, again and again, through history. Every sixty years, like I say.

'And the giants are always from our family, Ianto. From the family of the first giant, to be exact, who came to live up here on the mountain. Our family. But up till now, the giant has always been the grandson of the previous giant.

'And, at the same time, their companion, their very best friend – a girl – becomes an owl. That's you, Rose, of course.' Mr Williams glanced at her, eyes crinkling briefly in an anxious smile. 'Also, at the same time, Bleddyn appears. In the form of animals. And attacks them.'

'Why?' asked Ianto, shortly.

'Erm.' Mr Williams coughed. He raised his eyes to meet theirs, glancing from one to the other, guiltily. 'I can't remember, exactly. Tadcu said something about there being a curse, or a prophesy, or some such. And I think he said it was laid by Bleddyn.' Mr Williams paused, and his eyes flickered to the newspapers again, as if his mind was straining at the leash. 'Or . . . *ahem*, maybe he said it was his brother, Berwyn, the good king . . .' Then he started again, more certainly, 'But I remember for sure that every sixty years the place that hides the cave where the two kings rest – the wood, that is – comes into danger, and the giant and the owl and Bleddyn rise again.'

Berwyn, the good king. The mention of his name made Rose's spine tingle, and a warm feeling filled her. With all this horrible Bleddyn stuff, they hadn't thought of the other king. The good one. Surely he would be on their side, would help them, if he could—

Then she stiffened. Wait a minute. Rewind. *The wood . . . comes into danger.* Did he mean . . .

Yes, he did. 'And,' went on Mr Williams, looking down again, 'well, this is where I need to apologise. Again. This year, as you know, I sold the wood.'

'That's what started all this?' Ianto shook his head in disbelief, his frown deepening as he stared, incredulously, at his uncle.

Mr Williams did not reply.

'How could you do that, when you knew?' went on Ianto. 'When it was sixty years on from when it happened last time?'

'I . . .' his uncle started. Then he looked up and his face flushed red, his voice suddenly harsh, loud. 'Now, look, boy!' His hand shot out and he lunged forward, pointing angrily at Ianto. 'You want to try scratching a living up here, on your own in a tumbledown house – rain coming through the slates, chimney falling down. You want to live here through the winter, when you're all alone—'

'*All alone, all alone!*' interrupted Ianto, hotly. Their anger was quickening, sudden and blazing, like flames on dry kindling. Ianto was shouting now, stabbing his own finger back at his uncle. 'You're always moaning about being *all alone*. But you were the one who didn't write back to poor Gwenllian! You didn't have to be alone! And now we're supposed to feel sorry for you, despite the fact that you triggered the curse, and put me and Rose through all this danger . . . We had to figure it out for ourselves, because you couldn't even be bothered to warn us! Plus, selling the wood to the abattoir people! What? You really want to look out of here and see an *abattoir*? You think Rose and her mam want that? We could have helped you fix your house, but you didn't want help. Oh no. Much easier to feel sorry for yourself and make as many problems as you can for other people, instead!'

Stunned silence; Ianto breathing hard. Then Ianto surprised them both by leaping up, so suddenly that his chair fell backwards and clattered on the floor. Before they knew it he was storming towards the door, Del yelping and scrabbling in a skitter of claws on flagstones as he stumbled over her legs. Struggling with the bolts, he cried out in frustration, but he soon shot them open and was off, out the door, running into the dark night.

For a second, Rose and Mr Williams stared at each other. 'He's not wearing his shoes!' cried Rose, leaping up and grabbing both pairs of trainers from the stove, ripping out the newspaper balls, then slipping hers on to her feet as fast as she could. No time to tie the laces – she was bursting out of the door, running down the drive and calling out to Ianto.

Mr Williams was right behind her.

'Come back! Both of you! It's not safe out there!'

Rose breathed in cool, night air, stumbling towards Ianto, who was sprinting away in socked feet, slipping on wet cobbles. The clouds had dispersed now, and Rose was running towards a sky that was lightening to a brilliant, deep blue.

Ianto had reached the flag. Still running, he raised his hand to give it a little salute, then he turned and plummeted wildly down the steep, stony track.

'Ianto!' called Rose. 'Wait for me!'

But he didn't. He carried on running, arms out and windmilling wildly as he careered down the uneven track, wincing as his socked feet met rocky outcrops.

The next thing she heard was the rumble of an engine behind her. It was Mr Williams, in his battered, gunmetal Land Rover.

He drew level with her and leaned across to open the side door. She jumped in, wordlessly, slamming it behind her while the vehicle continued to roll forwards. Rose felt something warm and wet nudge her elbow and looked around in surprise. There was Del, standing up, shakily, in the back, poking her nose through the seats to be close to them.

They were not far from Rose's house now. And here was Ianto. He had stopped and was leaning forwards, breathing heavily, hands on knees.

Mr Williams hit the brake and leaned across Rose to open the door.

'Get in,' he said. And Ianto did, squashing up next to Rose.

She handed him his trainers, and they exchanged a glance.

No one spoke. When they got to Rose's, Ianto opened the door and stepped out to allow her to get down.

They stood for a moment, Ianto's tall silhouette dark against the lightening sky. Then he stepped forward and enveloped her in his arms, burying his face in her neck. Warm and strong – and so familiar, though he had never hugged her before. Surprised, she hugged him back.

He pulled away and watched as she carefully, quietly, opened her front door and sneaked inside. She turned and gave him a little wave before shutting the door behind her.

The Land Rover's tyres crunched down the track behind her and the sound of the engine retreated down the slope. She tiptoed to her bedroom and, fully clothed, still damp, fell into bed and deep sleep.

And here she was now. Still in bed. Her stomach rumbled and twanged, emptily. She grabbed her mobile – 12:45. No wonder she was hungry! Then the phone rang in her hand. It was Mum.

'Hello, love!' she said, brightly.

'Hi Mum.' Rose's voice sounded creaky and unused.

'What are you up to, then, on this lovely morning?'

'Well, I had a bit of a lie-in . . .'

'Good girl! First day of the summer holidays, eh? You enjoy it. Had lunch yet? There's left-over moussaka, if you fancy. And trifle.'

'Oh, yeah, that sounds good – thanks, Mum.' She paused, trying to think of something to say. Hard to make normal conversation, when your mind is full of shape-shifting sorcerers and long lines of giants and owls, stretching back to Celtic times. 'Um – how's the bakery?'

'Busy morning, love, very busy – Delyth and I are rushed off our feet, and we've already run out of wholemeal loaves. Just having a sandwich and a cup of tea now, out the back, while she holds the fort. Lovely, sunny day! Now, I was going to say something, and I've forgotten what it was . . . What was it? Help me, Rosie!'

'Mum, I have no idea.' Rose leaned over to open her curtain, then lay back again, enjoying the framed picture of the sunlit grass in the garden and the darker green of the wood beyond.

The wood! 'Hey,' she said, sitting up. 'I need to check the council website and see what's happening with the planning permission.' She was suddenly alert, nervous.

Mum gave a little gasp. 'Rosie – you're a mind-reader. That's exactly what I'd forgotten I was going to say to you!'

'Cool. I'll have lunch, and then I'll check it. And I'll text to let you know – OK, Mum?'

Rose showered and got dressed. As she tucked into a plate of cold moussaka and a slice of buttered bread, she tried to sift everything that she and Ianto had learned last night. So many questions, still unanswered.

Then, from her swirling mind, a thought leapt out at her, like a flying fish from a stormy sea. She caught it, and looked at it, and her heart stood still for a moment. It went like this.

So, every sixty years a boy from Ianto's family becomes the giant. But who, exactly, are the owls? How did she, Rose, fit into the picture? Were the owls connected somehow, too? What if – what if she was Gwenllian's granddaughter! What if Gwenllian was, somehow, Dad's mam – her grandmother?

Rushing back to her bedroom, she grabbed her mobile.

Hi Mum – what was Dad's mam's name, please? X

Then she finished her lunch, wiping the cheesy, tomato sauce from her plate with the last of the bread, but she could no longer taste it, her heart beating fast as she waited. Minutes passed, and there was no reply from Mum. Rose began to feel uncomfortable. Perhaps she'd upset Mum by talking about Dad – Dad's family – like this, out of the blue. Now she wasn't sure what to do. Should she text back and say sorry, don't worry about it, Mum?

Then, *ping*, came the reply.

Hello, love. She was Beryl – Beryl Morris. She died before me and Dad met, bless her. She sounded a lovely lady. X

Right. Rose felt herself deflate, like a left-over party balloon. Bang went that theory. She wasn't Gwenllian's granddaughter.

Then Rose felt mean. Mum had just told her about Dad's mam. Beryl. A lovely lady. Who deserved much more thought and kindness than this – this just thinking of her as a theory, then ruling her out.

She closed her eyes. 'Sorry, Mamgu Beryl,' she said, concentrating on sending good wishes to this lady – whom she had never met, nor even seen in a photo. 'When all this is over, I'm going to find out more about you, I promise. And I'll find your grave, if you have one, and lay flowers on it.'

Slowly, she opened her eyes, and felt better. As if lovely Mamgu Beryl was looking down at her with a smile.

She breathed in. Then she breathed out, slowly.

Now she needed to check the council website.

Rose realised, as she got its homepage up, that she had, sadly, come to dislike the council's website. She knew it was full of good and useful things but, for her, it was a source of horrible anxiety. She braced herself, and clicked first on *Planning* and then on *Application number: D4/27983*

Under all the familiar information, there, in front of her, were the words:

Outcome of Planning Application Meeting: *Application put on hold while developers organise archaeological survey of area.*

She read it again. To be sure.

So, she thought. The archaeologists will come, and they will look at the jumble of rocks and realise that they're the ruins of an ancient, megalithic monument. And then the cromlech and the wood around it will become a conservation area, so the company won't be able to build their abattoir. That was how it would work. *She hoped.*

She had done it. *She thought.*

But a little part of her was still worried. Had she understood the wording properly? She wished Miss Evans was here, to confirm that this was a good outcome. But she couldn't speak to Miss Evans now. Miss Evans was on her well-earned summer holiday.

So she texted Mum.

I think it's going to be OK – the developers have been told to organise an archaeological survey! X

And now, now it was time to go to work again. And, somehow, she had a feeling that it was up to her to organise things this time. To get Ianto and Mr Williams together again – knock their heads together, if necessary.

She phoned Ianto. When he picked up, she was about to start with 'Hi, it's me,' in English, as she always did. And then she remembered – they had spoken Welsh to each other last night. And not just because they were with Mr Williams, but naturally, between the two of them. Something she had always wanted to do, ever since she had learned to speak the language.

So she said '*Shw mae, Ianto – fi sy 'ma,*' instead. And he replied '*Rose! Sut wyt ti?* Rose! How are you?'

And it felt as natural as if they'd always spoken Welsh together. Rose knew, somehow, that they would do so from now on.

Ianto had called her by her name, too. He hardly ever did that. Only when things were very important. And speaking Welsh together was very important.

Despite everything, she couldn't help smiling.

26

Ten minutes to midnight, and Rose was waiting by the track outside her house, in darkness. She was carrying a small backpack that contained a torch, a bottle of water, a cheese sandwich, a fleece and a waterproof jacket. Just in case.

No spade this time. They'd left their spades at Mr Williams's last night, anyway. She'd wondered about bringing a kitchen knife, or one of Dad's hammers or something, but it had felt wrong. It would be horrible to carry a weapon like that. Anyway, she had a feeling it was illegal.

In her pocket was the ancient scroll of vellum. *The Thirty-Third Owl.* She couldn't wait to show it to Ianto and his great uncle, to hear what they made of it.

Then the low rumble of an engine interrupted her thoughts. Crunch of tyres over stone, approaching up the track from the village. She hoped that Mum was fast asleep inside, and did not hear it.

The Land Rover stopped, its headlights illuminating the track ahead. Ianto opened the side door and shifted over for her to step up and into the vehicle. Mr Williams nodded at her from the driver's seat and they carried on up the track. Rose looked behind to see that Del was in the back, balancing shakily and looking forward as best she could through the gap in the seats, part of the team.

Soon they were all tumbling in through the front door of

Mr Williams's house. He bolted it behind them and immediately busied about. There was a backpack on his bed, already half-full, and he was stuffing something else into it – what looked like climbing gear.

Del, sensing the tension in the room, was keeping nervously to his heels, almost tripping him up when he turned abruptly and strode to the seld, pulling open one of the drawers in its bottom half and sorting through the bits and pieces in there – pliers, a set of false teeth, an eye-patch, pens, batteries and fuses, until 'Aha!' – he found what he was looking for. He brandished aloft a see-through plastic compass on a cord, which he put round his neck.

Then he took up two climbing harnesses from the bed and threw one each to Ianto and Rose. '*Cymerwch rhain*,' he said. 'Take these. In fact, put them on now – where you can see what you're doing.'

They caught the ribbons of black webbing and stepped through the leg loops, then buckled them up at the waist. Rose looked at Ianto and he shrugged. Was Mr Williams expecting them to go rock climbing?

At that moment he picked up a long, stiff leather holster and threw it over his shoulder, doing up the buckle around his waist. The shotgun.

Then he lifted a heavy-looking loop of nylon rope and slung it across his chest. Now he looked like Indiana Jones – wearing a green John Deere cap instead of a brown fedora.

Ianto had picked up a hand-axe, about the length of his forearm, from the bed. He weighed it in his hand and gave its blade an experimental swipe in the air. His uncle turned and snatched it from him by the handle, glaring at Ianto. Then he tucked the weapon into his own belt.

Ianto shrugged, grinning. '*Werth trio*,' he said. 'Worth a try.'

He and his great uncle seemed to be back to normal, after last night's fireworks. That was something, thought Rose.

But she needed to get their attention.

'*Mae rhywbeth 'da fi i ddangos i'ch 'ch dau!* I've got something to show you both!' she said as loudly as she could, and she pulled out the little roll of vellum.

The two of them turned in surprise and hurried over. She uncurled the small parchment to reveal the black letters that covered its surface.

Ianto leaned over her shoulder and read aloud.

'*The Thirty-Third Owl*,' he said. Then he glanced at Rose, his eyes full of wonder.

She heard Mr Williams repeating '*The Thirty-Third Owl . . .*' quietly to himself. He was frowning. 'I know I've heard that before, somewhere. No matter. Go on, Ianto.'

Ianto continued:

'*Cave-coffined, two kings under earth – the bad and good –*
Sound Celt-crafted instruments of iron and wood.
Kin wakes kings. Iron breaks wood – for second birth.
King takes king; iron makes good – to end the curse.'

There was silence in the room. Then Del, crowding in at Mr Williams's leg, looked up at them with her mismatched eyes and gave a little whine.

'Where did you get this?' asked Ianto at last.

Rose told them how Dad had been given it by his grandmother, and how he had given it to her.

'Let me see,' said Mr Williams. He reached out and carefully took the parchment from Rose's hands, bringing it over to the table so he could examine it under the light. 'Vellum,' he pronounced. Rose nodded.

'I'd say it was cut from a book,' he went on. 'Look – the edges are a little jagged, like a knife was used.'

They gathered around him. He was right – the light revealed little snags.

'Medieval, I reckon.' Mr Williams turned it over to look at the back, which was blank.

'It's got to be about Bleddyn and Berwyn,' said Ianto, looking from Rose to his uncle with shining eyes. 'Coffined in a cave – one good, one bad – it's them!'

'Then it talks about them playing instruments. Made of iron and wood,' said Rose, excitedly. It felt so good to share the mystery. 'Like a harp, maybe – that's made of wood? But I don't know what instrument's made of iron.'

'Not sure,' said Mr Williams, frowning at the scrap of material, 'not sure it means musical instruments . . .'

Ianto grinned, cheekily. 'Hey, forget the gun, Uncle. Let's take your guitar and we'll sing to Bleddyn. That'll get rid of him, all right.'

'Hah,' said Mr Williams, distractedly. He was squinting at the words. '*Kin wakes kings*,' he quoted. He looked at Ianto. 'That's got to mean us, boy. We're the kin who wake Bleddyn.'

A little voice inside Rose said, *Maybe the kin means me. Maybe it's* my *family that wakes the kings. Kings . . .*

'Hey,' she blurted. 'It says *kings*, not *king*. But we only see one king – Bleddyn. We don't see Berwyn, the good king, do we?'

Mr Williams looked at her, and his blue eyes were sharp. He shook his head, slowly. 'No, we don't. It's always been Bleddyn.'

'Uncle – has Bleddyn ever killed anyone?' asked Ianto.

There was a beat of silence after this question. The words filled the cosy room with a sudden, ominous tension.

Mr Williams took in a breath, then he looked down at the newspapers on the table. *Uh-oh*, thought Rose. *He's going all evasive again.*

He looked up, exhaled, and said, 'No,' quietly.

Rose and Ianto let out the breath they hadn't realised they'd been holding.

'But,' he went on, 'that's only because, in the past, the danger to the wood was taken away.'

There was a pause.

'What do you mean, Uncle?' asked Ianto carefully, staring at him.

'Well, I was going to explain it last night, boy, but of course you got in a stew and stormed out the house . . .'

Ianto didn't respond, his eyes suddenly humourless and hard. Rose saw that he was clenching his fists at his sides.

Mr Williams met his great nephew's glare with one of his own. 'See, every sixty years, like I said, the wood comes into danger.

'Sixty years ago, when Tadcu and me had the fight with Bleddyn at the bog, Dad was short of money – as per usual – and wanted to sell the wood to the council. They were buying up land, hereabouts, to build council houses.'

'Why would your dad want to sell the wood,' questioned Ianto, 'when he knew what would happen?'

'Well, here's the thing, boy. He *didn't* know what would happen,' said his uncle. 'That generation – the in-between generation, who don't get to meet Bleddyn – never do know. Your dad now – Tegwyn. The policeman. He has no idea about the giants, about Bleddyn. And he never will have – because you, boy, are not going to tell him.'

Ianto frowned. 'Why not?'

'He won't believe you, that's why not. He won't believe you, but he'll interfere. Stick his nose in. Mess it all up. And then the whole thing won't get sorted out.

'Nah. That generation always think they know best. Always think they know better than old Tadcu – old Uncle, in my case – better than their own kids. Think the old stories are just made-up tales – Pah!' Mr Williams seemed to be warming up for a rant.

'So what happened with the sale of the wood to the council?' asked Rose, hoping to keep him on course.

'This is what happened,' he said and he cleared his throat, shifting into storytelling gear. 'The day after the adventure at the bog, Tadcu and me went to the National Eisteddfod to watch the Chairing of the Bard. As luck would have it, it took place in our town that year.'

Rose nodded. She knew that the Eisteddfod was a movable feast – it happened in a different place each year.

'And, of course, that was the year that Tadcu won. No one was prouder than I was to see him stand and take the stage to sit in his splendid chair, to witness the ceremony – the flowers, the great horn, the sword and the song. But best of all, you know what his bardic name was?'

Rose shook her head. Every poet who competed for the Chair entered anonymously, using a pseudonym.

Mr Williams's shoulders were jogging up and down now and, sure enough, 'Heh, heh, heh,' he wheezed. '*Y Cawr. Y Cawr!* The Giant! I ask you! Good old Tadcu.' He smiled fondly, shaking his head. To Rose's surprise, she saw tears in his eyes, which he wiped, suddenly and fiercely, with the back of his hand.

'He won,' he repeated, sniffing loudly. 'And that meant, along with the chair, he was given a good sum of money. And he came home, and he handed that money straight to his son, my dad. Told him he could take the wood off the market now. And we didn't see Bleddyn again after that. Danger had passed, you see. The secret of the cave was safe.'

'So,' Ianto had closed his eyes, concentrating, 'what happened the other times? Sixty years before that? When your tadcu was twelve?' His voice was clipped, strained.

Mr Williams looked at him, hard. But he cleared his throat and continued, 'Ah, now. That time, Tadcu's dad wanted to sell the wood – again. See, one thing about our family, boy – we've always made an honest living, but we've never been money-makers. Dreamers, more like. Farmers, and dreamers. Every man Jack of us.

'And that time – we're talking, what? 1901 – Tadcu's dad was set on selling the wood to foresters. Wanted to plant pine trees for pit props, they did.

'Tadcu, and his friend – my Mamgu, as it goes, but that's another story – turned into giant and owl and had their own close scrape with Bleddyn. As luck would have it, the very next day, his tadcu – the author of the book, of course – received his first royalty payment for *Chwedlau Cymru*. He made sure to give that money to his son, and the wood was saved again.'

Wow. Rose's mind was whirling backwards through the past, taking giant steps of sixty years.

'And the time before that?' she asked Mr Williams.

'Old Thomas Williams's dad was approached by a quarrying company. They wanted to mine the mountain again, for building stone. To cut down the trees in the wood and put up their buildings.'

'And how did that get resolved?' asked Ianto, tightly.

'Well, now. Old Thomas Williams's tadcu was another special one.' His uncle was shaking his head again now, in wonder. 'He was a preacher, a hymn writer. And, do you know, he walked the length and breadth of Wales, spreading God's message.

'As luck would have it, one of his followers – a rich widower – gave him a sum of money. Wanted him to buy a fine horse with it, so he wouldn't have to walk so far, preaching the word of the Lord. He was getting on, of course – he'd be seventy-two by then, as you know.

'But he didn't spend the money on a horse. He explained to this kind lady that he would use it to safeguard the wood, so that the people of the village had a place to find their God, in nature. And, as luck would have it, she agreed.'

For a moment Mr Williams looked lost in another age. Then he cleared his throat and his eyes focused back on the two of them.

'Now. Don't ask me about the times before that. Because if Tadcu told me, I can't remember. But I do know this pattern has happened again and again, back to that first giant and owl. And, as luck would have it, it's always been resolved. No one has ever died.'

'*As luck would have it . . .*' repeated Ianto. His fists remained clenched and so did his face, his brown eyes never leaving his great uncle's. 'But the luck's run out. It's too late. Because you have sold the wood to the abbatoir people. And you can't unsell something, when you've sold it, can you? They're going to build their abbatoir. This time, Bleddyn is going to keep coming after us. At some point, he'll kill us.'

Rose saw, to her shock, that tears were forming in Ianto's eyes.

Mr Williams looked shocked too. He stepped forward and grabbed his great nephew's shoulders, trying to pull him into a hug. Ianto, arms limp at his sides, submitted for a moment before pushing him away and turning from him, head in hands.

Rose wasn't sure what to do. Mr Williams came forward, awkwardly, as if to hug him again, but seemed to think better of it, and said instead:

'Hey now, Ianto, bach. No, boy! No one is getting killed. Not on my watch. See, that's why we're here now. We're taking the fight to Bleddyn. We're going to find his cave. And when we do, we're going to break his staff.'

Ianto took his hands from his face and turned to Rose. They stared at each other. What was he on about *now*?

'Yes – break his staff,' Mr Williams continued, nodding enthusiastically. 'That's all we need to do. Easy. No more giants, no more owls, no more Bleddyn. So, so – cheer up, bach. We're finally breaking the curse, boy!'

27

Ten minutes later, they left the house.

'Wait here,' instructed Mr Williams, leaving them in the yard while he hurried into the hay-barn, Del running at his heels.

Ianto turned to Rose. 'What do you make of all this?' he asked, in a low voice.

'I . . . well, I don't know. There's so much to take in.'

'Do you believe him, I mean? Believe all this stuff, about the sixty years, about this latest thing – breaking Bleddyn's staff?'

'Well, yes, I think I do. I mean, it kind of makes sense, doesn't it? And it all happened to him too, when he was young. I don't think he made that up – all that about the bog.'

'But he keeps throwing new stuff at us,' Ianto whispered, urgently. 'You think you're somewhere, then he pulls the rug from under your feet. He's put us in terrible danger – and, I know he's family and all, but I'm not sure I trust him. He's a total loose cannon. It's bad enough having to deal with Bleddyn, without a mad uncle to worry about too.'

Rose couldn't help snorting with laughter at that, despite the situation.

Ianto was looking at her, and she could see he was smiling through the darkness. She smiled back, trying to convey a sense of hopefulness to him.

'Wish it was just me and you, again,' he whispered.

'Me too,' she replied, remembering last night – battling

the boar together, running from the eagle, hiding in the wood. OK, it had been really scary. But they'd had to think on their feet, make decisions for themselves, and that had felt good. Now Mr Williams had kind of taken over.

'I guess we have no choice, for now,' she went on. 'And he's got a gun, at least.'

There was no chance to say more, because a giant tortoise was emerging from the barn, with Del trotting beside it.

Rose blinked. She was tempted to rub her eyes, like people do in books, but instead she screwed them up to try to see better across the dim, starlit farmyard. Once again, she longed for her sharp, owl eyes.

The tortoise ambled closer through the darkness, weaving its way around the old ploughs and prongs that littered the farmyard, and she saw that it wasn't a tortoise at all. It was Mr Williams – who else? – and he was carrying a coracle – a small, round boat, made of leather stretched over a strong, wicker frame – on his back. A strap across his chest held it to his body and he was carrying an oar that looked like a long cricket bat in the crook of his arm.

'What now?' groaned Ianto, under his breath.

Mr Williams heard this. 'Tadcu's coracle, boy! Used it to fish on the river, he did. But we need it now. It's going to come in handy, where we're going.'

'But we're heading for the cave, aren't we?' said Ianto.

'We surely are. Come on, you two.' And Mr Williams strode past them down the drive, showing them the rounded underside of the coracle. Del kept to his heels.

With a glance at each other, eyebrows raised, they followed.

A starry night sky, shot through by threads of long, silvery clouds, lit their way to the flag at the corner of the track. But instead of heading down the track, the rounded back of the coracle strode upwards, to the top of the mountain.

'Uncle!' hissed Ianto, jogging to catch him up. 'Where are you going? The cave's down in the wood!'

The coracle did not break stride, but continued to move up the slope.

'We know where it is, Mr Williams!' added Rose, trying to keep her voice low. 'I was trapped down there, before, and Ianto saved me! It's under the wood, near the stream.'

This time, the coracle did stop. And then it turned round so they could see his face, lit by cool white light from the sky. It wore a surprised expression.

Ianto and Rose scrambled towards him.

'You were trapped in the cave, bach? Are you sure, now?'

'Yes. Bleddyn led me down an earth tunnel, and then out into a stone cave. There was another cave around the corner, and I knew – I just knew – that that was where the two kings were. Where they *are*. And it was down in the wood. At the far side there.' Rose turned and pointed far out over the dark tree canopy that stretched below them.

'Then, last night, we found another earth tunnel, which turned into a stone tunnel, which led to the cave,' added Ianto. 'Or, at least, we felt sure it did. But Bleddyn, as a wild boar, chased us out before we reached it,' he went on.

Mr Williams let out a low whistle and turned to Ianto, frown deepening. He snapped, 'Why the heck didn't you tell me all this, boy?'

'You never asked! You never gave us the chance! You were too busy talking about yourself, as per usual—'

'Hey!' Rose surprised herself with the sharpness and authority in her voice. But she was fed up with all this bickering. 'Stop arguing, you two! It's not getting us anywhere. We have to work together –' She looked meaningfully at Ianto – 'and we have to share everything we know.' Then she looked, meaningfully, at Mr Williams.

To her surprise, both of them seemed to calm down, letting out long breaths.

'Sorry, bach,' said Mr Williams to Rose, from inside the shell of the coracle. 'You're right, of course. But – do you know how important this is? None of us have ever been near that cave! You're sure, now?' he repeated.

'Like I say, I wasn't in the actual cave, but one next to it. And Bleddyn disappeared round the corner into it, when he'd stopped being a mole. I *am* sure it was the cave. Somehow, I am sure.'

Mr Williams was shaking his head, looking at her. 'Something different is happening this time,' he said. 'Something stronger. And . . .' he hesitated, 'and you're right, bach. We're all equals on this trip, isn't it. One crew. And no, I haven't been sharing everything I know with you both.'

Then he turned to take in Ianto. 'I have to tell you, kids, I'm concerned. The pattern has changed. Like you going to the cave, bach.

'And no one has been attacked by Bleddyn before, when they're not in their owl or giant forms. I was pretty worried last night, I tell you, when I came up the mountain and found you both there, as kids, with Bleddyn as the eagle . . . That's a very dark turn of events. Very dark indeed.'

'So it's never happened before? Bleddyn attacking the owl and the giant when they're humans?' asked Ianto.

Mr Williams shook his head. 'Never heard of it, no.'

Suddenly, Rose felt the bottom drop out of her resolve. They were surely on mission impossible. How could they defeat Bleddyn, just the three of them?

Del sensed something of their concern and looked up, giving a little whine. Mr Williams put his hand on her head to comfort her.

And that gesture, so small but so kind, reassured Rose too. She turned to look at Ianto and, on impulse, she grabbed his hand.

Surprised, he turned to her. Then he smiled, and squeezed her fingers.

'Heh, heh, heh!' went Mr Williams, seeing their clasped hands. Then, 'We need swords for this really, but never mind. *All for one*,' he broke into English, putting his own hand out towards them, fist down –

'*And one for all!*' replied the other two, extending their arms to knock knuckles with him. Then they all lifted their fists triumphantly in the air like the Three Musketeers and joined in Mr Williams's laughter while Del jumped around in sudden excitement, ducking forward on her front paws with her behind in the air, giving a little bark.

Then Mr Williams turned his coracled back, and continued up the mountain.

Ianto started, 'Hey, Uncle, where . . .?' then he tailed off, giving up. He grinned at Rose, shrugged, and followed him upwards.

Rose joined him. Might as well. Mr Williams seemed to know what he was doing – good job someone did.

They climbed until they reached the large stone at the top.

Then Mr Williams unstrapped himself from the coracle and laid it on the ground. He placed the slim paddle within it then took off his backpack and rummaged inside, pulling out some carabiners and a climbing sling – a long loop of webbing, an inch or so wide.

'Give us a hand with this belay,' he said, and Ianto and Rose hurried over. Obeying his instructions, they placed the sling over the boulder and attached a carabiner to it, nearest the edge of the cliff.

'You two done any abseiling before?' he asked.

They nodded. Last year their class had spent a week at an outdoor activity centre in north Wales, doing abseiling and climbing and stuff. But not in the middle of the night. And not without instructors, safety ropes, helmets and gloves . . . What was Mr Williams expecting them to do? But there was no time to think – now he was throwing a carabiner each to Ianto and Rose.

'Clip these to your harnesses.'

They did so. Mr Williams reached into his backpack again, coming up with two small, solid metal devices, shaped like number eights with one large and one small hole. 'These are figure-of-eight descenders,' he said, handing them out. 'Clip them on to your harnesses – put the carabiner through the small hole.'

They did as they were told, then they watched as Mr Williams unslung the coil of rope from his shoulder and tied the end of it to the sling on the rock. He tied a big knot in the other end. The rope was only about a centimetre thick – was that enough to hold their weight? Then he strode to the edge and threw the coil over, shouting 'Rope!' He turned and grinned at them. 'Sorry,' he said, quietly now. 'Force of habit.'

Rose was desperately trying to remember how they'd abseiled on the school trip. Had the rope been this thin then? And how had they done it? She couldn't remember.

'Right,' Mr Williams went on. 'Come here, you two.'

He led them to the edge of the cliff. Del stayed behind, guarding the gear by the stone. He got down on his hands and knees and crawled the last two yards, then lay, so that his head was over the edge and he was looking straight down the sheer cliff of the mountain. The grey hair sticking out from under his cap blew up in a sudden breeze from below.

Rose and Ianto followed, and soon they too were lying flat, looking over the edge. Rose felt dizzy as the breeze hit her and her eyes fell down the rocky drop, into the darkness below. Suddenly she remembered Ianto's fall, crashing down the mountainside and landing with that terrible crack at the very bottom. She glanced at him. He was facing the drop, brown hair blowing in the wind. She couldn't see his face.

'See that hawthorn? About twenty metres down?' said Mr Williams.

Rose's eyes refocused, higher up the cliff. Yes, there was a dark shrub sticking out from the rock, somehow finding a root-hold in the sheer cliff.

'That's where we're heading,' he went on. 'The hawthorn hides a tunnel straight into the mountain. The remains of an old drift mine.'

He was backing away from the edge now, and the others followed.

'And this is how we're going to do it,' he was saying. 'Ianto, you're going first. Then you, Rose. Then I'm going to lower the coracle. And in the coracle will be Del. You two need to grab it and pull it into the tunnel. Del will be fine. Then I'm coming down. Got that?'

Mr Williams had thought it all out. How long had he been planning this? No time to ask, because already he was helping Ianto thread the nylon rope through the big hole in the figure of eight clipped to his harness. Then he and Ianto strode to the edge, Ianto walking backwards as he paid the rope out through his hands, his head twisted around to see where he was going.

'Hold the rope at your hip, boy,' said Mr Williams. 'Let it run through smoothly. When you're safely on the ledge below, release the rope and call "Rope's free!". Remember – feet apart, and lean back. Now then. Ready?'

Ianto's feet were on the edge of the drop now, where wind-clipped grass gave way to thin air. He was leaning out over the abyss, his face tight with concentration. If he was feeling any nerves, he wasn't showing them. One hand on the rope above the figure of eight, to steady it, the other on the rope dangling below, holding it at his side. He nodded. Then, after quickly flexing his knees, his feet on the grass, he began the descent, clambering over the edge a little awkwardly, then holding himself taut as he found his feet, leaning back and walking himself down, jerkily at first, then more smoothly, until he had disappeared completely.

Rose joined Mr Williams to lie at the top again, looking down, and watched as Ianto's head dropped below them, legs stretched forward and bent a little at the knee, walking himself down the sheer cliff, letting the rope out with his right hand as he went.

Soon, Ianto had reached the hawthorn. They heard him cry out as he was briefly entangled in its thorny embrace. And then he scrambled about and disappeared from view. After a bit, they heard him shout 'Rope's free!' and Mr Williams tugged at it to make sure it was slack.

Rose was filled with stomach-churning fear. She tried to say something, but no sound came out. She stared at Mr Williams with her mouth open, like a goldfish. She knew, all at once, that she could not do this.

But, somehow, her body wasn't listening to her mind. Somehow, her body knew what it was doing, and it took over. Mr Williams was looping the rope through the figure of eight attached to her harness. Then she was backing towards the drop, eyes fixed on his, as he murmured, 'Good girl. Now you're there. Grip the rope tight, down by your hip.'

Her heels were over the edge. The draft blew up from beneath her, the air cool and damp-feeling. Now she remembered how it felt – to lean out, backwards, over a precipice. It was unnatural, terrifying. Her eyes gripped Mr Williams's, who was calmly helping her to kneel on the edge and slither over it, so that her feet were now on the sheer rock beneath the thin, clinging layer of earth at the top. She was leaning back, supported by the harness and the rope. She held the rope to her hip with her right hand – the braking hand, she remembered. Her left hand gripped the rope above, and so did Mr Williams's. Again, she thought how thin the rope was.

As if he could read her mind, Mr Williams said, 'Don't you worry about the rope, bach. It might not look it, but it's strong enough to hold your mam's car.

'Off you go now,' he went on, letting go of the rope.

And off she went. Or, off her body went. Her mind had gone somewhere else now, eyes wild, locked on to Mr Williams's. She had no choice. They all had to do this, they had to keep going.

And before she knew it, she had left the top of the mountain and Mr Williams with it and she was facing the sheer cliff face, moving down it, using her feet, spread apart about two feet – in the way that she remembered from last year. But too quickly, too jerkily – she was bouncing now – *Slow down!*

And with that thought, her foot slipped and she lost balance, swinging inwards towards the cliff, bashing her shoulder then swinging back, spinning on the thin rope so that she was facing outwards in mid-air, towards the darkened, moonlit hills. The fear came back, shoving her head beneath the surface of a sea of shifting terror. And the cliff, the rope, the harness – everything – was distorted with terror.

'Rose!' Ianto called from below. She looked down and saw his upturned face, white through the darkness. His eyes were the only still point in her fear.

'You're all right,' he went on, nodding encouragement. 'Keep going. Easy does it. Remember, the rope and the mountain are your friends.'

She wrenched her eyes from his to look forward, and saw the cliff coming back to her, its great mass looming. This time she put out her feet so they met the rock as gently as possible, to keep control of her movement. And the mountain met her halfway this time, and held her, while she shuffled her feet apart, then began to walk again, carefully stepping down its surface. Letting herself down.

'Down, down, down,' she said aloud, not caring if anyone heard, as she controlled the rope through the figure of eight and descended. Now it was working. She was doing it. She was pushing with her feet against the cliff, leaning back, going down, down, down.

But she was still very glad when she reached the hawthorn and Ianto grabbed her waist and pulled her inwards to safety, past the thorny branches of the shrub. She was shaking, and Ianto had to remove the rope from the figure of eight for her.

'Rope's free!' called up Ianto. The two of them watched as the rope slithered back up the sheer mountainside. They were standing just inside the entrance of a tunnel, beyond the ledge. Looking behind her, Rose saw stony darkness. And heard their sounds – shufflings, clinking carabiners – distorted within it.

But no time to think about the tunnel, because now the coracle was being lowered down the side of the mountain. Mr Williams had made a sling of webbing which held the coracle like a baby. Small enough to drop at an easy pace without catching the cliff's sides, its descent was smooth. From below they could not see Del within the little boat.

Soon, however, the coracle was upon them, and the sheepdog's head appeared, peering over the side, eyes wide, ears back.

Together, they clasped the coracle and pulled it past the hawthorn, doing their best to keep it upright and stable. It was tricky, and a couple of branches broke. Del was standing up inside, legs shaking as she balanced, like they did in the back of the Land Rover. The entrance to the tunnel was not very wide, but there was enough room for Ianto and Rose to pull the coracle with Del inside it to safety. Then she and Ianto busied about untying the rope and taking off the sling and Ianto called out 'Rope's free!' for the final time.

Del looked brave and nervous all at once, whining faintly as she stood up in the boat, watching the two of them with big eyes – one pale and one dark in the half-light.

When they'd freed the coracle, Rose couldn't help herself. 'Good girl, Del, bach!' she said, flinging her arms around Del's warm, furry body. But Del slithered from her embrace and jumped from the coracle to stand on the ledge, looking up for her master. She whined a little as the figure of Mr Williams came abseiling smoothly and quickly down the cliff face towards them.

When he reached the ledge he undid the rope and left it hanging down below the cave entrance. Del gave a little bark and a single lick of his lowered hand. Her tail was wagging. But only a little. She wasn't an over-the-top kind of dog.

Rose glanced beyond Mr Williams, back up the mountain to the lip of grass at the top. It seemed a very long way. *How are we going to get up again?* she wondered. *You can't abseil upwards.* Only a really experienced rock climber could climb the cliff face – it had almost no ledges or toe-holds. And they couldn't go downwards, because that was more sheer rock, and they didn't have any spare rope . . . unless Mr Williams was carrying some in his backpack? Maybe he was.

Or maybe they were burning their bridges as they went.

She turned to join the others in the tunnel entrance.

'How's the crew? OK?' asked Mr Williams, looking round.

'We are.' Ianto answered for all of them.

'Right, then.' Now his great uncle pulled three thick bands with a torch on the front from his backpack. 'Put these on,' he instructed, strapping one over his cap then flicking the switch.

Soon the tunnel about them was randomly illuminated by three swinging spotlights. Now they could see that it sloped down, gently, before them. Its floor, walls and ceiling had been hewn out of rock, and the rough, hacked-at stone on all sides shone and glistened with damp. Around the entrance the tunnel sprouted green with mosses and small ferns, which petered out quickly as the tunnel descended into grey, stony darkness. There was a particular smell here – sharp, mineral, strange – but not unpleasant.

Once Mr Williams had strapped the coracle to his back, holding the oar in the crook of his arm, he turned to them. The coracle knocked the stony sides of the tunnel as he did so, and he winced and ducked as wood hit stone.

'Now,' he said. And he looked at Rose and Ianto. 'We

talked before about sharing things. Well, I'm going to share something with you, now. Here it is. Bleddyn can't make rock open and close like he can earth. So the only sure way to get to the cave is through the rock. Right?'

Rose thought about how Bleddyn had opened and closed earth tunnels at will, to trap them or to lead them in the wrong direction. But the rock of the tunnel and the cave had not changed. So that made sense to her, kind of.

'How do we know this tunnel will take us to the cave?' asked Ianto.

'Well, we don't, for sure,' admitted Mr Williams. 'But I know there's a network of tunnels down here, and I think it's reasonable to assume we can get to the caves under the wood this way. Known about this old drift mine since I was a boy, and about the mineworks here – more tunnels, going all over, honeycombing the mountain,' he continued.

Honeycombing the mountain. What a strange idea, thought Rose, looking about at the slick, grey walls of the tunnel. The mountain that, from the outside, looked utterly solid, had been tunnelled through and through, looted for stone. Like a piece of rotting wood, eaten out from within by grubs.

'And, yes, it was Tadcu who told me about it –' he went on, anticipating Ianto's next question – 'but I've never come down here myself to explore. You need a crew of people to do it, and I never got one organised. And then – I kind of forgot about it as I grew up.'

He cleared his throat '*Ahem*' and it echoed up and down the tunnel. He raised his eyebrows at the sound, then continued, 'But I guess I was always planning this. Knew exactly how I'd do it – what we'd need, how to prepare.'

'So why the coracle?' asked Ianto.

'You'll see, soon enough,' said Mr Williams, smiling cannily now. 'That is, if Tadcu was right. And I've no reason to doubt him – no reason at all.'

And with that he turned his coracled back, ducking to avoid scraping the roof, and set off down the tunnel with Del picking her way over the rocky floor at his heels.

Rose came next, then Ianto brought up the rear – the four of them, heading down into the very heart of the mountain.

28

The rock-hewn floor beneath their feet was uneven and slippery with damp. Water was everywhere, but never in quantities enough to make a drop, to drip down from above. Instead it shimmered silently all around in the light of their headlamps.

Then Rose saw something sparkle and flash, from a line in the rock beside her. A seam of gold! It was sandwiched, pressed down by the grey stone around it. She grabbed Ianto's arm, who reached out to touch it, in wonder, and Rose hissed, 'Mr Williams!' The coracle stopped and turned, awkwardly, in the tunnel. 'Look at this! Is it gold?'

Mr Williams examined the seam in the light of his headtorch. 'Not gold, no,' he pronounced. 'No gold in this mountain. Fool's gold – sure to be.'

'Fool's gold,' repeated Rose, touching it herself, now. It was cold and wet and as sparkly as a fairytale princess's necklace.

Mr Williams looked at her and gave a little chuckle. Then he said, 'Igneous rock. That's what was mined here. Mined in prehistoric times, for axe-heads. This is going back – oh, five thousand years, mind. When the cromlech was first built. Then the mountain was quarried again, more recently – three hundred years ago or so – and that was done on an industrial scale. That's how the side of the mountain fell away, to expose this drift mine. So, just think – this tunnel was made by prehistoric miners. People way, way older than Bleddyn and his brother.'

His eyes sparkled, like fool's gold, in the darkness.

Then he turned his coracled back and they continued on their way.

The tunnel stretched before them, dark and damp. Ianto strode silently behind her, and Rose felt the weight of the mountain pressing upon them as they moved further downwards and inwards. It became harder and harder to imagine the world outside of here – the world of open sky and green grass and trees. But though there was a strange atmosphere down here, it wasn't a scary one. It felt, thought Rose, as if they'd all gone back in time. As if they were part of the company of prehistoric miners, and those miners were still working, all around them—

Crack! A loud, sudden explosion of sound, echoing about the tunnel, froze the four of them. Like the snapping of a huge piece of wood. And again: *Clack!* – making them jump this time, like stringed puppets. Resounding, sharp – as if a massive tree-trunk had fallen to hit another, then a wooden clattering, like an old-fashioned rattle, followed by a rushing noise, *Whoosh!* as if all this had triggered a small avalanche of scree. Which died to a whisper and then – silence.

The sounds had come from all around them, impossible to place. Mr Williams turned round to face Ianto and Rose, as slowly and as quietly as he could. Del turned with him. All four of them were braced for more sounds, holding their breaths, their eyes wandering about the tunnel.

Even Del held her head to one side, mouth closed, eyes

unfocused. Then she licked her chops and gave a little whine, looking up at Mr Williams.

'Bleddyn?' asked Ianto, in a whisper.

Bleddyn had to put in an appearance at some point, Rose thought. She wondered what he would be, down here. This had sounded like something big – an elephant, perhaps, pushing down planks with its broad forehead, collapsing complex scaffolding with a kick . . .

'Not Bleddyn. *Y cnocwyr*,' whispered Mr Williams, looking about the tunnel roof. 'The knockers. It's the knockers. We're all right.'

Ianto and Rose looked at each other. *The knockers?*

'Little people. Underground people. Like the *tylwyth teg* – the fair folk. Some say they're the ghosts of miners who died in accidents. Need to treat them with respect. Show them we mean no harm. Anyone got any food?'

Rose nodded and took off her backpack, pulling out the tin-foil-wrapped cheese sandwich.

'Break a piece off, bach,' said Mr Williams. 'And leave it somewhere for the knockers.'

Rose carefully placed a corner of the sandwich on a narrow ledge, making sure that there was a little piece of cheese within it.

'That's grand,' said Mr Williams. Then he turned and continued on his way, Del trotting just behind.

Rose and Ianto looked at each other, again. Ianto took in a deep breath then shook his head as they set off behind Mr Williams, leaving the piece of sandwich behind them.

* * *

An hour or so later they were in the same tunnel but had passed many ways off it – smaller tunnels, low-roofed, twisting out of reach of their headlamps. Mr Williams ignored them all and continued down the main tunnel. He didn't explain his decisions, and it was hard to ask when all they could see of him was the back of a coracle.

Soon Rose became aware of a change in the air. Was it draughtier? Colder? Damper?

Yes, it was all three. She was wearing her fleece, but she wondered if she needed to put on her waterproof, too. They trudged forward and then, suddenly, Ianto and Rose found themselves barrelling into the back of the coracle, which had stopped abruptly. They could not see around it to know why. Del wriggled between Mr Williams's legs to have a recce in front.

'Aha!' said Mr Williams triumphantly, his voice echoing strangely. Then he stood aside, and they saw that the tunnel had opened out so they were standing on a ledge, a ledge that crumbled into smaller stones to become a small, semi-circular beach that jutted out into a still, black expanse. An expanse which caught the light of their headlamps and reflected back, coldly.

An underground lake of still water. They could not see to the other side. Just water. Black and immobile, as if made of glass.

Looking up, Rose's head torch illuminated a rocky ceiling, shaped roughly like the inside of a dome.

'*Now* you see why the coracle?' asked Mr Williams, turning to Ianto with a grin. 'Always be prepared. You a boy scout?'

'No,' said Ianto.

'You should be, boy. Keep you out of mischief.'

'Whatever,' said Ianto, stiffly. 'Listen, Uncle. Do we really know where we're going? We could be heading in the opposite direction to the cave. And the further we go, the further it is to get back. I mean, is it safe down here? Prehistoric mineworks, underground lakes – the knockers? How do we know the knockers are friendly?' Then he paused, frowning, as if realising that he sounded ridiculous. 'I mean, if that noise we heard really *was* the knockers. Maybe it was a roof caving in. Maybe the whole thing is unstable – the honeycomb. We could be setting it off, making it collapse around us. We could get lost down here. Trapped.'

Ianto was working himself up. His hands, gripping the straps of his backpack, were white with strain.

Mr Williams gave him a hard stare. Then he shrugged off the coracle, placed it on the beach and grabbed the compass that hung round his neck.

'That's where *this* comes into play,' he announced, brandishing it in Ianto's face. 'If you two are right about the whereabouts of the cave, it's due south-west of here. So we cross this lake to the other side, then we take whichever tunnel heads in that direction. Unless, of course, you've got any better ideas?'

There was a pause. Then Ianto dropped his eyes. 'No,' he said, quietly. He sounded defeated.

'Rose?' asked Mr Williams.

Rose shook her head. 'No.' Then she added, 'But I am worried about Bleddyn. Is anyone else here wondering why he hasn't appeared yet?'

Ianto didn't reply but looked away across the lake, his dark eyes inscrutable. Mr Williams's grin left his face, returning it to the default setting of anxious. 'I know what you mean, bach – we do need to keep on our toes. But I reckon what he's doing is waiting for us. Keeping his powder dry. Why come to us, when we're coming to him?'

Waiting for them. In his cave.

Not a pleasant thought.

But in the meantime, they had a journey to make. And it seemed that Mr Williams had, once again, thought it all out.

He pointed straight ahead, over the black water. 'That's where we're heading,' he said, 'and this is how we'll do it. We can't all fit in the coracle together, so we're going to take turns. Ianto, Rose – you'll go first. Reckon the boat will hold your combined weight. Ianto – you'll leave Rose on the other side, then row back here. Me and Del will cross next to join Rose, leaving Ianto here. Then, you, Rose, will collect Ianto and the two of you will row back to join me and Del. All clear?'

'I think so,' said Rose, looking at Ianto. He didn't respond, but she heard him draw in a breath, and then he nodded.

Mr Williams showed them the slim oar. 'The person sculling the boat sits at the front, right? But to keep it steady, you need to describe a figure-of-eight in the water.'

Mr Williams held the oar with both hands and drew figure of eight after figure of eight in the air, illuminated by three headlamps like spotlights on a magician's trick.

Then Mr Williams pushed the little coracle off the beach and held it steady while Rose and Ianto gingerly climbed in. The bottom of the boat was criss-crossed with slim laths of wood, between which dark, tarred leather stretched. As Rose stepped into it and felt it give a little under her feet, she realised just how lightweight it was.

But it was a sturdy little craft, tough. Built for purpose.

Rose settled, cross-legged, at the back of the coracle and held both sides with her hands. Ianto sat on the narrow bench that stretched across the boat towards the front. The coracle rocked a little and sank in the water, settling on the shallow, sloping shelf just beyond the beach. It was like sitting in an empty bathtub. Then Ianto seemed to come to his senses and he turned to her, oar in hand. 'Did you want to row?' he asked.

'No,' she replied. 'You go first. I'll learn from your mistakes.'

When Ianto did not reply but turned his back, she went on, 'That was a joke by the way, Ianto.'

Ianto jerked his head around. 'Huh? Oh, yeah.' Then he looked forward again, out across the water.

Something was up with Ianto.

Mr Williams pushed them off, standing with boots ankle-deep in the lake. The coracle was almost round, but not quite – the front of it, the bow, was wide and flat, and the sides of the back tapered inwards and a little upwards, so that it looked back to front. But it moved smoothly forwards when Mr Williams let go, sinking deeper the further it went, until the wooden rim of the coracle was, maybe, six inches above the surface. It would not do to rock about on this little craft.

Ianto gently plunged the oar through the dark, glassy surface and made neat figure-of-eights which pulled the boat forwards at a steady rate. Rose looked back and saw Mr Williams standing on the beach with Del at his side, arm raised to wave them off. Then she looked ahead and her head torch illuminated nothing but black water. The other side wasn't visible, yet. They seemed to be moving through the water without a ripple, without a splash. Like floating on air, not water.

'Ianto! Let's take the coracle down to the river, when all this is over,' said Rose, spontaneously, and her cheerful voice echoed about the cavern.

There was a pause, while Ianto continued to scull. Then '*When all this is over*,' he repeated, in monotone.

Oh dear. There really was something wrong. 'Ianto, what's the matter?' Rose asked.

'Apart from being stuck underground with a bunch of knockers, a mad uncle and an evil shapeshifter? Oh, nothing at all,' he responded, staring ahead.

For some reason, Ianto's dark mood made Rose want to laugh. 'Hey, remember – *the uncle and the knockers are your friends*,' she said, quoting back what he'd said to her earlier.

Ianto didn't reply. Suddenly Rose stopped wanting to laugh. Now she wanted to hug him. But she couldn't, because she'd rock the boat.

'Ianto,' she said, instead. 'Try not to worry. We're doing everything we can. And we've got each other, remember? Me, you, Mr Williams and Del. The Four Musketeers.'

This time, Ianto did twist round to face her, the oar

poised still in the water. And he managed a smile, but his eyes didn't smile with his mouth. They seemed sunk in his head, and full of fear, and then he stopped trying to smile, and spoke. 'Look,' he said, urgently. 'I've got to tell you – I hate being underground. It's making my skin crawl. And the further we go, the worse I feel. Like I'm being suffocated. And so I can't think about what's happening, about being under the mountain, deeper and deeper in, because if I do, I'm a goner. I think I'll die.' He was stumbling over the words as they poured out. 'I reckon it's because of being a giant, sometimes. Because I keep thinking, what if I turn into the giant, down here? I'd never get out again. I wouldn't fit through the tunnel. I'd be stuck . . . down here. Squashed – like, like, a seam of fool's gold. It's making me panic, when I think about it. So, so – I *can't* think about it.' He turned back and continued to paddle, head down, desperately concentrating on every stroke of each figure eight.

Rose remembered how she had felt, abseiling down the mountain. Remembered too, the abyss that had opened before her when she'd thought about Dad.

She knew that this kind of panic was unbearable. And poor Ianto had been feeling it, down here. But he'd kept quiet, soldiering on in his own bubble of misery.

She reached out and put her hands against his back. He turned his head, quickly, and said, 'Thanks,' in a very small voice, then faced forwards again. And then he sniffed, and his back shook, and she realised that he was crying, the oar held still in the water, the boat idling in the lake.

'Ianto,' she said, her hands still on his back. 'I won't let anything bad happen to you. I promise.'

He turned back to her, his face shining wet with tears. And then she watched his expression changing, a puzzled frown growing, his mouth opening and his eyes refocusing beyond her.

'*What . . .?*' he said.

Whipping her head round, Rose saw a small, round ball of pulsing blue flame emerge from the entrance of the tunnel and float through the air, moving at a rate that was neither fast nor slow. It drifted past Mr Williams and Del, who were sitting together on the beach. Taken by surprise, Del jumped up and barked wildly, the sound echoing about as the blue light spun out beyond her and over the water, casting its cold reflection downwards, so that it seemed as if two blue flames were moving over the lake – one above and one below water. And the light shone upwards too, on to the craggy ceiling of the cavern, illuminating, briefly, its nooks and crannies, then passing on.

The flaming, blue ball was heading straight for the coracle.

29

'Duck!' shouted Rose, and Ianto came tumbling off the bench, the two of them cowering together in the back of the rocking coracle, hands covering their heads.

A second later, they felt the inside of the boat fill with cold, blue light. And then the strange illumination passed silently away, over them, onwards.

Rose opened her eyes and lifted her head, and so did Ianto. They saw the ball of blue fire continue its stately journey across the lake. It reached the other side, where there was another rocky beach, just like the one behind them, and another tunnel entrance. It mounted the beach, a foot or so in the air, then disappeared into the tunnel. They caught a quick glimpse of the tunnel's rounded, rocky interior, then it disappeared as the mysterious sphere curved out of view.

Darkness again. Nothing but the light of their head torches. Looking around, Rose could see Mr Williams, still sitting on the beach with Del. He didn't call out to them to ask if they were OK, to ask what the heck had just happened. Strange.

Ianto spoke first. 'What was that?'

'I have no idea. Do you think it was the knockers, somehow?'

'Could be. Maybe they were trying to show us the way to the cave?'

It was good to hear Ianto sounding more like himself. Interested. Alive.

'At least it didn't harm us,' she said.

Ianto sculled towards the beach on the other side. Thanks to the blue light, they knew which direction to aim for through the darkness. And soon they saw the beach again – lit by their headtorches this time. Gently, Ianto used the oar as a punt and pulled the coracle on to the sloping expanse of beach. Rose stepped out, water seeping over the top of her trainers as she scrambled up the slope to dry rocks.

'Will you be OK here, on your own?' asked Ianto.

'I'll be fine. Off you go.'

Ianto pulled the coracle about. Then he set off again, faster this time, steering the little craft through the water like an expert. He disappeared into the darkness in the middle of the lake, and she was all alone.

She sat down at the top of the beach. Behind her was the tunnel entrance, down which the flaming blue ball had disappeared. She did not want to step into it before the others were with her, did not want to look down it.

Before long, a voice called over the water: 'Ahoy there!'

'Hello, Mr Williams!' she called back, trying to keep her voice low.

She strained her eyes, and then she made out a small white headlight approaching through the darkness. Rose thought again how amazingly quiet the boat was on water. No wonder coracles were good to fish from.

Mr Williams was sitting comfortably in the prow, sculling away. Behind him was Del, standing up, piercing the darkness ahead with her alert stare.

Mr Williams beached the boat and stepped out of it, Del

bounding over its side behind him and splash-landing before hauling herself out and shaking her shaggy coat all over them.

'Give over, lass,' he said to her, chuckling. 'Now then.' Mr Williams turned to Rose, handing her the oar. 'What's this nonsense about blue lights?'

'Didn't you see it? It came out of the tunnel and flew over your head, then over the lake – over us, in the coracle – and off down that tunnel.' She pointed at the tunnel mouth behind them. How could he not have seen it?

But as she spoke, she saw Mr Williams's face fall, the bravado melt away. The blue eyes that stared into hers, lit by her headlight, looked suddenly lost. Then he averted them from her altogether, looking down at Del, who had come close to stand by his leg.

'Del saw it,' remembered Rose. 'She was barking.'

'I . . . yes, she was, bach – you're right.' There was an awkward silence. Then Mr Williams looked up again. 'Well, never mind. I'm sure it was nothing to worry about. Nothing to worry about at all.

'Hey! We're wasting time here – that won't do. Off you go, bach. Go and collect your boyfriend.'

Rose felt her face grow hot with embarrassment. 'He's not my—'

Her protest was cut off by an explosion of laughter from Mr Williams. Then he helped her into the coracle and pushed her off before settling himself on the beach with Del at his side.

Rose was soon figure-of-eighting herself over the lake towards the other shore – the oar, the wood worn smooth and shiny by generations of Williams's hands, light and responsive under hers.

Presently she saw a light ahead. Ianto's headtorch. And soon she was punting the coracle up the stony slope at the foot of the beach.

'Last leg now,' she said, as he got in the back and sat down, arranging his long legs in a cross-legged position. 'OK if I row us back?' she went on.

'Go ahead,' he said.

As they left the beach behind them, Ianto said, 'Uncle Thomas didn't see the blue light.' He was speaking in that monotone again.

'I know. I don't get it. It flew right over his head!'

Ianto was quiet for a moment. Then he said, 'You know what it was?'

'What?'

'*Cannwyll corff.*'

A shiver ran down Rose's spine. 'A *what?*'

Ianto translated into English. '*A corpse candle.* A light that appears the night before someone dies. It usually goes from the door of their house to the cemetery, or –' Ianto paused – 'or maybe just to the place where that person's corpse lies.'

He sounded so matter of fact. About something so horrible. Rose stopped rowing and turned round. To see his face blank and tight-looking.

'Why didn't you tell me this when we saw it?' she asked. Her mind was scrabbling to make sense of this new horror.

'I didn't know what it was. Uncle just told me. But he

didn't want to believe it. He thought I'd made it up, or was imagining it.'

So that's why, when she'd confirmed that she'd seen it too, he'd looked so frightened.

Rose stared into Ianto's brown eyes, and started, 'Who . . .' and then stopped, feeling horrified that she'd said that word, said anything at all.

Neither of them spoke again on that final journey over the lake.

30

Leaving the coracle pulled well up on the beach, the four of them entered the tunnel mouth on the other side of the lake.

No one said a word. Even Mr Williams had given up on being cheery now. They trudged forward down the sloping tunnel, Mr Williams at the head. It felt good to have him with them, rather than separated by the base of the coracle. Del stuck to the side of his left leg as if obeying the pull from a powerful magnet. Before, she had moved forwards to look ahead or come back to check on Rose and Ianto, but now she never left her master's side.

Every now and then they came to a dark, open mouth, leading off from this main tunnel. Peeping inside, these usually proved to be another tunnel – smaller, with a lower roof. Sometimes they opened out and a larger space was glimpsed within, a hollowed-out gallery, stone stolen and carted away, up and out and into the world above.

Mr Williams, consulting his compass, ignored all ways off and continued ahead.

No sound but their own breathing, their own steps and shuffles.

Then, 'All right, crew?' said Mr Williams, stopping suddenly in the tunnel. Ianto and Rose jumped in surprise. His voice sounded so loud within the deadening, underground space.

'All right,' Rose and Ianto replied together.

Then, tentatively, Rose started, '*All for one . . .*'

'*And one for all,*' they all chimed together. This time there was no laughter. But their voices sounded bravely under the mountain.

They set off again, but after a couple of steps it was Del's turn to freeze, causing them all to pull up short. She cocked her head to one side, a low growl vibrating through her body, before springing off like a released greyhound and sprinting down the tunnel ahead of them.

'Hey! Del! *Heel!*' barked Mr Williams, breaking into a run to follow her with Ianto and Rose fast on his heels.

The light of three jogging headtorches revealed Del's back legs and tail, and they heard the clicker of her claws on stone as she disappeared around a curve. She was after something – something swift that they could not see, could not hear.

The three of them rounded the bend, panting with exertion, and the tunnel straightened out before them. Ahead, Del was sprinting into darkness. But this time Rose caught a glimpse of a small, dark mass scuttling wildly ahead of her.

A rat.

'*Del!* Heel, girl!' yelled Mr Williams, but she was blind, deaf, to anything but her prey. And then, suddenly, she and the rat disappeared.

No more skittering of claws on stone. A startled yelp. Then silence.

As she ran, breathlessly, through the tunnel, Rose could see nothing ahead of her. What had happened? The image of the corpse candle, floating over the dark water of the lake, entered her mind like an uninvited guest.

Mr Williams was running ahead of them, still calling out wildly – and then they saw him pull up short, lean forwards, swear loudly and scrabble backwards, opening his arms to stop them passing.

'Whoah!' he cried.

His voice echoed hollowly, like the cry of an owl. Reaching him, panting breathlessly, they saw they were standing at the end of the tunnel on a ledge that was maybe two metres deep. Below them was a long, wide abyss. Their headtorches reached the other side, illuminating a sheer stony wall and another ledge, beyond which the tunnel continued. It was, perhaps, ten metres to the other side. There was no bridge.

As Mr Williams's exclamation faded, they became aware of another sound. Del, whining thinly and pitifully. From below them, from inside the abyss. Whines which echoed wretchedly about the space, and which grew in desperation and fear to howls, until the entire space was filled with her agony.

The three of them edged forwards, getting on to their hands and knees and then lying, as they had on top of the mountain, to look down the sheer drop. Many metres below them, about the same depth they'd abseiled, two shining eyes reflected back and Del's howls reached a new pitch. Rose could make out the white patches of her fur, could see that she was standing, legs shaking in fear, on a ledge. Beyond her the abyss sank further into deep darkness, a bottomless pit.

'Del . . .' cried Mr Williams, almost to himself. He

sounded bewildered. At her master's voice, Del raised her head and howled even louder, even longer, then the sound disintegrated into a sharp, heart-rending whine.

The seconds ticked by, and no one moved. Rose realised that she was waiting. She was waiting for Mr Williams to tell them what to do. Tell them how they were going to save Del, get out of this fix.

But he was silent. His head hung down, eyes locked in desperation on his dog's.

Rose turned to Ianto. He looked back at her. Then he shuffled backwards and stood up, announcing, 'OK, Uncle. We're going to get Del out of there, right? You got any more rope in that backpack?'

Mr Williams turned his head to look at him, then shuffled back and stood, taking off his backpack.

'I . . . yes, boy, I have. What's the plan?' His voice shook as he pulled out another coil of climbing rope.

'I'll abseil down to her,' said Ianto, grabbing the rope and swiftly tying a knot in the end. 'I'll put her in a sling, then you can pull her up. Then you'll drop the rope again and help me up, using a figure of eight. Looks like there are enough footholds down there. OK?'

'Yes. Yes, lad. Good plan.' Mr Williams delved again, desperately, in his backpack.

'We'll need two slings,' said Rose. 'One to belay, then one for Del.' She looked about for a secure belay.

Mr Williams froze. 'We've only got one sling,' he said. 'The one we used for the coracle.'

He turned to her, his eyes wide in panic. He seemed

unable to function, unable to think.

Rose took this in. 'We can use our harnesses to carry Del, Mr Williams,' she said. 'Ianto can put my harness over her front legs and your harness over her back ones. That should work.'

Mr Williams turned his anxious eyes to Ianto, who nodded.

Together, they found a spike of rock – part of the tunnel's side that jutted up, just inside the entrance. They examined it carefully – knocking it to make sure it was not hollow, scanning it with their head torches to see that it had no cracks. Then they fixed the sling around it and tied the rope to the sling, passing it through the figure of eight attached to Ianto's harness so that he could lean back, pulling at the belay to test its strength.

'Feels solid,' said Ianto.

With that, he abseiled swiftly away from them and into the abyss, looking downwards at Del until his feet reached the ledge beside her. Del had stopped howling now and was whining quietly, breaking off now and then to lick her lips. Her eyes were fixed on Ianto.

Lying as she was with her head over the edge, Rose saw Del meekly allowing Ianto to lift her legs and fit the harnesses. Then he tied the rope to the harnesses and looked up.

'Pull her up,' he called, tugging on the rope.

As her paws left the ledge, Del hung in the air above the depths. She was completely silent now and did not struggle, even as she caught her back and head on rocks that jutted out as she was slowly, jerkily, hauled up the side of the abyss by Mr Williams.

The rope ran over the ledge as he pulled. That had to be wearing it out, thought Rose. She glanced up at Mr Williams. Suddenly, he looked every one of his seventy-two years. His face was strained with effort and tension. His eyes were hazy with fatigue and fear. But even now, he managed something comforting for Del.

'Nearly there now, girl. Have you out of there soon.'

And they *were* nearly there now, but there was a hitch at the very lip of the ledge. Progress had stalled, and Del was hanging just under it.

Then to Rose's alarm, Mr Williams stepped forward to within half a metre of the edge. The rope jolted and Del fell back a little way, letting out a sharp yelp.

'I'll grab her, Mr Williams, if you pull,' called Rose, urgently.

Then she understood. He could not pull her over the ledge without hurting her on the rock. So he was stepping forward further now, leaning out and over the drop to lift Del clear. But he was too far forward, too near the abyss . . .

Del hung for a moment, head down, frozen in fear above the void, while Mr Williams's arms strained and then, suddenly, here she was, with them again, and Rose leaned forward and grabbed at her, tumbling backwards to safety, suddenly lost in her furry, shivering body.

Rose unclipped her from the knotted end of the rope. She shouted 'Rope, Ianto!' and when he responded with an echoing call of 'Right-o,' she threw it over the edge to him.

Mr Williams stepped from the edge towards them, a huge smile breaking on his face. He reached out his arms to embrace his dog.

'Come here, Del!' he said, in a voice filled with relief.

Then came a movement from just inside the tunnel. Rose whipped her head about to see something small, dark and vicious.

The rat. It sprang high into the air, claws extended and teeth bared, at Mr Williams.

Who shouted, threw up his arms to protect his face – and stepped back, over the edge of the abyss.

31

As he fell, Mr Williams grabbed at the rope. Rose saw it tensing, tightening against the belay as he screamed out in agony, the thin nylon shredding his bare hands as he plunged downwards.

Ianto was shouting too, from below – but Rose could not make out the words.

Mr Williams could not hold the rope. It sprang back a little, as if the tension had been released. He had lost his grip, and now he plunged, helplessly, into the void.

The unbearable sound of his screams cut off, suddenly, in mid flow, echoing briefly around the chasm.

Then there was silence.

Rose made out a small patch of disturbance in the air over the void, like pixelated interference on a screen. Bleddyn. Of course, the rat had been Bleddyn.

Rose buried her face in Del's fur, unable to process what had just happened, right in front of her. She had been unable to do anything. Unable to stop it. It had happened so fast . . .

'Rose!' Ianto was shouting.

She lifted her head. 'Stay!' she said to Del, who was shaking in fear. Surprisingly, she obeyed.

Then Rose crawled to the edge and looked over. Ianto's white face appeared beneath her.

'I'm coming up, OK?' he called. 'I've got the rope.'

'Ianto – I'm not strong enough to lift you.'

'I know that. Listen. I'm going to tie the rope to my harness. You need to clip a carabiner to the belay and attach a figure of eight to it. Undo the rope and put it through the figure of eight. Pull it through as I climb, keeping it tight. There are footholds here. I'll be OK.'

'Right,' she said, her voice shaking as she turned and fumbled in her backpack for a carabiner and her figure of eight.

Soon she was all set, her hands gripping the rope above the figure of eight, holding Ianto.

'Ready,' she called, trying to steady her voice.

It was awful not to be able to see Ianto, not to watch him as he used his arms and legs to reach up and around the rock face, testing holds here, pulling himself up, finding the next toe-hold. But he had to be doing OK because the rope was slackening, as he climbed. And bit by bit, she was tightening it.

Then a cry came from beneath her, and the rope below the figure of eight tensed suddenly. What had happened?

'Ianto – are you OK?' she called.

'*Argh* – yes. Yes, I am.' He was panting, and his anxious voice echoed about the chasm. 'Just lost my footing.' He must have fallen away from the rockface, must be dangling in thin air, above the drop. But Rose, and the figure of eight, were holding him while he found his feet again. Rose could see, from the length of the rope she'd pulled up already, that he had to be nearly there now.

'You're doing great, Ianto,' she called, watching the edge and wishing she could do more to help.

And then, finally, his bare hands – flecked with blood,

grazed and cut by rock – were gripping the ledge. She tightened the rope as he struggled upwards, pushing from toe-holds below as his hands scrabbled for purchase on the ledge, hauling himself out of the chasm. Soon his head appeared, face grim with effort and strain, and then he was pulling up his legs, first one knee then the other, until he was on all fours at the edge, panting, head down. Rose pulled up the slack on the rope for the final time, then rushed towards him.

'Stay back!' he commanded, lifting his head in alarm, stopping her in her tracks while he crawled towards her, then stood.

He looked exhausted, done in. He unclipped the rope and they collapsed together, Rose supporting him as best she could, at the entrance to the tunnel.

Then they wrapped their arms around each other and wept – great, heaving sobs pulled up from the depths of their souls.

Presently a furry body with a wet nose nudged between them, and they wrapped their arms around Del too, drawing her in. She cried with them, lifting her head from their embrace to howl pitifully.

Their mingled grief echoed about the chasm. But from below, from where Mr Williams's body lay, came deadened silence.

Perhaps an hour passed. Perhaps two? Rose and Ianto had no tears left. And no words. They sat, slumped, still clinging to each other. Looking down, Rose saw that Del had fallen asleep across their laps.

Suddenly she realised how tired she was. Dead tired.

Ianto must have felt the same, because he reached up and gently switched off her head torch. Then he extinguished his own. And the three of them were plunged into the deepest darkness that Rose had ever experienced.

In a way, it was comforting.

They fell asleep within seconds.

32

Chock! Clack! Two great smacks of wood on stone. Echoing out. Then more sounds. The creak and groan of wood straining under pressure; wood adjusting, giving. Then – *Crack!* – breaking.

Echoing notes of wood on wood, wood on stone, mingling all around like a huge symphony, performed in a great hall by giants using glockenspiels and double basses and kettle-drums . . .

Where was she?

And then she remembered, and her heart stumbled and fell down.

She was in this dreadful place. And Mr Williams – Mr Williams had . . . she screwed up her eyes, tightly. But open or closed, it made no difference down here in the pitch dark.

She reached out and found Ianto's shoulder. His fingers clutched her hand and held it tight. He was awake, too. He was listening. She put the other hand down to find Del's head. There she was – the sleek, silky fur between her ears. Rose felt a warm, wet tongue lick her palm.

The strange sounds continued, with their heavy, off-beat melody.

'The knockers,' Rose whispered. Ianto squeezed her hand, again.

Then, gradually, the wooden notes faded away until with

one last, echoing *tap*, they ceased.

The three of them sat in silence, waiting for more sounds – which did not come. Now there was nothing but their own, halting, breathing.

Presently, and as one, Rose and Ianto reached up and switched on their headlamps.

In the sudden, flaming torch beams, Rose and Ianto saw this.

A rickety wooden bridge, made of short planks tied together with rope and fixed at both ends with thick, strong stakes, driven into the rocks. It stretched from the far edge of the abyss, over the long drop, to reach their ledge. A bridge to the other side.

And on the other side something lay, waiting for them, on the stony ground before the tunnel entrance. It was a stretcher or a bier, with two wooden handles at either end.

Lying flat on the bier, arms folded over his chest, was Mr Williams.

33

Without a word, the three of them scrambled to their feet. Stepping on to the wooden bridge they hurried over it, not daring to look down, the planks creaking and the bridge bowing, swaying as they ran.

Ianto was the first to reach the other side. As Rose hastened off the bridge she pulled herself up short and, hesitantly, joined him. He was looking down at Mr Williams stretched out on his bier. Next came Del. Tail down, head down, she hung back, wide eyes fixed on her master.

Then Ianto gave a small moan and hung his head, bringing his hands up to cover his eyes.

Rose had felt a little surge of hope, earlier. But looking at Mr Williams now – the anxious, lined face so still and pale, eyes closed – she knew that the life had gone out of him.

As one, Rose and Ianto knelt at his side. Rose noticed that Mr Williams's cap had been placed on his chest, under his hands. There was no sign of injury on him.

Ianto took off his backpack and reached inside it. He pulled out an apple and, gently lifting Mr Williams's hand from the cap, put the apple into it. Then he bowed his head, still holding his uncle's hand. The apple, green and red, a living fruit, seemed to glow beneath the white fingers.

Rose watched Ianto. She wondered what she could give to Mr Williams. Something precious. She pulled the little roll of vellum from her pocket then, tentatively, she lifted his other hand and placed the englyn within his cold, curled fingers. Then she closed her eyes.

And thought: *Mr Williams, I . . .* but the thought dried up. There was nothing there. It was simply too awful, and too like Dad.

Del plucked up her courage and stepped forward now, to gently lick her master's cheek. She whined, and looked up, beseechingly, at Rose and Ianto. As if asking them to wake him.

Now Ianto reached forward and very gently took his great uncle's head in his hands. Lifting it with great care, he slipped the cord from around his neck, ruffling Mr Williams's grey hair. Then he tenderly laid the head back down.

The compass.

Ianto turned his pale face to Rose. She nodded, and he slipped the cord over his own head.

Then, once more without a word, Rose and Ianto got to their feet and bent to grasp the wooden handles on the bier – Ianto at his head, Rose at his feet.

And together with Del they set off through the tunnel entrance on the other side of the abyss – the four musketeers.

34

They were in another tunnel now – dark, dank, chilly. *Cold as a tomb*, thought Rose. Her mind rambled around the words. *Tomb* was so very like *womb*, in English. And both were small, enclosed places – but one was for death, and one was for birth.

It was easier to think about words than to think about where they might be heading. And to think about what had happened in the abyss to Mr Williams.

This tunnel was much like the one that had led to the abyss, and the one before that, that had led to the lake. Every now and again, when they reached a way off or a fork in the path, Ianto and Rose carefully put Mr Williams down and consulted the compass. South west. Heading south west. Heading for who-knew-what, south west.

Along the way, Rose and Ianto hardly spoke, and Del trotted silently beside her master.

As they marched through the mountain, heading deeper and deeper into rock, Rose thought about Mr Williams. Glancing down at the hands that clasped the apple, the englyn and the cap; and at his boots, worn at the heels and sides, she was overcome with sadness. Mr Williams had been lonely, up on the mountainside, on his own. He had lost touch with Gwenllian, his best friend in the world. He had kept his stories within him – until now. He had made plans to break the curse – and at last he had started to enact those plans. But now, those stories and those plans, finally revealed, had killed him.

And all the stories within him – how he had loved telling stories! – were gone, like tears in rain.

His hand-axe was still tucked into his belt. Mr Williams had been armed to the teeth – axe, gun – but it'd done him no good in the end. His face, anxious and still, made Rose want to weep again. What was the point? What was the point of anything, of trying to do anything? You were just going to die, whatever you did – sooner, or later.

It was very hard, down here, to think about the world outside. Was it even the same time, out there, under the moon, or the sun, and the sky? They might emerge to find that they'd gone back two thousand years, to the time of Berwyn and Bleddyn. Or further – to the age of the prehistoric miners, the builders of the cromlech.

But if they ever did get out of here, and if it did happen to be the world and the time that they knew – the world that contained Mum and Ianto's family, and the summer holidays, and everything – how on earth could she and Ianto explain what had happened? How Mr Williams had died? How come they were bringing him home on a bier? It didn't bear thinking about.

And so on they went, down the endless tunnel. The cave must be close now, Rose thought. We've walked for miles and miles. We must be under the wood now, surely. But the tunnel wound on, curving about, straightening up . . .

Until, suddenly, they were there. The end of the road.

Everything had to end some time. Nothing went on for

ever. But it seemed incredible that they were here, nonetheless. If, indeed, they were here, or there, or wherever.

Who cares? flared a weary, dangerous voice inside Rose. But as soon as it spoke, she snuffed it out. She pulled back her shoulders and held her head up. They had to carry on and finish this. They *would* carry on and finish this. They were going to end the curse. For Mr Williams.

'For you, Mr Williams,' she whispered down to him.

The tunnel had come to an end. Their headtorches revealed a wooden door, built (by the knockers?) of slabs of ancient, dark wood, its top curved round to fit the shape of the tunnel. Thick, iron hinges attached it to the stone at the side, and a black iron ring was set into the middle of it as a handle.

Ianto turned his head to Rose and they both nodded. Del stood, alert, looking from one to the other. She knew something was up.

They set down the bier. Ianto checked the compass. Then he reached out and twisted the heavy iron ring to open the door.

35

In the split second before the door swung open, Rose was tempted to leap forward and slam it shut again. It would be a trick. It would be another deep drop, and they would tumble into it to be crushed at the bottom, like Mr Williams. Or an ocean of water would thunder through, sweeping them all away, flooding the honeycomb. Or maybe the door hid a solid wall of stone. And they would have to troop all the way back again.

The hinges were smooth and soundless, and the wooden door swung heavily inwards.

And immediately, they were hit by a wall of chaotic sound, cutting into it mid-flow. The deafening bellow of a war-horn, the thundering of frantic hooves, the screams of horses and of men. Crashing through undergrowth. Sharp metallic thrusts of slashing, stabbing, iron on iron. A great roar – of men, of explosively burning wood.

All this, all together, in one great onslaught.

Rose and Ianto had crouched down, their hands over their ears. Del had pushed herself between them and had lifted her head to howl, the sound lost in the flood. The barrage of noise rushed out of the door and echoed, whooshing, down the tunnel. Like a time capsule, compressed, waiting to explode.

Finally released. After two thousand years.

And then it stopped. A smell of burning wood lingered

around the dark, half-open door, then that, too, disappeared.

Dazed and shaken, stumbling to their feet and lifting the bier once more, Rose, Ianto and Del stepped through the door to the other side.

Into a high-ceilinged cave that was littered with stones and rubble. It seemed empty, at first. But as they strode towards the centre of the space their headtorches picked out something in the far corner. Something that reflected back white, and something that sparkled brightly.

'Fool's gold?' whispered Rose, as they carefully put down the bier and hurried over to it.

It was not fool's gold. It was the real thing. And Rose realised that there was nothing to compare to real gold. Shining, deep yellow, like a newly-opened buttercup.

A battle helmet. A splendid, glittering thing, fit for a king. Iron, for proper protection, with gold banding to mark his rank, dividing the helmet into four sections and decorated all over with intricate, overlapping markings. A gold band came down over his nose too, and encircled the tops of his eyes, so that they looked like thick, golden eyebrows.

Thick, golden eyebrows over two empty black holes, in a shining white skull.

A row of flawless white teeth hung down from the skull, and a matching set jutted up from the open jawbone beneath.

The rest of his bones curved together in a crouch. Delicate toe bones, finger bones, had separated out and spread like small fans over the stone floor. Strong, long thigh bones remained in place. Ribs like the laths of the coracle.

Rose shivered. And found tears pricking at her eyes, again.

Another death. A terrible murder. An innocent man – the good king.

Then she saw that beneath the bones there was something long and rusty, and more gold – a sword: short, stout at the top, tapering towards the tip, with an ornate, golden grip and cross-guard.

'Over here,' came Ianto's voice, low. He was standing close by, looking down.

She tore herself from King Berwyn to see another skeleton. This one lay on its side, jaw hanging loosely down, backbone arched in agony.

No helmet. No sword.

But a dark length of wood – shining in their torchlight with the polish of age or use; plain, deeply old, nestling within the finger bones as if he had just opened his hand to let it go.

'The staff,' Rose breathed, meeting Ianto's wide eyes with her own.

Del had left Mr Williams's side to join them. Now she stood over Bleddyn's bones and stared down at them. Rose saw the fur on her back stiffen and stand up. She yapped, then growled, her animal eyes – one blue, one brown – fixed on the skull.

'Let's do it, then,' said Ianto. He turned from Bleddyn's body to look for a tool.

A tool, thought Rose. *Offeryn*, in Welsh. And suddenly the words from the englyn ran through her mind: *Sound Celt-crafted instruments of iron and wood.*

They had thought that 'instruments' meant musical instruments. But, as in English, the Welsh word for instrument didn't just mean musical instruments. It also meant instrument in the sense of 'tool'. And weapons were tools, weren't they? The tools of a soldier, of a king, of a sorcerer? Did the englyn mean Bleddyn's wooden staff and . . .

'Berwyn's iron sword,' she whispered, aloud.

Ianto looked at her sharply, then down at the rusted, golden-hilted weapon on the ground, glimpsed under the good king's bones. He hesitated. She could see that he did not want to disturb Berwyn.

Instead, he strode to the bier and kneeled at his uncle's side. Gently, carefully, he prised the hand-axe from his belt.

Then he stood, hefting it in his hand and swinging it through the air before him. Rose remembered him doing the same thing back at Mr Williams's, when they were setting out. The heavy steel of the head cut through the air as if it was working on its own, as if Ianto's hand was merely following it.

Moving quickly forward, drawn by the axe, Ianto raised it above his head to bring it down, hard, on to the very middle of the ancient, wooden staff.

A great crack – sharp and sudden as a shot from a gun – as steel met aged hardwood; and the staff broke into two pieces, the thin, sharp edge of the axe chiming loudly as metal met the stone beneath, throwing out sparks.

Ianto stood back and Rose and Del edged to his side, bracing themselves.

The skeletons before them remained still. The staff lay in two pieces, cut cleanly through. The sword's golden hilt glinted from beneath Berwyn's bones.

A familiar feeling swept Rose, and she closed her eyes to allow it to happen. She was condensing, coming apart and forming again, settling into shape. She lifted off and beat her wings, manoeuvring neatly and swiftly in the air.

It was a relief to leave behind the heavy body, full of grief.

Opening her eyes, hovering above the floor of the cave, she saw the place anew in brilliant detail. The headtorches had disappeared, but there was a new, glowing source of light. It was coming from the golden bands on Berwyn's helmet.

Next to her loomed the giant, Ianto. His head was only feet from the ceiling of the cave. He turned to her and she flew up to flutter before his eyes. He smiled, holding out a finger for her to perch on. Then he lifted her to his shoulder and she stepped her clawed feet – once, twice – then tucked in her wings and blinked.

Del was looking up at them from far below. She gave a sudden, short bark, which propelled her momentarily into the air, as if she was trying to join them.

Then, from behind them, came a sound. A small, sharp *crunch*. The three of them spun around.

To see Mr Williams, sitting up on his bier and munching hungrily into Ianto's apple.

36

They watched in amazement as Mr Williams ate the glowing green and red fruit in three bites, core and all. He chewed. Then they saw his cheeks flush pink as an apple and his hands turn brown and strong again, like apple-tree bark.

'Best apple I ever had,' he murmured, swallowing and staring ahead with unfocused eyes. 'Best cup of tea, too . . .'

Then he uncurled his hand to reveal the roll of vellum. He muttered, 'The Thirty-Third Owl.'

With that he looked up at Rose. His bright, blue eyes met the owl's round, dark ones. 'That's you,' he said to her, clearly. 'I remember now.'

He put the englyn in his pocket and fixed his cap securely on his head. Then he stood up and stepped off the bier, patting his belt and looking about in confusion.

'Hey!' he said finally, glaring accusingly at Ianto. The giant was still holding the hand-axe – which looked tiny now – between his thumb and forefinger.

Ianto gave a little start, then he bent down to hand it back.

His uncle reached up and snatched the weapon from him, tucking it back into his belt. Then he remembered something else, and one hand reached round to pat his back.

His shoulders began to shake. 'Heh, heh, heh, heh . . .' he chortled, shaking his head in wonder. 'Knockers,' he said, affectionately, when he could speak again. 'Knockers took my gun.'

Next, he put his hands on his knees and leaned forwards, addressing his dog.

'Del? Don't you know your master?'

As if she had been waiting for his invitation, Del sprang forwards, her tail wagging in desperate, wriggling joy. She stood before Mr Williams, fairly shaking with happiness, then gently reared up so her forepaws reached his chest.

Ianto turned his head to stare at Rose. His eyes sparkled with questions, and with joy. And so did hers, in reply. What had happened to bring Mr Williams back from the dead? Was it eating the apple?

Then the words of the englyn came to her: *Iron breaks wood – for second birth . . .* Had he been born again, when they broke the staff?

Was everything finally, *finally* falling into place? Had they broken the curse?

They turned back to Mr Williams, because he was addressing them now. 'What are you two staring at?' he said, hands on hips. 'No time to stand about, boy!'

Striding past them to the skeletons, he took in the bones, the gold-banded helmet, the sword and the broken staff with a long, low whistle. Then he turned, and his face was shining with excitement.

'Well! Well, well. You broke the staff. *Broke the staff!*' He thrust his fist in the air in triumph then, bringing it down, continued to shake it at them, his blue eyes glinting in the light from the golden helmet. 'You know what this means, don't you? Bleddyn's a busted flush. End of the curse – end of Bleddyn, sure to be . . .'

But the animation in his face fell away as a sound reached them from the opposite corner of the cave. They turned as one, silently, to face it. And here it came again.

The thin, terrified whimper of a child. At a glance, Rose realised that the corner was not a corner, but a dark corridor, leading on, leading upwards, into another space.

37

The four of them took off for the corner: Rose lifting into the air to lead the way; Mr Williams sprinting over the cave floor like a twenty-two-year-old, Del at his side; and Ianto striding across in three long paces.

Rose turned and hovered in the air to watch Ianto edge, sideways, around the bend. For a moment he was stuck, the jagged rocks of the tight curve trapping him. She heard him moan in pain. Then he wrenched himself free and stumbled into the other cave.

It was the same cave that she'd fallen into all those days ago. But the ceiling that Ianto had knocked out to rescue her was intact. It seemed higher than before. It had to be, because Ianto could stand in here now. Perhaps Bleddyn had sealed the roof again, but with a layer of earth this time? And it was dark in here, shadowy, though the light from Berwyn's helmet filtered in, dimly, from next door.

Mr Williams and Del were standing stock-still, staring ahead.

A giant spider web, spun of thick, ghostly-white strands, was strung untidily across the middle of the cave. It vibrated lightly as Ianto let out a sudden, deafening roar of recognition.

For wrapped neck to toe in thick, silk binding, like a tiny mummy wound into the very centre of the web, was his sister Cerys.

She was facing outwards and her wide, desperate eyes were darting about in terror, taking in the newcomers. When Cerys saw Rose she cried out, struggling within her bonds and closing her eyes tight shut.

Mr Williams spoke, stepping swiftly towards the web. His voice was shaking. 'Cerys, darling. Don't worry. We're here now. We're going to get you out of here.'

Her eyes opened to meet Mr Williams's. '*Wncl! Helpwch fi*—' she cried. 'Uncle! Help me—'

Her voice cut off as she glanced to her left. Rose heard a soft scratching and turned her head to the sound. Something was emerging from a crack in the wall, next to the web. Something long, like a jointed, flexible stick. It extended into the cave and the very end of it flickered, feeling the air. Then another limb pushed out from the crack, lifting high before coming down on to the web, denting the surface and making Cerys shiver in her bindings. Before the four of them could move, the long, arching legs were joined by six more. In a sudden, shocking burst of speed, the bloated body of a giant spider, fully two metres across, scuttled from the crack in the wall towards its prey.

So much for a busted flush, thought Rose.

The spider's head was fused to its thorax, and drooping behind both was a big, sacky abdomen, from the very end of which silk leaked in a grey dribble. Fast as lightning, long front legs pulled Cerys towards it, then hind limbs swiftly gathered her up and held her tight against its body – its huge, furred fangs poised above her, waiting to plunge.

Then it turned its beady, round eyes – arranged in four

matching pairs of different sizes – to its audience. And all were black and swirling blankly.

Rose, Ianto and Mr Williams had frozen in place. They could not move to help Cerys without endangering her life.

But, thought Rose, we're *all* hostages now. Because if Bleddyn killed Cerys, then he would himself be killed, instantly, by the three of them.

Deadlock.

Cerys was soundless now, her face pulled into the spider's thorax. She looked like a doll, or a new-born baby, in its arms.

Then Rose realised that one of them was missing. Where was Del? She flapped higher to reach Ianto's shoulder and look for her. The spider's eyes followed her movement and the legs tightened around Cerys's body, the fangs skimming the hair on her head.

Ianto let out a moan. His fists were clenched at his sides, his whole body tensed, while Rose scanned the shadowy cave for Del, keeping her head as still as she could so as not to draw the attention of the spider.

And then she saw her. A flash of white and black fur, up against the far wall of the cave, behind the web. She was on her outrun, sprinting silently on soft paws, circling swiftly. Just as she did when she rounded up sheep.

Del had a plan.

Rose watched through the net curtain of raggedy cobweb as Del reached a point at the back of the cavern and fell straight down from running to lying, head facing front, watching the body of the spider with intense concentration.

Then she was creeping forwards on her belly, soundless –

until her paw slipped and a piece of shale clinked out of place.

At the sound, the spider quivered. Still grasping Cerys, it scuttled upwards, backing up to look behind it.

Then everything happened very quickly. Rose flapped from Ianto's shoulder as the giant bent swiftly to grab a boulder, drop it, pull back his huge, booted foot and belt it at the spider in a powerful, bending strike that hit the creature's huge abdomen with a liquid, splatting squelch.

Del was leaping forwards at the same time, jumping high to grab the edge of the web in her strong jaws, pulling at a thick strand of silk like a loose thread on a knitted jumper. As she retreated, growling and worrying at the fibres, the entire net unravelled before her, its cargo of pulverised spider and wrapped child tumbling down to the cave floor.

In a second, Mr Williams had sprung forward to catch Cerys – just as he had Rose the night before. Cerys, wrapped in her cocoon, fell into his arms. Then he turned and sprinted from the cave, followed swiftly by Ianto.

So only Rose and Del were there to see what happened next.

Because the spider was not finished yet. It had fallen to the floor on its back, legs crumpling lifelessly. But as Rose hovered silently above she saw, from out of the ripped balloon of its body, hundreds – thousands – of tiny spiders, scattering noiselessly out of the wreckage. They moved as one across the cave floor, fangs held high, ready to strike.

And they were after Del. She stood her ground, at first, and moved her head to growl and bark at the lapping tide before her. But when they did not recede, she yelped and turned tail, soon cornered by the wave at the back of the cave as the spiders flowed forward.

Rose was already winging her way towards Del.

And she was remembering something Mr Williams had said. *When Bleddyn makes himself into more than one animal . . . you take one out, you take them all out.*

Handy advice.

Now she was hovering, wings busy, head held still in the air, over the tide of spiders. She could see each tiny one in pristine detail – and they were all perfect replicas of their parent. Rose dropped like a stone, head up, claws extended, and landed hard on one of them, her large eyes closing instinctively for a moment as, with a tiny crunch, she stamped the life out of it while Del cowered against the far wall, yelping as the wave reached her.

In the next instant the whole lot of them disintegrated into a low cloud of filthy black smoke, filling Rose's beak with foul-tasting matter.

Del sprang forward to attack the cloud as it rose upwards through the cave. It evaded her lunges, drifting free. Gathering itself into a long ribbon of darkness, inserting its end into the crack in the wall, it drew in its length and whipped in its tail to disappear completely.

Rose winged from the cave with Del hurrying beneath her, around the curving corner, down into the other cave, the cave of the skeletons, where they found their companions.

38

The cave was still lit by the golden bands of Berwyn's battle helmet. Was she imagining it, or was it shining even more brightly now? In its light, as she flapped forwards, she could see the huge bulk of Ianto, crouching in the centre of the cave over his great uncle, who was sitting on a low rock holding Cerys in his lap.

Mr Williams was unwrapping the ragged bindings from her body, tearing at them with his hands to free her. Soon, like a butterfly emerging from a cocoon, Cerys stood up, shrugging off the last of the grey threads. She was a little shaky on her feet – and she looked very small and young. She was blinking rapidly, doing her best not to cry.

Unable to hold himself back, Ianto leaned forward to embrace her, his hands extended. She gave a little squeal and threw herself backwards, burying her face in her great uncle's chest.

Mr Williams chuckled, looking up at Ianto.

'Hey,' he said gently, to Cerys. 'That's no way to treat your brother.'

Cerys's head shot up and she turned, tentatively, to study the giant.

'He's Ianto?' she whispered, in awe.

Ianto made a little 'Umph' noise, and smiled.

Cerys looked him up and down.

'Why doesn't he talk?' she asked.

'Well now. Giants don't say anything, you see,' explained Mr Williams.

'Bendigeidfran did.' Cerys was talking about the heroic giant from the stories of the Mabinogion.

Mr Williams chuckled again. 'You're right, bach, he did. But, well, Bendigeidfran was a special one.'

'Ianto's a special one, too – even if he doesn't talk,' said Cerys, and she left her uncle's lap to clamber on to the giant's knee.

Very gently, Ianto picked her up. She was only a little bigger than his palm. He lifted her to his face so that they were eye to eye. As he gazed at his little sister, safe within his hand, a tear the size of a tennis ball fell from his eye. At the sight of it, an answering tear, tiny in comparison, fell from Cerys's. She leaned forwards, arms outstretched for a hug. Ianto lifted her so that she could sit on his shoulder, where she wrapped her arms about his neck.

Silence in the cave, for a moment. Then Rose flew forwards to join them. Cerys looked up, screamed shrilly, then turned to bury her face in Ianto's neck.

Why was Cerys afraid of her?

'What's the matter, bach?' asked Mr Williams. 'This is Rose – she's your friend.'

'She's not my friend! She *acted* like my friend. But then she brought me down here . . .'

From the safety of Ianto's neck, she raised her head and bravely held Rose's gaze this time.

Rose held her breath, hovering at a safe distance.

What could have happened?

Cerys continued, 'You came to our house last night, and you were screeching, like you did the time before. You woke me up, and I wanted to follow you, because I thought you were my friend. But I knew that Ianto would want to come too. So I went to his room, but he wasn't there – he'd stuffed clothes under the duvet to make it look like he was.'

Cerys turned from Rose now, as if she couldn't bear to look at her any more. She looked down to address her uncle. 'Then I thought that Ianto was in trouble somewhere, and the owl wanted me to rescue him. I got dressed, and I put my torch in my pocket. I went outside and there was the owl, sitting on the lamppost, like before. It flapped away towards the wood. I went after it, but when I got to the wood I felt frightened. It was so dark in there. I thought I should go back and get Dad. But then the owl spoke to me, in my mind. It said "The king. This way." And then I thought I was doing the right thing. Because, I don't know why, but when it said "king" I thought it meant Ianto.'

That old chestnut, thought Rose, descending to land next to Mr Williams.

Ianto started, and hung his head for a moment. Then he bent his ear to listen keenly as his sister continued.

'I was running through the wood. The owl was flying so fast in front of me it was hard to keep up. I was still frightened. I felt as if something awful was going to happen to me. And to Ianto. Then I tripped and fell down into the dead leaves. And it was like the earth gave way beneath me. I found myself in a tunnel. I stood up and put on my torch, and I walked along the tunnel, going downwards, but the owl had disappeared. It was just me. I didn't know where I was going . . .' Cerys's eyes had grown wide, and she let out a sob.

She swallowed, and continued.

'And then the tunnel came to an end, suddenly, and I fell down into a big stony cave. The tunnel closed up behind me. I was trapped. I could see the big spider web, shining in my torchlight. I looked about for Ianto. But there was no one there, no one at all. Then the giant spider came out of the crack and – and . . .' Cerys slumped against Ianto's neck and buried her face.

Ianto raised his hand and gently stroked her hair with a fingertip.

Mr Williams cleared his throat. '*Cariad bach*,' he said. 'Little darling. You've been very brave. And you've found Ianto now. And me, and Rose, and Del! And we're not, any of us, going to let anything else bad happen to you.

'But listen, bach.' Mr Williams spoke very firmly, so that Cerys pulled her head from the safety of Ianto's neck to face him. "The owl that came to your house last night wasn't Rose. All right? Rose has been down here the whole time, with Ianto and me. The owl that came to the house was a sorcerer called Bleddyn. The bad king. He was pretending to be Rose, to make you do what he wanted. And he also became the giant spider.'

Cerys's tear-stained face nodded. Rose could see that she understood. Her eyes moved cautiously down, to meet Rose's. Rose jumped up, flapped in the air and, quietly, called '*Ke-wick*.'

Cerys smiled a wobbly smile at her.

Mr Williams, watching the two of them, said, ‘Good. Now then. Let’s get out of here.’

And they all rose and turned as one to the wooden door.

To find that it had disappeared. That they were surrounded on all sides by stone walls.

39

The light that was pulsing behind them from the golden bands on Berwyn's battle helmet increased in strength, growing brighter and brighter, so it was almost as if the cave roof had opened and burning, mid-day sun was pouring in.

They turned to face the source of the light, and . . . well, what Rose saw was this.

Bleddyn's skeleton, the broken staff, there, spread across the floor as before.

But next to it, from Berwyn's skeleton, a new, glowing body was uncurling and stretching upwards, like a growing stem topped by a bright bud, about to burst into flower. Finally, the figure lifted its head, and she saw that it was Dad. His yellow hard hat was shining golden, giving out the light of a small sun. In his hand he clasped Berwyn's sword – no longer rusty, but gleaming wrought iron, keen-edged. Dad stepped away from the skeleton like a lizard might leave behind a cast-off skin.

Without thinking, Rose took off and flew straight to him. She would not let him go this time. She approached at speed, and it was as if she was flying into the sun – a warm glow clouded her vision, overcame her. She wanted to lose herself, lose herself in Dad. She stretched out her feet to grip on to his shoulder, to embrace him as Cerys had embraced Ianto, and . . .

Her feet, her whole, feathered body, passed right through him and out the other side.

'Daddy!' she cried, but all that came from her beak was '*Ke-wick!*'

She manoeuvred lightly in the air, adjusting to fly back to him.

He was there. He was so real, so himself. She flapped, determinedly, to reach him again.

Her claws extended, reaching out more determinedly this time, to land on his shoulder. She entered the glow, his aura, but she missed him. Again, he was not there.

She wheeled in the air to try again. She would keep trying. Like a moth, battering itself against a bulb.

Once more, she passed right through him.

'Rose,' called Mr Williams from behind her, gently.

And she understood, although she didn't want to understand. She had always understood, really. This glowing figure was Dad, but it was also not Dad, not really. Dad was dead. And although Mr Williams had come back to life, Dad would not. He would not live again, although somehow, he was here, now. And it was wonderful to see him. Wonderful, and also . . . very sad.

So she gave up and flapped back on weary wings, landing on Mr Williams's shoulder. Which was solid and bony. Mr Williams turned his head to look at her. He seemed surprised but he did not shrug her off.

Like them all, Cerys was staring, awestruck, at the glowing figure.

'Who is that?' she breathed.

'That's the king. The good king,' said Mr Williams quietly, taking off his cap. There was a catch in his throat as he said, 'Berwyn.'

'Berwyn.' Cerys repeated his name, in wonder.

And again, Rose understood. She was seeing Dad, and they were seeing Berwyn. It all made sense . . . kind of. Who cared, anyway. She knew, for her, it was Dad, always Dad.

Dad strode towards them. It was as if he did not see them, quite. His dark eyes seemed focused somewhere beyond. They made way for him, then closed together behind him as he passed. As they watched, he walked straight into the wall they were facing, and as he did so the rock opened, leaving a wide, high-ceilinged channel. One that Ianto could fit into easily.

As they trooped behind Dad – the giant with the little girl on his shoulder, the old man with the owl on his, the dog trotting beside them – the walls of the tunnel lit up, fading behind them into darkness as they moved ahead. Rose swivelled her head to look back, and saw that the rock was closing up behind them, just as it was opening before Dad, before the good king. Like being in an air bubble that moved through the solid stone as if it was water.

That should keep Bleddyn at bay, thought Rose. Because she knew – they all knew – that he was still about. He was merely regrouping.

Cerys, from her perch on Ianto's shoulder, was chattering to her great uncle. She seemed to have recovered from the terrible time in the spider's web. But Rose knew it was not as simple as that, and that Cerys would carry this story inside her for the rest of her life. Then, as if she'd read Rose's mind, she announced,

'When all this is over, Uncle, I'm going to write it all down, as a story. I think I'll call it *Cerys and the Owl*. Or maybe *Cerys and the Defeat of Bleddyn* or – hey, Uncle! What about *Cerys and the Good King*? I can't decide, at the moment. I need to sit down and think about it properly.'

'Sounds good, bach,' said Mr Williams. 'Always write things down. Then you remember them.'

Rose glanced sideways at him. He looked pensive. He too had another story now – the story of dying a terrible death deep underground, then coming back to life.

Now she heard a different kind of chattering coming from in front of them. The echoing, subdued roar of water flowing rapidly over stones. An underground river?

Ianto had stopped, suddenly. Rose opened her wings to lift off from Mr Williams's shoulder to see why.

Sure enough, they were now at the stony bank of a wide, underground river. At the edges the water ran shallow, over stones and solid slabs of rock. But in the centre it was a dark flowing mass of deep, rapid water. The good king was walking across it as if over solid ground, his boots skimming the surface, leaving a set of wet footprints which disappeared almost immediately as the water flowed swiftly on. He reached the other side and continued through the solid rock as it opened before him. He did not look behind him.

And now, the rock behind them was moving up, to push

them along. They had to cross the fast-flowing river – and there was no time to make plans. Rose would be fine – she could fly – but—

Swiftly, Ianto lifted Cerys from his shoulder and set her down beside him. Then he leaned right out over the river, so that his hands reached the far shore, making himself into a bridge.

Mr Williams gasped, and said '*A fo ben, bid bont,*' quietly to himself. *He who wants to lead must be a bridge.*

Then, holding Cerys's hand, the two of them ran lightly over his great nephew's legs, back and arms to the other side, Del racing behind them and Rose flying above.

And just in time, because the good king was striding ahead and the river was closing up behind them. Ianto scrambled to his feet, his legs splashing into water as he hauled himself out and stepped once more into the high tunnel, his boots squelching. Cerys was reaching up her arms for a lift, and he bent to scoop her up and put her back on her shoulder-perch. She clung, gratefully, to his neck.

'Hey, Uncle! I know what I'm going to call my story, for sure,' she said, looking down at him with excitement. '*Cerys and the Giant.*'

'Very good, bach,' chuckled Mr Williams.

Now the good king was moving upwards ahead of them. A set of deep, stone steps had been cut into the rock. They looked ancient and ceremonial. The king strode up them, easily, lightly. As they approached, Rose saw that it was a long staircase, the top shrouded in darkness.

They began to climb, following the king. The steps were

wide and high, stretching upwards and, presently, they began to take their toll on Mr Williams and Del, who were running out of puff. Soon they were standing to take their ease – Del panting, Mr Williams with hands on hips. Then they continued, Del bounding up ahead, then turning to watch as her master mounted the steps behind her.

Ianto strode easily upwards ahead of them, Cerys riding on his shoulder. The roof began to lower the higher they climbed, though, so that he soon had to crouch. Eventually he put Cerys down while he climbed the last few steps on all fours, Cerys clambering up beside him.

Rose flew overhead, so that she was right behind the good king, or Dad. Now she couldn't tell, from the back, which he was. The battle-helmet's golden bands glowed so brightly that it could also be Dad's hard hat – or not.

The stairs had come to an end. Above the glowing helmet was a final, giant slab of rock, balanced in the air on four other tall boulders. And beyond those, to Rose's amazement, was the dark night sky, already brightening towards the east to a deep, deep blue.

40

The five of them emerged from the stone structure, breathing in fresh, night air, full of the green, living scents of the wood. But this was not the jumble of stones, partly covered in earth, but the cromlech as it had been when first built – the cromlech as it was before Bleddyn had caused it to collapse on the first owl and giant, long centuries ago.

Around them the wood waited, silently, as if for a play to begin. And they seemed to be the actors, on the stage. But they didn't know their lines. They glanced at each other. Rose flew back to perch on Mr Williams's shoulder. Del was pressing against his leg. Cerys was back on Ianto's shoulder, gripping his neck. They were all silent now, even Cerys.

And the good king, Berwyn, was facing the entrance of the cromlech. The seconds ticked by. Like the rest of them, and the trees all around, he seemed to be waiting for something, or someone.

Then it arrived.

A deep rumbling from beneath the earth and then, suddenly and with great force, a torrent of black matter shot upwards from below, hitting the huge roof stone of the cromlech and pouring out and upwards over its sides, until an immense black cloud hovered over the whole clearing, pulsing and thickening above them, blotting out the stars.

Soon a succession of dark shapes appeared in the sky, as if

Bleddyn, or the force that powered him, could not decide what to be. Rose saw the eagle, momentarily, before it split into thousands of smaller forms – starlings? – that joined together to become one, huge mole. Which broke to form rats, scurrying in the sky, that became bats, beating their wings just once before gathering themselves to make up the wild boar, with fearsome tufted mane and curved fangs.

Next, as if overcome by angry, swirling energy, the whole thing reverted back to the cloud of dark particles, spinning furiously and drawing itself out like a thick, black ribbon, filling out into a round-bodied snake. The giant snake slithered and coiled in the sky as a flat, dead-eyed head formed, from which a forked, flickering tongue flared out.

Rose felt suddenly angry herself. Furious at the way that Bleddyn had used the forms of all these beautiful creatures – moles, rats, spiders, bats, snakes – and turned them into frightful things. Before she knew it, she had launched herself into the air at him, crying out in fury. She would not let him continue. She would stop him, or she would die trying.

The snake before her coiled and then shot forwards, mouth open, fangs bared, with a speed and power that stunned Rose. Before she had a chance to think, she was gripped within its jaws, high up in the air, beyond even Ianto's reach – Ianto, who had thrust Cerys at Mr Williams and was jumping off the ground, trying to grab her from the air. Now he was clambering on to the cromlech and stretching up from there, but she was still too high for him. From below she could hear his roar and make out Mr Williams's cries, but not his words. And then all sound ceased, because the snake had swallowed her whole.

She had closed her eyes, braced for death, but now opened them, cautiously. She was surrounded by darkness. It was as black in here as the inside of the mountain. She was inside the snake, inside Bleddyn.

Inside Bleddyn? Really? And despite the situation, she wanted to laugh, at how ridiculous that sounded. What was this all about? Bleddyn had lived long, long ago, and he had died long, long ago. What they were seeing now, what they had been seeing, this last week – all these creatures, formed from dark matter – were not really him. How could they be? Whatever they were, they were inconstant, always changing, made up of tiny particles, that were changing all the time themselves. The whole thing, a great swirling chaos, brought together to resemble a form, to resemble something. But really, truly, impermanent.

And so, she realised, with a flash of wisdom, are we. We're all made up of tiny particles, buzzing around each other, arising, passing away, so fast we don't even know it. What's there to be afraid of in that? Nothing. Nothing to fear. Nothing to fear, from anything.

And whether I live or die, thought Rose, *that's the truth.*

The shimmering darkness around her seemed to still, and then to pulse lightly, as if it was listening to her thoughts. Then she remembered Mr Williams's story. What his tadcu had said to him when he was stuck in the bog.

They aren't real starlings, Thomas. They're substanceless, unreal – remnants of an old, old spell which cannot persist. Think of good things, Thomas, boy, think of good things.

Too right, Tadcu Williams, thought Rose. Because when you realised the truth, all that was left was to think of good things. To be kind, and to be grateful for others' kindness. Dad came into her mind, unbidden. Ordinary Dad, reading to her at bedtime. She felt choked with love at the thought of him. And of Mum. And of all her many friends – Miss Evans, and Cerys, and Mamgu and, of course, Mr Williams and Ianto and Del. The Three Musketeers.

She was filled from top to bottom with love and gratitude for them. The love extinguished the fear, like darkness flees when a light is switched on.

Then, all at once, a single word ran through her mind, in the same way as those other words had, days ago – so long ago – when the mole had spoken to her. This time it said 'Enough.' And it was not the word, not the language, but the meaning, that was impressed upon her.

Then the black tomb, or womb, that she was held in convulsed, and she was vomited out through the mouth of the huge snake into the night sky, tumbling through the air until she found her wings again.

Tearing away from the black cloud that was already re-forming behind her tail-feathers, she plummeted back down to her friends who were staring into the sky in alarm.

Landing with a little thud on Mr Williams's shoulder, she raised her own eyes to look skywards.

And to realise that the curse was truly ending here, because Bleddyn was stretching and contracting into what must be his final shape, surely. A wolf. His final shape, because of his name. For Bleddyn is another word for Blaidd

– which means Wolf. Bleddyn was becoming a bleddyn.

He was almost as big as a Shetland pony, loping supplely, gracefully, through the sky, bounding down towards them as if he was running down the slope of an invisible mountain on strong, padded feet, sharp claws cutting through the air. As he approached, she saw his beautiful amber eyes, the thick fur that covered his body and his short, upright ears – in colours from white through grey to brindling brown along his back and down his magnificent, bushy tail.

He was almost upon them now. Rose glanced at Berwyn, the good king, to see that he was standing as before, still and alert, in front of the cromlech. His expression, beneath the glowing battle helmet, was calm as he watched his brother descend from the sky.

In seconds, Bleddyn had landed on the roof of the cromlech. Then he sat, lifting his muzzle so that his back was a perfect, straight line from tail to nose, pointing towards the sickle moon that shone above the clearing. He opened his lips to let out a long, mournful howl. The sound filled the valley and echoed back again, before dying away. To Rose, it rang with weariness, regret, and deep, deep sadness. A shiver ran down her feathery back.

Del, who had been fidgeting at Mr Williams's side, could not resist this. She lifted her own head to give an answering call, full of her own hidden longing. It was as if she was paying homage to her ancestors.

Bleddyn took no notice of Del. Lowering his head, his majestic eyes focused entirely on his brother, who stood motionless before him on the ground, sword sheathed at his belt, hands at his sides, fingers slightly open.

Silently, the wolf curled back his lips, wrinkling the skin on his nose so that four pairs of long, white incisors were revealed, and startlingly red gums and tongue. The thick fur that ridged his back and neck stood up, making him look even bigger as he got to his feet and crept forward along the long roof stone.

And then he uncoiled and sprang at his brother from the top of the cromlech, opening his mouth and lunging for the bared neck of the good king.

But Berwyn had prepared for this attack. As swift as lightning, he reached around with his right hand to pull the iron sword from its sheath and to raise it, tip first, before him. And then, like a strange performance in which two dancers know exactly which moves to make – graceful, sure, Bleddyn fell upon the extended sword.

His weight – the weight of a heavy, full-grown male wolf – impaled him entirely, and Rose saw the tip of the sword, bright red – red as his gums and tongue – protruding from the upstanding fur on his back, before Berwyn stepped back and, with a practised jerk, withdrew his sword, allowing Bleddyn's body to slump, dead, to the ground.

Instead of disintegrating into foul black smoke, blood, bright red against the snow-white fur of his neck and underparts, gushed from the wound in the wolf's chest. Berwyn's sword had ripped open his heart.

The little company of Rose, Ianto, Cerys, Mr Williams and Del stood stock-still, silent, staring at the brothers.

Rose saw, with a start, that Berwyn was quietly weeping,

tears rolling down his cheeks from his dark eyes and into his beard, his shoulders heaving with subdued sobs. He knelt to wipe the bloodied blade on the grass and then stood again, sheathing the sword before drying his wet face on his sleeve.

Then his eyes, dry now in his solemn face, focused forward towards the cromlech once more, as his brother's body slowly drained of blood beside him.

The audience shuffled a little. Rose saw Mr Williams glance down at Cerys, who was holding his hand tightly. She looked up at him with wide, unsmiling eyes, then turned back to watch the king.

Ianto was gazing ahead at the brothers, as if in a trance.

And then came a sound from the far side of the wood, over by the stream. Thundering hooves, approaching at a wild gallop; and a crashing through undergrowth until, all at once, a magnificent black steed burst into the arena of the clearing. As one, the five of them shuffled backwards, to give this spirited creature space; but the good king stood his ground, his eyes following her rapid approach.

She pulled up before him with a jerk – her long legs prancing, rearing her noble head, wide eyes looking down at her master, shaking her long, shining mane. Upon her back was a thick, red cloth – no saddle, no stirrups – and about her head was a simple bridle, adorned with gold and red enamel fittings.

She danced a few steps on light, skittish hooves next to Berwyn, then took off again, wild-eyed, as if the energy that fired her would not allow her to stand still.

Now Berwyn sprang into action, sprinting at her side

then, in one smooth movement, wreathing his left hand around her mane and lightly bounding from the ground and up, on to her back. Straight-backed, easy, heels gripping her sides, he grasped her reins and pulled her about, so that the next moment they were cantering back to the cromlech.

And here the audience gave a collective gasp. Because, lying on the grass where the bloodied body of the wolf had been, was a full-grown man. A man dressed as the king was, in long tunic, trousers and boots. As he got to his feet they saw that he held no weapon in his hand and wore no helmet on his head. He, too, had a beard. And he looked like his brother, the good king, only younger, slighter, less sure of himself.

And he looks like Dad, too, thought Rose.

Wheeling the horse about with a firm, one-handed grip, Berwyn leant down to grab his brother around the waist. Bleddyn reached up and, while the horse skittered about on the spot, settled himself behind Berwyn on her back and wrapped his arms tightly around his brother.

The noble horse pawed the air with her front hooves and, as Berwyn and Bleddyn leaned forward and Berwyn dug his heels into her sides, she let out a loud, neighing cry and took off at a disciplined, rocking canter, moving anticlockwise around the edge of the clearing. The audience of five shifted quickly to give her free passage, moving towards the cromlech at the centre of the circle.

It was like watching a circus act from the very middle of the ring, as the horse with the two men on her back circled round and round them. Then Rose realised that the brothers were changing. Gradually, naturally, the beards disappeared, the muscular height diminished. Berwyn's helmet and the sword at his side melted away. They were growing younger. Time was turning back for them until, while the horse continued to circle the clearing, lap after lap, the transformation stopped and what they saw were two boys – aged, maybe, twelve and eleven. Freshfaced, dark-haired, slight but strong, the older one took the lead with a sure hand, pulling his horse in at the very edge of the clearing.

Bleddyn's young face shone with a mixture of excitement and fear, and he clung hard to his brother's back. Then Berwyn dug his heels into his horse's sides to let her have her way.

She had been waiting for this. Head forward, nostrils bared wide and tail streaming behind her, she raced at full gallop across the centre of the clearing. Her head was stretched before her, legs reaching out almost as far then tucking in beneath, eating the turf, throwing up divets of earth as she went.

The boys crouched as one, clinging to her and shouting with exhilaration. They thundered past the cromlech in front of Rose and her friends then plunged into the wood, crashing through the undergrowth, the boys' shouts growing fainter until, as they watched, the horse and her riders emerged at a gallop from the edge of the wood and up, out on to the track to the top of the mountain.

Then, diving from the sky to join them, was the silhouetted outline of a small, sharp bird of prey. Although the sun was yet to appear over the horizon behind them, with her keen owl-vision Rose knew that it was a kestrel.

The kestrel descended swiftly to land on Berwyn's

outstretched arm as the horse galloped on, up the mountain, past the ruined house. Rose saw him lean forward to kiss the bird and then, all at once, the horse had reached the very top of the mountain and was leaping out over the edge. But she didn't fall. She continued to gallop through the night sky, her hooves powering through air, onwards and upwards, westwards, to where the sky was darkest and the stars shone brightest until, eventually, the beautiful black horse and her cargo of brothers and kestrel disappeared completely.

41

Rose found herself transforming. She closed her eyes as the feathers drew in to become skin, clothed in trousers and fleece, the wings to become arms, the short, feathered legs and claws extending to become human legs and feet. She felt heavier now – and fuzzier. When she opened her eyes, the sharpness had gone from her vision, so that she strained to see clearly in the early-dawn darkness.

Next to her was Ianto, a boy again.

Mr Williams, Cerys and Del were staring at the two of them with open mouths. Rose smiled, realising that they must have been quite a sight. She glanced at Ianto, and he was looking at her and smiling too. Impulsively, she reached out and hugged him tightly, filled with affection and relief. Before she knew what she was doing, she had planted a kiss on his cheek. Immediately he shifted and planted one back, on hers. They pulled apart, a little shyly now, and smiled some more.

'Woooo!' said Cerys, who had been watching avidly.

Everyone laughed.

And then they held still, because from somewhere, deep in the darkness of the wood, an owl hooted as if in reply: 'Woo-hoo-hoo-hooo!'

The leaves rustled gently. Then came the response, sharp and loud, clear as a bell – 'Ke-wick!'

It sent a shiver down Rose's spine. It was as if two friends were greeting them, telling them that all was well with the wood once more.

As the sounds faded into the shushing of the leaves, Mr Williams spoke.

'Well, crew, I know I've said this before, and I've got it wrong – got a lot of things wrong, as it happens –' he chuckled – 'but I think it's safe to say, after that little show, that the curse is finally ended.'

'Yay!' said Cerys, her small fist punching the air in triumph. Everyone laughed again – laughter that was full of relief, full of a kind of craziness.

Then, '*Group hug*,' said Ianto, in English and in a corny accent, and everyone formed a little circle with their arms. Del wormed herself between their legs, and barked with excitement in the middle of them.

When they'd fallen apart, still chuckling and looking about at each other, Mr Williams gave a little start and pulled the rolled-up englyn from his pocket, peering at it in the half-light.

Helpfully, Cerys got out her torch and shone it on the words. 'What is it, Uncle?' she asked curiously. Then she edged around him to read it out loud:

'The Thirty-Third Owl.

Cave-coffined, two kings under earth – the bad and good –

Sound Celt-crafted instruments of iron and wood.

Kin wakes kings. Iron breaks wood – for second birth.

King takes king; iron makes good – to end the curse.'

There was a pause, then Cerys said, 'Oooh!' in awe,

looking around at them with wide eyes. 'I don't understand it all, but I think I understand the last line. *King takes king; iron makes good – to end the curse.* That's what we saw, isn't it? We saw the good king kill the bad king with his iron sword, making all the bad stuff into good. And they ended up being friends again, didn't they? I really enjoyed that bit.'

Rose and Ianto shared a smile at this.

It has all happened as the englyn said it would, thought Rose. *But we had to actually* do *it all, to understand it.*

Then Rose remembered something. 'Mr Williams, when you came back from the dead, you looked at me and said "The thirty-third owl. That's you. I remember now." What did you mean?'

And she straightaway regretted her question, because Cerys turned to her great uncle in concern, grabbing both his hands and pulling on them to get his attention. 'Uncle! Did you *die*?'

'Er, yes, bach. But only for a little while. Right as rain now, I am. A change is as good as a rest, as they say.'

Cerys seemed to accept this, examining him carefully and nodding. But she wanted more information. 'But what was it *like*, Uncle?'

'Ah, well – hard to say. Course, the knockers looked after me . . .'

Cerys's eyes grew wide again. 'What are the *knockers*?'

'Well, bach, that's another story. For another day.'

Then Mr Williams turned to Rose. 'Yes, Rose. I did say that, and I do remember now. You are the thirty-third owl. And you are the most important one of them all, Tadcu told me. He said that you would be the one to break the curse. See, if you count forwards from the very first owl – that is, from Celtic times, two thousand years ago – there's been one every sixty years since. So, you are the thirty-third owl of all.'

She was only the thirty-third owl? It didn't seem like enough, to stretch back all that way, almost into pre-history. That was only a few more people than were in her class at school.

She did the sums quickly in her head. OK, so it looked as if she was the thirty-third owl. So what?

'But Ianto is the thirty-third giant too. Why isn't that special? And I didn't really do anything. All of us fought Bleddyn to break the curse, in the end. All of us. Even Del.'

And then came a voice, solemn yet light, as if it came from a songbird. It sounded from amongst the trees behind them.

'*Bydd y drydedd dylluan ar ddeg ar hugain yn arbennig achos bydd hi o deulu'r ddau frenin.*'

'The thirty-third owl will be special, because she will be the descendant of the two kings.'

42

They all whipped around to face the voice, but could see only dark trunks and the moving, whispering shadows of foliage. Rose was frozen, stunned. Because she had known, as soon as she'd heard the chiming voice and taken in the meaning of the words, that it was true. Somehow those two kings – the good and the bad – were related to Dad, related to her. She knew it in her bones. Because, after all, her bones were made up of the same material – the same material as Dad's, as Berwyn's and Bleddyn's.

She gasped, thinking of her recent encounter with those bones, those skeletons. But there was more to it than that, of course. She knew there was. There were all the other ancestors in between, as part of the mix.

She peered into the darkness, looking for the source of the portentous words, desperate to know more. Before she knew it, she was running towards the trees. And it seemed that Del felt the same, because she was soon overtaken by a sprinting dog. Then she realised that Ianto was behind her too, calling to her to be careful. And Cerys, shouting breathlessly, 'Wait for us, Rose!'

In the meantime, Del had disappeared into the wood, as if she was after a sheep that had dared to stray.

Before Rose reached the trees, a figure emerged from the shadows at the edge of the clearing, with Del zig-zagging behind it, driving it back to the pack.

It was a small figure. It moved gracefully and unhurriedly towards them on small feet, and it seemed unconcerned by the sheepdog that was harrying it forwards. It was carrying a wicker bag in its hand.

'Mamgu!' cried Rose, Ianto and Cerys together, and they ran to her, enveloping her in hugs. Then Del herded them all back to Mr Williams who was standing next to the cromlech, staring in amazement at the sight of his sister.

'Hello, Thomas,' said Mamgu. She looked as calm as ever. She was wearing sensible trainers and a warm, padded coat over neatly-pressed jeans. She put down her bag, then kneeled to reach inside it. 'I should think you're all ready for a cup of tea and a biscuit,' she said, in her sweet, kind voice.

'Never mind tea and biscuits. What on earth are you doing here?' exploded her brother. Mamgu ignored this, pulling out two large flasks, a collection of plastic cups and a packet of Hobnobs.

Suddenly, a cup of tea and a Hobnob was the one thing Rose wanted most in the whole world. When had she last drank anything – or eaten anything, come to that?

She watched fondly as the small lady poured steaming, milky tea into mugs, which Ianto passed around with the opened packet of biscuits.

Then she remembered the sandwich in her backpack, with the corner she'd torn off for the knockers, and she pulled it out and unwrapped the foil. And she realised that Del was watching her, watching the sandwich, intently, her head on one side and a little dribble of saliva falling from her lip. Del must be hungry too. She held it out and the dog took it delicately, gulping it down in two bites.

In the meantime, gripping the cup of tea that he was too distracted to drink, Mr Williams watched his sister, shaking his head. Eventually, he spoke again.

'So. How long were you hiding in there?'

Mamgu, grasping her own cup of tea, looked up to meet her brother's eyes. Then she took a sip and said, 'Mmmm.'

Biting into her Hobnob, she chewed carefully and swallowed. Then she said, 'I've been here a few hours now.

'I woke up in the night. I think I heard an owl. And I had a feeling, a very strange feeling. I crept upstairs to check on the children, and I saw that Ianto and Cerys had gone. Siriol was sleeping peacefully, thank goodness. So I dressed, packed up these tea things, and headed to the wood – I didn't know what else to do. And I waited over there, under the trees. It was quiet. As if the wood was waiting for something very important to happen. I waited too. I was frightened. Not for myself, but for all of you. I prayed that everything was going to plan – that the curse would be lifted.

'And then I saw something amazing. I thought to myself, *I'll never see anything more mysterious and wonderful in my life.* The earth peeled away from the great stones in the middle as if it were a carpet, rolling itself up on all sides. And then the four enormous stones, the ones that form the sides of the cromlech, slowly stood up again, of their own accord. At the same time, the roof-stone, the biggest of them all – weighing tons, surely – floated up into the air, as light as a feather, and came down to stand flat upon the other four.'

They all turned to look at the cromlech, as good as new –

rocks clean of earth, of lichen, standing as if it had just been made – which it had, in a way.

'I thought I would never see anything more amazing than that cromlech, remaking itself,' Mamgu went on, looking round at them all with her clear, blue eyes. 'But then I did. I saw Berwyn, the good king, in his shining golden battle-helmet and with the bright sword at his side, step solemnly from the cromlech. And then, one by one – oh, it was such a relief to see you all! – out you all came too. And, of course, I saw that Ianto and Rose were in their forms as giant and owl.' She smiled at Ianto and Rose.

'And then I saw the dark cloud that was Bleddyn. I saw him swallow you in the air, Rose, then spit you out again.'

She looked at Rose and shook her head, as if in awe, then continued, 'Finally, I saw Berwyn kill Bleddyn, and the two of them grow young again – to the time before the darkness grew within poor Bleddyn. I saw them ride away together on Berwyn's magnificent horse.

'In other words I, too, saw the curse come to an end.

'Because, the three happenings happened. First you, Rose—' she turned to her – 'the thirty-third owl, the owl who is the descendant of the two kings – came into being, waking both kings. Not just Bleddyn, but the good king, Berwyn, for the first time in nearly two thousand years.

'The second happening was the destruction of Bleddyn's staff with an iron tool and, with that, the giving of new life to its owner. I'm guessing that tool was yours, Thomas?'

Her brother nodded, a frown creasing his brow. 'My hand-axe. It was Ianto who did it. Thank you, by the way, boy.' He looked at Ianto, who raised his eyebrows, surprised to be credited. 'It was steel actually, not iron,' Mr Williams went on, 'but I guess that works just as well. Go on,' he said, and there was a note of challenge in his voice, a hint of sulkiness. 'What was the third happening, then – seeing as you know it all so well?'

'You ought to know what the third happening was, Thomas,' she said. But Thomas remained silent, watching her and holding his undrunk cup of tea on his crossed arms.

Mamgu stood her ground, staring up at him stoutly. She said, 'The third happening was the killing of Bleddyn by Berwyn, using his iron sword. Those three things, happening one after the other, finally broke the curse, as foretold by our family for generations.'

Mr Williams looked at the ground for a moment. Then he looked up again, murmuring, 'Yes. That's how it went. The three happenings – of course. Now I remember.'

As they watched, the frown deepened between his eyes. 'What I don't get,' he said, slowly, addressing his sister, 'is how *you* know all this? About the thirty-third owl, and the curse, the three happenings – everything. Tadcu told it all to me. Only me. Not you.'

'Oh, Thomas!' his sister replied, in exasperation. 'You weren't paying any attention to Tadcu, were you, that night in the barn, on your twelfth birthday? When he was trying to tell you all these important things. I could see you weren't. You were fiddling with bits of hay, you were flicking through the book, you were doing anything but listen to him. Just like you always do when anyone tries to tell you something. Probably thinking about your new bike, or Gwenllian—'

'Wait a minute!' interrupted her brother, incredulous. He'd uncrossed his arms, forgetting his cup of tea, which slopped, steaming, down his front. 'You mean to say, *you* were there, too?'

'Yes. I was in the barn – hiding behind the hay, near the doorway. When you and Tadcu didn't come in for supper, I went out to look for you. I peeked round the barn door and saw you both in there, heard you talking. I sneaked in and hid. And I heard it all. But more importantly, I *remembered* it all – unlike you.'

For a few long seconds, Mr Williams continued to stare at her in silence. Slowly at first but gaining in frequency, jolts of energy pulsed through him and his shoulders began to jerk up and down like a puppet's. Rose waited. Only a matter of time now— Yes. Here it was: 'Heh! heh! heh! heh! heh!'

When he could speak again, he wiped his eyes and said, 'My little sister. Always poking her beak in. Always listening behind doors . . . heh, heh, heh. Fair play to you. *Fair play to you!*' And with that, a sudden burst of affection hit him and he grabbed his sister, hugging her hard, lifting her off her feet and spilling her half-drunk cup of tea into the bargain.

When he'd put her down again he held her at arms' length, smiling down at her upturned face.

Mamgu gripped his arms firmly and smiled back – a little sadly, Rose thought. She didn't seem to notice the spilled tea that was slowly staining into her coat. 'Yes, Thomas, you're right,' she said, and her voice shook a little. 'I *was* always poking my beak in. But I was only seven at the time. And you were so much older. I adored you. I *was* always following you about, because I wanted to be your friend. But you weren't interested in playing with me. Tagging along and listening in was the only way I could be part of things.

'It's not easy being a younger sister, you know.'

There was a pause. Then, 'Poor Mamgu!' said Cerys, her eyes shining with sympathy, wrapping her arms around her grandmother. 'I'm a younger sister, too,' she confided to her, 'and I know *just* how it feels.' Then she looked pointedly at her brother, narrowing her eyes to challenge him.

'Hey!' Ianto said. 'Not guilty. We're *always* playing together.' And to demonstrate he began a mock-boxing match with her, which ended up with him tickling Cerys until she was doubled up and squirming with laughter.

When Cerys had recovered, she said, 'Don't worry, Mamgu. At least you knew what was going on.' Then she turned to the others and proclaimed, 'Mamgu always knows *everything*.'

'Not everything,' said Mamgu, still looking at her brother. 'I don't know what will happen with this wood, Thomas. This precious wood. Not now that you've sold it to the people who want to build the abattoir. The curse may be broken, but the wood is still in great danger.'

'Ah . . .' Mr Williams looked down, suddenly taking great interest in the inside of his empty plastic cup.

Then, 'Well,' he went on, slowly, 'apparently someone went to the council planning meeting and threw a spanner in the works.' He looked up, and this time his eyes met Rose's. She stared back, her heart beating suddenly fast.

'Who?' said Ianto. 'What did they say?' Then he followed

his uncle's eyes and looked at Rose, puzzled.

'Oh, apparently they made an objection to the building of the abattoir, on the grounds of there possibly being a precious, ancient cromlech in the middle of the wood, or some such nonsense. So I hear, anyway.'

Rose gulped, but she held Mr Williams's blue eyes. And then she saw them twinkle, saw his mouth twitch up in a smile. What was going on? She smiled back, nervously.

'No *possibly* about it, Uncle,' said Ianto, gesturing behind them at the cromlech, which stood, solid and magnificent, in the centre of the clearing. The first streaks of pink, dawn light reflected off the great stones, bathing it in a golden glow. 'If the cromlech wasn't visible before, it most certainly is now. No one could miss this huge great megalith. But who made the objection?'

It was time to come clean.

'Me,' Rose said, quietly, still looking at Mr Williams.

Mamgu, Cerys and Ianto gasped and turned to her in astonishment. Ianto whistled. 'I *knew* it! That's why you wanted to borrow the book and the map,' he said. 'Good for you, Rose!'

'Yes, well done, Rose fach,' said Mamgu, reaching out to squeeze her arm. 'That must have taken a lot of courage. And a lot of work. Well done.'

Rose glowed with their praise. It was good that it was out there now – the truth. She had opposed the planning application. And it looked as if, it looked as if – she might have succeeded!

But Mamgu hadn't finished. 'The thing is,' she continued,

and her tone was despondent now, 'these abattoir people might not be able to build their abattoir, but they'll still own the wood. And who knows what else they might do with it? They might even build the abattoir around the cromlech, or something dreadful like that.'

Mr Williams looked at her. Then his shoulders began to jiggle once more, jerking his arms up and down. '*Heh, heh, heh, heh,*' he went, and this had to be the loudest, most uncontrollable of all his bouts of convulsive laughter. Everyone stared at him, puzzled. What could be funny about the situation with the wood?

Eventually, he was able to enunciate some words. 'I didn't – heh, heh, heh – I didn't – heh!' Then he cracked up again, tears streaming down his face.

Hands on knees, he made a superhuman effort to control himself. He broke off, took a deep breath and spluttered out, quickly as he could, 'I-didn't-sign-the-contract!'

Then he let himself go completely, breaking into more peals of breathless laughter, his face screwed up with the effort of it all.

'You— you what, Uncle?' Ianto was frowning in disbelief.

Mr Williams looked at him. His shoulders, suddenly, stopped heaving. He said, clearly this time, 'Didn't sign the contract. Kept putting it off. Couldn't bear to. It's sitting on my table. Been there for months. Hidden under newspapers now.

'Didn't sign it.

'The wood's still mine.'

43

Rose awoke to find herself in bed. The sparrows were cheeping outside, and the swallows were twittering from the telephone line. Mum was singing, too, in the kitchen – singing along to the radio.

All at once she sprang upright, wondering what stressful thing she had to do today. And then she sank down again, as the realisation came that there was nothing she had to do today, no stressful thing lying ahead – for now, anyway.

Because it was Sunday. The first Sunday of the summer holidays. And they had broken the curse. They had battled Bleddyn for a week and, finally, they had seen him go. And by that stage, amazingly, they had all wished him the very best.

She could tell it was late – lunchtime, maybe?

But then, she had gone to bed late – or more like early.

It had been around five a.m. when she'd finally sneaked back into the house, into bed. Mamgu, Ianto and Cerys had walked her home, then headed down the track to their house. Mr Williams had strode back up to his tumbledown farmhouse, Del at his side. He had whistled tunefully all the way, and the cheery sound, like a blackbird's song, had drifted down to them as he climbed, the rays of the rising sun glowing on his back.

Rose hoped that every one of them had had a good sleep, like her. And that every one of them would have a good day today. Restful. Peaceful. With a feeling of achievement, after all they'd been through. After sorting everything out.

Or, almost everything.

On the way back to her house through the wood, Rose had asked Mamgu more about her ancestors, the two kings. Because it had occurred to her that, as far as she remembered from *The Return of the Kings*, neither Berwyn nor Bleddyn had children.

'*Ti'n iawn, bach.* You're right, bach,' Mamgu had replied. 'But, according to Tadcu, they had a younger sister. The Princess Erwain. You are one of her descendants.

'Apparently,' Mamgu continued, 'Princess Erwain had many adventures of her own. Tadcu said that a book was written about her in medieval times: *Llyfr Erwain – The Book of Erwain.* But that book is lost now. So it's often referred to as *Llyfr Coll Erwain – The Lost Book of Erwain.* Historians and storytellers have been searching for it for hundreds of years.'

So, this Princess Erwain was her and Dad's ancestor. Rose was itching to find out more about her and, already, she knew that she was going to join the search for the lost book.

But there was something much more important than this. This whole, long week had taught her many, many things. But here was the most important one of all.

She and Mum needed to talk about Dad.

They needed to share their memories of him, together. They needed to do the garden together and remember him by uncovering the roses, and pruning them, and feeding them, like he used to. That would be a good start. And then they needed to take a trip to his home town, and put flowers on his mam's grave – *Beryl, a lovely lady* – and see if they could find any more of his relatives and talk to them – talk to them about Dad, and then stay in touch with them.

Find his family. Be part of it.

But first of all, they just needed to talk about him, and maybe write things down. Because when you wrote them down, you remembered them. And then they were there for your children, and your grandchildren . . .

She could hardly wait – she wanted to do it right now, and she almost sprang from the bed again. But the lazy, Sunday feeling held her in place for a little longer, enjoying the leafy patterns of the sun on her duvet and the warmth of the soft bedclothes, while Mum continued to sing in the kitchen. It was lovely to hear her so happy. Happy . . .

Then Rose realised something else. She needed to tell Mum about this week. About becoming an owl, about her adventures with Ianto and Mr Williams and Del, and Cerys and Mamgu. Mum had to know everything. She didn't want to keep secrets from Mum. She wanted to tell her everything that had happened.

And the best way to tell Mum everything, Rose thought, was to write it all down, and give it to her as a proper story, to read in her own time. Otherwise, she just didn't know where she would start.

Phew! Write the whole, complicated story? Remember everything, explain everything, colour it all in with detail? Make it as scary and exciting and sad and joyful and magical, as it was? Could she do that?

Well, why not? She'd already done so many things that

had amazed her, things that she'd never imagined she'd be capable of. Doing the presentation to the council meeting. Fighting Bleddyn. Actually killing him, twice. Abseiling in the middle of the night. Going underground. Seeing Mr Williams fall to his death, and then live again. Ending the curse.

And facing the abyss inside her by thinking about Dad, by looking at her memories of him. By actually *seeing* him. Perhaps that had been the most difficult thing of all.

Of course she could write the story.

Then, suddenly, Rose thought of something she could tell Mum straight away. Not just *could* tell her straight away but *had to* tell her straight away. And this time she did spring out of bed, running from the room in her pyjamas and bare feet, bursting into the kitchen, where Mum was busy at the stove, the kettle steaming and whistling softly and the frying pan before her sizzling and giving off the delicious aroma of mushrooms frying in butter.

Mum turned, smiling, in her apron. 'Hello, love—' she began, but she got no further.

'Mum! The wood is safe! Mr Williams didn't sign the contract – and he's not going to. He's not selling it. We're going to be all right. Everything is going to be all right!'